Your Home for Multi-Genre Reading Entertainment.

ADVENTURES

Your Home for Multi-Genre Reading Entertainment.

COPYRIGHT ©2023, OFFBEAT PUBLISHING, LLC

All rights reserved. No part of this publication may be reproduced, distributed, or transmitted in any form or by any means, including photocopying, recording, or other electronic or mechanical methods, without the prior written permission of the publisher, except in the case of brief quotations embodied in critical reviews and certain other noncommercial uses permitted by copyright law.

This publication includes works of fiction. Any resemblance to actual events or persons, living or dead, is entirely coincidental.

ISBN: (PAPERBACK) 978-1-950464-35-7
ISBN: (EBOOK) 978-1-950464-36-4

---

*COVER PHOTOS:
STARTING AT TOP, FROM LEFT TO RIGHT:
JANE WITHERS, JOSEPHINE BAKER,
BARBARA STANWYCK, CLARA BOW,
DOROTHY DANDRIDGE, JOAN BLONDELL,
SUSAN HAYWARD, JANE RUSSELL,
YVONNE DECARLO, LAUREN BACALL,
ROSALIND RUSSELL, MUCHIKO KUWANO.

WWW.OFFBEATREADS.COM

ADVENTURES

Your Home for Multi-Genre Reading Entertainment.

SPRING, 2023   **ISSUE #7**

WHAT

THE ARTIFACT	1
A JURY OF HER PEERS	153
SOUTHWEST SCENARIOS BY DARRYLE PURCELL	178
A LITTLE JOURNEY	181
COVER STORY BY ELMEDINA HOTA	190
THE INCIDENT IN GALLOWAY'S QUARTER	203
FOR ADDISON	245

WHERE

ATTENTION WRITERS:
OFFBEATREADS IS ACCEPTING SUBMISSIONS!
EMAIL MANUSCRIPT WITH YOUR CONTACT INFO TO:
OFFBEATREADS@PM.ME
PUT "SUBMISSION" IN SUBJECT

EDITOR'S NOTE

OUR TEAM IS PROUD TO PRESENT ANOTHER STUFFED RAG FOR YOUR PERUSAL. Five complete stories are ahead, three of which are brand new, never-before published originals. Two comics from Darryle Purcell are in this issue. In one, Darryle appropriately jabs at disgraceful Hanoi Jane, who fairly recently showed her ignorance and hypocrisy. In *Dark Corners* you can tease or torment emotions with poetry by Elmedina Hota. Speaking of Elmedina, she was given a green light to briefly explore a time long gone. If you are interested in fashion and glamour from early to mid 20th century, feel free to skip ahead to the cover story.

It's a fact: each era and generation comes with its own set of problems. So, of course, any thorough study of a period from the 19th or 20th century may objectively note those problems. However, here there is not enough space to mention any and all points one might choose to consider, and that is not our purpose here anyway. This cover story is intended to briefly touch on a time when beauty and glamour were authentic.

When I look at today's fashion, I want to put it in quotes: *"Fashion."* The "fashion" of today seems to have three pathetic motives: to expose as much of the body as possible, to see how outrageous it can be, and provide a fix for an already conceited ego. I admire a woman's body as much as the next person, but dresses that are barely existent only flaunt. The prevailing attitude is, "Look at me, I'm elite, wealthy, and you must recognize that and give me attention. I'm sexy." This clawing for attention is actually a turn-off. There can be no beauty when an actress on the red carpet flaunts her very recent bikini wax in a revealing dress, for example. Doing something for attention is childish.

In my opinion, real sexiness also comes from having class. Today, there are very few if any examples of class. Fake smiles, bad acting, kowtowing to trends, and standing on popular political soapboxes in order to stay popular and get work in Hollywood—none of these are attractive. *(Yet, people fall in line, loving the craziness, praising the fake. This is no surprise when our ill culture has forgotten what a life with real meaning means; people fill life with things that offer false meaning.)* **With exceptions**, today's Hollywood stars are shallow attention-seekers. Not a whole lot is real. Each moment is planned carefully to promote each event and star, and the star in turn dons fake excitement in appearances and movies to stay relevant. To me, that's ugly no matter who it is. It hasn't always been this way. Sure, being popular among the fans of film was a good thing, but stars during the Golden Age of Hollywood were once revered for who they were, and for the *real* talent displayed in films—and yes, the *real* glamour. They were seldom if ever elevated because they acted outrageously and fell in line with politics.

You'll enjoy Elmedina's look back. It showcases and discusses rather than harshly criticizing as I have. In fact, I hope you enjoy everything this issue offers. Take it with you and choose to read for a few moments instead of grabbing your cell phone for another possibly compulsive waste of time. Your brain will thank you, and so will we.

Yours,

Robert Kimbrell

THE ARTIFACT
BY DAVID ROGERS

THE ARTIFACT

BY DAVID ROGERS

PROLOGUE

Here's how one of the weirdest days of my life started.

It felt like morning, though I saw no windows or clocks in the room. A fluorescent light tube buzzed overhead. Someone was knocking on a door. I sat up in bed, feeling completely lost and confused, until memories of the evening before came flooding back. I kept hoping they would disintegrate the way bad dreams do when you wake up. They did not.

I was in a small room that reminded me of a college dorm. Not that I had ever lived in a college dorm, though I hoped I soon would.

More knocking, and the door opened. A young woman wearing a lab coat looked in. "I'm Jeanette," she said. "Dr. Eisenberg's assistant. He wants you in the lab in half an hour." She stepped inside.

"I'll also be making sure you have everything you need." She looked around and checked the closet and chest of drawers. "I see you didn't have a chance to pack. I'll get you some clean clothes. You just have time to get dressed and eat. Maybe shower, if you're quick about it. Facilities are in there." She gestured behind me. "I always knock before I come in, but I would appreciate it if you wear pants at all times, except in the bathroom. Some things I just don't need to see any more of."

She left as quickly and efficiently as she had arrived.

How did I get there? It started in 1922. Well really, thousands of years before that, but in November 1922, long before anybody I knew was born, a British archeologist named Howard Carter, along with some of his colleagues, discovered and opened the tomb of an ancient Egyptian Pharaoh named Tutankhamen. You've probably heard of the good pharaoh, popularly known as King Tut. Many books, movies, and television shows have documented the tale, with varying degrees of fiction often added to boost sales. Fictions aside, large quantities of invaluable artifacts were removed from the tomb, without respect for the dead or proper acknowledgement of Egyptian cultural heritage.

One more artifact, besides those Carter and his associates proudly carried away and put on display in museums, was unwisely removed. That item has never been written about or even had its very existence publicly acknowledged, until now.

This is the story of that artifact. Or the part of the story that changed my life, anyway, and led me to meet Dr. Eisenberg, Jeanette, and others I could have lived happily ever after without knowing. It's a long story, and I wouldn't believe half of it if it hadn't happened to me. These events led me to understand why those who delve into secrets of the dead should proceed with much circumspection, utmost caution, and great respect.

CHAPTER I

"**I** need you to hold something for me," the woman said.

"No, better not." I'm not old enough to remember September 11, 2001. I hear that's when the world lost its mind for a while and then realized people should be more careful with airplanes, especially big ones. Also, somebody needed to watch what people carry onboard. Why that wasn't obvious before 2001, I don't know. I do know you don't take a package from a stranger in the airport. In case you forget, they play the announcement on the PA every fifteen minutes.

"I'll make it worth your trouble," she said. "How's fifty bucks sound?"

"No way."

"Okay, a hundred. Just to watch this box for a minute."

This encounter was getting too weird. I looked around and wondered if I should find a security guard or TSA agent and report the incident. Or was this a test? Was she a bored agent trying to trick me into doing something silly?

The call came for economy class to board the flight from Detroit, Michigan, to Louisville, Kentucky.

5

"Gotta go," I said, trying to get up, but she was standing right in front of my seat, where I had been looking out the window watching planes land and take off.

The strangest thing about the woman was her eyes. A curious shade of light blue. Another odd quality that took me a moment to pinpoint – the eyes did not blink. Not once. I later learned certain medical conditions can stop people from blinking, but at the time, the constant stare just creeped me out. It reminded me of that Poe story "The Tell-Tale Heart" and how the narrator must have felt about the old man with the supposedly Evil Eye.

"It's nothing dangerous. Not illegal," the woman said, not stepping aside. "I do need to get it out of this airport, though." She pushed the box, brown cardboard sealed with duct tape, about half the size of a shoebox, into my hands.

"Sorry, gotta go." I stood, squeezing past her and pushing the box away. As I started to walk toward the gate, I saw myself getting off the plane in Louisville and carrying her package down the long passage. Clearly, I was in Louisville: pictures of Mohammed Ali and racehorses decorated the walls. And in my hand I held the package the woman had tried to give me.

As suddenly as the vision began, it ended. I was back in Detroit.

"Are you all right, sir?" a gate agent said. I realized I was standing between rows of seats in the waiting area, near the line of people waiting to board. I had apparently been blocking the way, staring out the airport window while seeing myself in Louisville. People were giving me strange looks and squeezing past.

"I'm fine, just a little dizzy." I turned and sat back down, looked around, and did not see the woman who tried to give me the package. The line to board the plane was shortening. I took out my phone, checked to make sure my boarding pass was on the screen, and got in line. My backpack felt a little heavier, but I thought nothing of it. I must have been distracted by that strange episode.

I STARED OUT THE WINDOW, MARVELING AS THE WORLD ROARED BY FASTER AND faster and then fell away beneath the plane. I hadn't been on airplanes often enough to be bored by the experience.

| THE ARTIFACT

By the time the plane leveled off and the fasten-seat-belts light went out, my seatmate, a tired-looking forty-something business type, had already closed his eyes for a nap. I pulled my backpack from under the seat in front of me, opened it to get my book – Stephen King's *It* (I was on my third trip through that epic) – and saw immediately why the pack felt heavy and lumpy.

The woman must have taken advantage of what I was calling an *episode*, not knowing a better word for seeing myself somewhere I wasn't, to slip her package in my backpack. The vision – maybe that was more accurate – had apparently blinded me to my surroundings and given her the chance to put the package in my bag.

There was no doubt. It was the same cardboard box sealed with duct tape that she had tried to put in my hands. It looked just big enough to hold an electric can opener. There were no labels or writing on the box.

I zipped the bag shut without taking anything out, and left it sitting between my feet and wondered what to do. Tell the flight attendant? What if the box held some sort of contraband? Something that would alert K-9 security dogs when I got off the plane?

Or worse. Could it be a weapon or bomb? I leaned forward, closer to the bag at my feet. Was it ticking? If so, I could not hear it over the noise of the plane. But why would it tick? Surely electronics would have replaced gears, even in homemade bombs.

But how could she have gotten anything like that past security? *There are ways,* said a little voice in my head. *Bribes, blackmail, a security screener who missed something …*

In the end, I decided to do nothing. Tell no one. If the box contained something dangerous, what could be done? Land the plane so I and the package I wasn't supposed to have could be ejected, inspected, and interrogated? I didn't think there was anywhere to land a commercial jet between Detroit and Louisville, anyway. Maybe Cincinnati, but, by air, that was almost to Louisville. Best to sit quietly and hope for the best. And avoid K-9 dogs in Louisville. There were dogs in the Detroit airport, and they apparently hadn't been a problem for Miss Blue Eyes, as I was starting to think of her. But maybe she just got lucky.

On my way out of the Louisville airport, I recalled the flash of images I'd had in Detroit, myself walking along the concourse with the package in my partially unzipped backpack. No chance of that happening. I had not unzipped the bag since I saw what it held, and I surely wasn't going to open it while I was inside the building.

A security agent and a dog appeared far down the concourse. I ducked into the bathroom, found a stall, and waited impatiently for several minutes. When I came out, no dog was in sight. I continued to the parking lot and found a narrow, grassy spot on a traffic island, under a small tree, where exit lanes from I-65 led into the airport.

I took out my phone and pushed the button to dial Lonnie. She answered on the fifth ring.

"May I speak with Leonora, please?" I said.

Brief pause. "Who is this?"

"I'm calling to tell you about exciting news in medical research. Did you know you could earn quick cash by—"

"Stop it, Linc," she said. "And don't call me Leonora."

Leonora was the name on her driver's license, but she was not fond of it.

"Okay. I was wondering if you could do me a favor."

"What kind of favor?" she asked cautiously.

"Come pick me up at the airport?"

"I'm kind of busy now, and I have to work at the museum this afternoon. Can't you call your mom?"

"Well, yeah, but she won't leave the office till four. I'll be stuck here for hours. Please?" I hoped I sounded confident, not whiny.

"There are cabs, Uber. …"

"Too expensive. Unless you can loan me some money?"

She sighed, then laughed. "Okay, Linc. You're not that poor, but you are persistent. Where exactly are you?"

"First lot on the left. I'll be standing at the curb so you don't have to pull in and get stuck at the gate. And I owe you, big time."

"Darn right you do."

I LOOKED AROUND. THERE WERE NO PEOPLE IN SIGHT EXCEPT OCCASIONAL passing cars. Drivers were occupied with parking in time to get through security and catch their flights. They paid me no mind. I knelt and unzipped the pack, and, keeping the box out of sight, just in case, pulled at the duct tape that wrapped it tightly. My Swiss Army knife would have been handy then, but, of course, I had left it at home so it wouldn't be confiscated at security.

Prying my finger into a gap, I saw the smooth, flat top of a silver-colored object. I pushed the flaps wide open, tearing cardboard away from the tape, and, keeping my hands mostly inside the pack, withdrew the object.

The object was just the size to fit in the box. Again, its rectangular dimensions reminded me of an electric can opener, but the front – where the can would go if it were in fact a can opener – had a round dial about three inches wide, two small lens-like protrusions, one red and one green, that I assumed were lights, and a button the size of my fingernail. Beside the button was a single word: *ON.* The dial reminded me of an old-fashioned radio, with a knob in the middle and a red pointer extending outward. Clockwise around the outside of the circle, however, instead of radio frequencies, were words: *Hours, Days, Months,* and *Years.* The indicator arrow pointed to the *D* in *Days.* A minute past twelve, if the dial were the face of an analog clock.

Without thinking about it too much, perhaps because I knew I would do nothing if I hesitated, I pushed the *ON* button. The red light flashed briefly, followed by a steady green light. I immediately grew dizzy, as I had in the Detroit airport. The parking lot disappeared, and I saw Lonnie. She was walking out of the Uptown Theatre, me on her left and Julie on the right. Lonnie held both of our hands as we walked across the parking lot in bright afternoon light. All three of us looked happy, smiling.

As quickly as it came, the vision flickered and was gone.

"*The Creature from the Black Lagoon,*" I said aloud, and looked around. The lot was almost full of parked cars, no people in sight except a couple of travelers, three lanes over, who towed rolling bags and seemed intent on their own destinations.

ADVENTURES TO GO |

The marquee said Creature from the Black Lagoon *was playing*, I said again, this time only to myself. My mother and Lonnie both loved black and white movies from the fifties or older – especially fantasy, horror, and science fiction. I had thus endured – and learned to love – a fair number of them. I found the robot in *The Day the Earth Stood Still* scarier than any imaginary primordial monster, perhaps because it was easier to believe the robot might exist and could turn up anywhere. The poor Creature, on the other hand, was busy minding its own business, threatening no one, until the humans came and started trouble.

10

CHAPTER II

I spotted Lonnie coming around the curve, zipped the backpack, and stood up, ready to jump in when she stopped.

"Working on the masterpiece?" I asked, noticing her hand on the steering wheel. A few flecks of color still dotted the back of her hand. I knew she was occupied with a big canvas, sort of an abstract landscape. "More Van Gogh than Van Gogh" was how she had described her mental image of the way it should look in the end.

"Coming along great. Until I had to stop and play taxi driver."

"Like I said, I owe you. But you didn't *have* to come pick me up – you got a chance to do a friend a favor. Anyway, how about if I pay, next time we go to the movies? Popcorn, the works."

"What, you mean on a date? Or just repaying a favor?"

I considered my words carefully. "Whatever you want it to be, I guess. I mean, a date sounds good to me."

"You guess? Way to sweep a girl off her feet." She smiled though. "There's nothing good playing now. I checked yesterday. But *Creature* is playing this weekend. One screening only." Lonnie glanced at me as she spoke. "What, surely you're not that terrified of a movie monster?"

11

"No, it's not that." She must have taken my surprise as anxiety over seeing a monster movie. "*Creature* is not nearly as scary as *Casablanca*. I mean, Nazis – they were real. And therefore a lot scarier than fictional monsters, or robots from space, which could be real but weren't, as far as I know."

"You looked like you saw a ghost when I mentioned the movie."

"It's just … I had … I've been having these flashes. They're like deja vu, except it's the future. In Detroit, I saw myself leaving the Louisville airport, and then just a while ago, I saw us going to see *Creature*."

Lonnie stared at me. "The road!" I said, pointing at traffic. Now, obviously, was not the time to also tell her someone had put an odd package in my bag. Or that the package seemed to contain a magic box that let me see the future.

"What do you mean, you 'saw' us?" Lonnie asked, glancing in the mirror and signaling to exit the interstate.

"It's probably nothing. I must have seen an announcement on the theater website, and that triggered the image in my head. Really, just deja vu. Except about the future, not the past."

Lonnie merged onto the street and stopped at a red light. "I know you well enough to know when you're not telling me the whole story, but okay. Keep your little secret, for now, if you want." She tucked a strand of stray hair behind her ear.

"I'm not–" I said before the car behind us honked. Lonnie still stared at me. "Green light," I said. "And you can give me the X-ray vision all you want, but it was just a weird mental moment. Nothing to get excited about."

"Like I said, keep your secret if you must," she said, accelerating through the intersection. "How was Detroit? Think you'll go to school there?"

"Probably not. Too expensive, unless I get a scholarship. And Detroit is okay, but not better than Louisville. I'll probably go to U of L. I can study architecture here, too. Then we can still, you know, go to the movies. Or whatever. You know, on a date. Or date*s*." I emphasized the *s* and watched her face in profile and thought I saw a little smile at the idea of my sticking around. *Don't read too much into it*, I told myself. "The Detroit Mercy campus has a really cool clock tower, though. You should paint it."

"Go to Detroit just for a clock?"

"Clock *tower*. But no need to go there. Just look it up online. You could do a Salvador-Dali-type version – you know, desert scene, the clock melting down the side of the tower."

"You know what that would look like?" Lonnie asked, laughing.

I didn't know what she meant. I must have looked confused.

"You know, an erect … thing, with fluids dripping off it? Think Freudian."

"Oh," I said, probably flushing. "Sounds like you're thinking Freudian enough for both of us. But what's wrong with a double meaning or two?"

"Nothing. Not a thing," she said, pulling into my driveway. That strand of long reddish-brown hair fell across her cheek again. She tucked it behind her ear once more and glanced at the dashboard clock. "I really have to get to work."

I knew how important her job at the Speed Art Museum was to her. She wanted to work full-time there after college, because, she often said, artists don't necessarily make a lot of money. I suddenly wanted very much to kiss her. Not that we really had that kind of relationship. We'd known each other since middle school and had always been friends. Sometimes she felt more like my sister than a girlfriend. But today, with no makeup, wearing ripped jeans and an old paint-speckled white T-shirt, she looked very much like someone you'd want to be a girlfriend, even though it felt sort of weird, too. All of which would take too much time to explain, right then, even if I knew exactly how to explain it to myself. Plus, I knew she liked girls. Not that she was a lesbian, I thought. Just open-minded. Or maybe she was a lesbian, but she was definitely … interested in a lot of possibilities, too. Her adventurous spirit was one of the things I liked about her.

Not that I would have put it into those exact words, or any words. "Adventurous spirit" is what an older person says when they look back at what it felt like to be seventeen.

So all I said was, "Okay, thanks for the ride. We'll text about the movies?"

She nodded, putting the car in reverse. "Right, text. Bye!"

13

CHAPTER III

My mom was at the desk in her work area between the kitchen and living room when I came in. Ours was your typical modest, older middle-class house in the suburbs – stairs on the left when you came in the front door, and to the right, living room, etc. Mom was (and still is) an attorney, specializing in environmental law. So it's not like we're rich. She works for the EPA.

It looked like she was still immersed in reading legal precedents on her current case. It involved land development and air and water pollution. She'd been working on the same issue for months. I'm proud of my mom, but I get lost in the details when she talks about work. Plus, the cases all sound pretty much the same to me – somebody wants to build an apartment building or mall, but they have no plan to avoid killing more trees and more fish in the river where the sewage will likely wind up. People have to live and buy groceries somewhere, argues the rich guy or big corporation that wants to bulldoze acres of fields or trees and pave what used to be a park or pasture or forest. Maybe so, goes my mom's counterargument, but there are better ways to make that happen, ways that don't wreck the planet. And so on. Meanwhile, the human race goes on making more people who will require more space and resources.

| THE ARTIFACT

She glanced up when I came in. "Hello, Linc. How was Detroit?"

"Okay. I thought you'd be at the office."

"I was. But I came home early. I can read just as well here, and I thought you might need a ride."

"Lonnie picked me up."

"Oh. She's a nice girl." That's Mom's lawyer-ish way of avoiding saying anything substantial. I know she doesn't dislike Lonnie, but she wants grandkids, and she doesn't think Lonnie is the mommy type. I'm not sure she is either. Not because she might be gay. That's one of the silly prejudices you hear – gay people can't have kids, or shouldn't have kids. Actually, *silly* is too nice a word for that kind of attitude. Let's try *mean* and *stupid*. Mom is neither mean nor stupid, but she knows some people just don't want to have kids. Most of the time, I'm not sure I want the job of being a dad, either. Or, sometimes, I *am* sure – that I don't. At least not for a long time.

"So the college was just okay? You don't sound too enthusiastic."

"I'm thinking I'll probably want to stay close to home for a while. And I don't want to borrow a lot of money for school."

"I'll find the money. You go where you think is best for you."

"Okay, Mom. I'm kind of tired. Can we talk later?"

She nodded and turned back to the computer. I knew she meant what she said about going where I wanted for college, even if it cost more. Like I said, we were not rich, but proving she could be a great single mom was always a sore spot for her. Or maybe not exactly sore, but a point of honor, anyway.

My dad had been a soldier, an Army Ranger. He was killed in Afghanistan when I was too young to understand what the word "Afghanistan" even meant. My mom was bitterly opposed to the war and his participation in it. I asked her once why she married a soldier if she didn't like war. She got a far-away look in her eyes and said, "It's complicated, Linc. You don't necessarily choose to fall in love."

I kind of knew what she meant about falling in love and choosing or not choosing. It just happens. You like who you like. You love who you love.

15

Whatever the thing was that I carried upstairs to my room, I had to face two facts: it was weird, and it was probably dangerous. And a third fact: it wasn't mine. It had ended up in my possession, but someone – maybe Miss Blue Eyes herself – was likely to want it back.

A fourth fact: it gave flashes, or visions of the future, but that future was not carved in stone. Not exactly, anyway. In the Detroit airport, I had seen myself carrying the package through the Louisville airport as if it were nothing remarkable, instead of what I had actually done – keeping it in my pack and trying not to look suspicious.

In addition to the facts, a question. Why hadn't I turned it over to security and told them the whole story? I told myself that, by the time I got to Louisville, I was implicated. I'd carried the box all the way from Detroit, and the story of feeling dizzy and seeing the future and being surprised to find the thing in my backpack – well, would the TSA buy that story? I wouldn't believe it myself if it hadn't happened to me.

Upstairs, I put my pack on the bed, pulled the box out, removed the object from the box, and set it on the desk. The dial was like an eye, watching me. Waiting for something.

I picked up the box and examined it more closely, left, right, and upside down. Aside from the dial, the two lights, and the on/off button, it was unmarked, made of what looked like black plastic and aluminum or stainless steel. Or maybe the silver-colored parts were shiny plastic, too. No labels, no serial numbers. No vents for a cooling fan. Nowhere to plug in a cord. No battery compartment. Didn't it need a power source? Maybe it pulled magnetic energy out of the air.

I put it back on the desk and stared, trying to figure out what else was odd about the object. After a moment, it came to me – there were no seams, no screws, nothing to indicate assembly. Not even any recessed holes for screwdrivers, the kind you've seen if you ever tried to take an old stereo apart – holes with warnings beside them that say, "Do not remove cover. Risk of electric shock. No user-serviceable parts inside." The box looked like it was made all in one piece. Or as if it had been laid, like an egg.

| THE ARTIFACT

It was just a matter of time until I pushed that on/off button again, so I decided to get it over with.

The red light lit up for a moment, and then the green one. *Green is for go?* I speculated. The box made a quiet hum, like an amplified speaker not connected to an input signal. This time I felt a mild electric shock. Or it seemed like an electric shock. *What kind of plastic conducts electricity?* I wondered, quickly pulling my finger back. The hum continued. I pushed the button again, after only a couple of seconds. The lights went out, and the hum stopped. The flashes of future events had happened when my hands were on or near the object, so I avoided touching anything but the button. I'd had enough visions – and shocks – for now, and I already had enough to think about.

Naturally, a lot of those thoughts were about Lonnie and the half-truth I had told her, how I'd had a flash of us going to see *Creature* with Julie. I needed to tell her the whole story. Even if she thought I was crazy. I had to come clean. Calling it *coming clean* pretty much explains why I had to tell her. The box could show me things she might consider private. Secret, even. For instance, she had told me, once, that she thought Avril Lavigne was way sexier than Britney Spears, and that led to a whole conversation about how important it was to be open to feelings, regardless of gender or other people's prejudices. So I knew she liked girls, but it wasn't as if she felt safe announcing the fact to the world just yet. Her family would not be happy, and it wasn't like people don't still get attacked, verbally or otherwise, for being who they are.

If I didn't tell her, it would feel like spying. And I liked her, the way you like someone you think about in those dreams – and daydreams – where anything can happen. Anyway, this object – it was the kind of secret you have to tell your friends. At least one of them.

CHAPTER IV

T he next morning, I called Lonnie. "Meet me at Willow Park?" I asked. She agreed. I stowed the magic box in a Louisville Free Public Library tote bag of my mom's and headed out.

"I HAVE TO TELL YOU SOMETHING," I TOLD LONNIE. "AND SHOW YOU SOMEthing. But you can't tell anybody." We sat at a picnic table in Willow Park, which was about halfway between her house and mine.

"Gossip? Great! Who doesn't love a juicy tidbit?"

"No. Not gossip. And I'm serious. You can't tell anybody. Absolutely no one."

"Right. You're secretly a spy from North Korea, sent to infiltrate the U.S. art scene. Starting from Kentucky. No one will get wise to that strategy."

"I mean it."

She looked at me and didn't say anything for a moment, tucked that strand of hair behind her ear the way she always did when she was thinking, and asked, "Okay, if it's such a big secret, why tell me?"

"Because …" I wanted to say *Because I love you*, but that was a whole other talk. "Because we're friends, and because it's about you."

"Okay, Linc, spill." She sounded very no-nonsense now.

I took the magic box from the bag and put it on the plank seat between us. I told her the whole story of Miss Blue Eyes at the Detroit airport. I recounted how I saw myself carrying the box through the Louisville airport. I told her about the mental image of us at the movies with Julie. "Okay, this is where you tell me I'm crazy," I finished.

"I would if I didn't know you. And know you don't play this kind of joke. There's obviously only one thing to do."

"Toss this thing in the river?"

"No, silly. Test it. Apply the scientific method. One strange event doesn't mean much by itself. Two strange experiences might just be a coincidence. But a third time – that would have to mean something."

"Test it how?" I asked.

"Try to get it to give you another flash, or vision. Whatever. So how does it work?"

"How would I know?"

"Okay, then. Let's start with the *on* button."

"I did that already. It makes a faint hum, which you could miss if you're outside and there's wind or traffic."

"So let's hear it."

I pushed the button, and the red light flashed once and stayed dark. The green light glowed steadily. Lonnie inclined her head toward the box.

"Fair warning – it gives you a little shock if you touch the sides while it's on," I said.

She drew back. "What, like an electrical shock?"

"I guess. A mild one. There's no cord, obviously, and I don't see where you could put batteries in it, or even connect a USB charger. It's not like it knocks you out or anything. Just one more weird thing about … whatever this is."

The noise of a passing car faded, and she leaned closer to the box again and nodded. "I hear it. Like a stereo that's not playing anything. Does it have a speaker?"

"No. Not on the outside, anyway. What you see is what you get. Lights, dial, on/off button."

ADVENTURES TO GO |

"And the times when you had the flashes, or premonitions, the lights were on?"

"The first time, who knows? I discovered the box was in my backpack after I got on the plane, and I didn't even know I had it. The second time, in the parking lot, the green light was on. It seems like the red light flashes and goes out, like a warning that you have turned it on. Or maybe it just tells you the box is not ready to work yet. Then the green one stays on, as you see."

"And did you say or do anything? Ask it a question? Turn the dial?"

"Are you kidding? I was too freaked out by having carried a package from a stranger onto an airplane. I was still wondering if it was a bomb or box of drugs."

"Let's test it then," Lonnie said. "Set the dial for one day ahead. Let's ask it a question."

"About what?"

"I don't know … the winning lottery numbers," she suggested. "Or how old we'll be when we die. Who the next president will be."

"Now that I think about it, there are a lot of things I don't want to know about. Like death and future politics. If it's good news, well, it will be a good surprise. If it's bad news, what can you do about it?"

"If you are going to be run over by a bus, that would be worth knowing, just to avoid it."

"Which raises a question – all kinds of questions, actually," I said. "How much of the future can we change?"

"Enough to make a difference. Say you do see yourself getting hit by a bus in the future. So you look out for buses and make sure it never happens. Not stepping in front of a bus should be one hundred percent up to you. Free will and all."

"Some people don't believe in free will," I pointed out. "We are who we are, and we are either cautious and look where we're going, or we forget. And then there's the Oedipus story, the play we read in sophomore English. Knowing the future doesn't mean you can avoid it. Oedipus is told he is destined to kill his father and marry his mother. He's determined to not let that happen. But his efforts to prevent the tragedies are what cause them. He can't avoid his fate."

20

| THE ARTIFACT

"Maybe some people question free will and fate, but everybody likes money. So, then, lottery numbers?"

I nodded. She was right, I decided. Some small voice in the back of my head told me this was crazy, that I should put this thing in the back of my closet and wait for its owner – or previous possessor – to come and ask for it back, but when you're seventeen, you don't always listen, not even to the voices in your own head. Or when you're seventy-seven, I suppose, if curiosity is strong enough. "Okay," I said, and turned the dial to the *One Day* mark.

"Do we say our question out loud, or just think it?" Lonnie wondered.

I shook my head. "Dunno. I hope it's not like a genie, and you get only three wishes. I had my hand on the box before, so maybe we need to touch it."

We reached at the same time, and our hands came in contact before mine was on the box. I felt a different kind of tingle from touching Lonnie, and then the familiar mild zap from the box.

Nothing happened for a few moments. I opened my mouth to speak. I was going to say maybe the box was only an odd sort of computer hard drive, when the premonition washed over me. The park, the picnic table, Lonnie sitting beside me – they all vanished. I saw a lottery ticket with a series of numbers scratched off. Quickly, despite the dizziness, I started memorizing the numbers.

A few seconds later, the premonition faded.

"Did you see it?" I asked. "Them, I mean – the numbers?"

Lonnie said nothing. She was busy writing on her hand with a pen she had pulled from her pocket. She paused and said, "What did you see?"

I told her my numbers, which she also wrote on her hand. "We didn't ask an actual question," I said. "Not out loud, anyway. So I guess it just shows you something related to what you are thinking about."

"That's odd. They're different," she said, holding her left hand up for me to see and tucking the strand of hair with the right.

"Maybe they're both winners?"

"I guess. For different amounts, you suppose"?

I shrugged. "Beats me. I have never bought a lottery ticket in my life. My mom calls it the idiot tax."

"Well, this once, I guess we should pay it."

21

"Right. In the name of science. It's the only way to be sure of the outcome."

"Don't they announce the numbers on TV, whoever wins?" Lonnie asked. "We'd know these are winning numbers even if we didn't buy tickets."

"Okay, but how silly would we feel if they were, and we let somebody else win?"

"And you think we will win?"

"One way to find out," I said. "But I think … it can't be this easy, can it?"

"Doesn't seem like it should be. We don't know the whole story. What this thing really is. Who made it? Why? And why did someone put it in your bag at the airport?"

"When you put it that way, we are probably crazy for even turning it on."

"All I know is, there's no free lunch," Lonnie said. "Somebody always has to pay the piper. And a dozen other clichés. Or think of the Ring in Tolkien's stories – there are consequences for using it."

"Can the machine read minds, or did it just hear us talking about lottery numbers?" I wondered. "It somehow had to know what we were thinking. If it can read minds, that by itself is a fair-sized price to pay. Who knows what else it knows about us, now? Maybe it's beaming all our secrets to a spy satellite, even as we speak."

"If that's the case, you're going to have to stop watching porn and using my Netflix password."

"I never … use your password," I said. This was Lonnie I was talking to. Maybe the box knew my secrets, or maybe it didn't, but she did. "Anyway, we have no idea if these numbers are any good. I saw a ticket with these numbers scratched off, but I didn't see any checks with my name or your name. Or any big stacks of cash. Did you?"

She shook her head. "No, but this is an experiment, remember? Let's go buy some lottery tickets."

So that's what we did.

CHAPTER V

On the way home, after we bought the tickets and said our see-you-laters, I got lost. I couldn't remember which street to turn down to get from where I was to our house. Keep in mind I had lived in the same house in Louisville my entire life, and had been to Willow Park dozens of times. Hundreds, probably. And the store where we bought the tickets was only a few blocks away. I'd been there many times, too.

Nevertheless, I had to use maps on my phone to find my way. I guess I was lucky I remembered I had a phone and how to use it.

It was like forgetting your own name.

As soon as I got home, I called Lonnie, told her what had happened to me, and asked if she had had any similar problems.

"Not that I remember," she said. "I've been making a list of questions about the future – where do we go to college, what will my major be, will I get married, etc."

"Now we know what the price for getting answers to those kinds of questions is. Or one of the possible prices, anyway," I said. "See the future, forget the past." Under normal circumstances, Lonnie's mention of the

ADVENTURES TO GO |

word *married* would have inspired a chain of questions that might or not be asked out loud – married to who? Did she think of me that way? Or Julie? Or some hypothetical person she had not yet met?

"I hope it's worth the price," Lonnie said. "For you. Like I said, I don't think I've forgotten anything. At least, I remembered how to get home."

"I didn't forget anything when I saw brief flashes of the future before, though," I said. "Maybe it was because I didn't have an actual question in mind. No charge if you don't ask for anything."

"How do you know you didn't forget anything the first time?" she asked.

"I don't remember forgetting anything."

"Do you remember forgetting the way to your house?"

"No, I just ... didn't know. Though it came back to me when I looked at the map. So at least some of the memory losses are temporary."

"Exactly," Lonnie said. "Memory is like a book. You don't know if there's a missing page until you open the book and see it's gone. I guess if you're lucky, you find where the torn-out page went. Did you ever have a goldfish?"

"You know I did, when I was in seventh grade." I had told her often about that fish, how much fun it was to watch it swim around, feed it, wonder what it was like to be a fish.

"What was its name?"

"I don't know. I don't think it had a name."

Silence.

"Hello?" I said.

"Winnie the Pooh."

"What about him?"

"You named that fish Winnie the Pooh. It was a joke. You wouldn't have forgotten that. Not unless something made you forget."

It was Lonnie's turn to ask if I was still there.

"This is getting a little scary," I said.

"A lot scary. I wonder if the effects are cumulative. You've been exposed to the machine more than me. Maybe that's why I don't seem to have forgotten anything. At least nothing super important."

"Yet. That you've noticed. What if you've forgotten how to brush your teeth?"

"Do what? To my what?"

24

"Brush your teeth," I repeated.

"Brush my teeth? What does that even mean?"

"Oh, no, what have we done?" I felt a sense of dread building.

"Hey, just kidding. A little joke. I remember all about brushing. Also rinsing and flossing."

I was too relieved to be mad. "Okay. But not funny. Forgetting things you know you should know is … it's too much like losing your mind."

"Maybe you should store the box somewhere outside the house," Lonnie suggested. "In the tool shed. Or a locker at the bus station."

"It's probably harmless if it's not turned on."

"Or maybe it's like radioactive elements. They don't have on/off switches. How can you be sure?"

"I'm not," I admitted. "All we know for sure is there's a lot we don't know. Anyway, let's hope the amnesia is temporary."

We talked a little longer and said goodbye.

I SLEPT AND DREAMED OF A LONG, NARROW, CURVING CORRIDOR WHERE JACK-in-the-boxes kept popping open and shouting "Surprise!" at unexpected moments. As the corridor went on, the boxes got bigger and bigger, as did things that popped out of them. There were doors, but each door led only to another corridor with more boxes. The last box was too big to step around, and when the leering figure popped out, teetering and bouncing atop its spring, it was a great-white-shark-sized Winnie-the-Goldfish-Pooh.

"You have giant teeth," I said.

"The better to eat you with!" The fish dived at me.

I awoke to sunshine and birds singing.

CHAPTER VI

When I went down for breakfast, Mom was looking at aerial views of woods on the internet. She was still at home because it was Saturday, though she would probably go to the office later.

"Nice trees," I said. "Why are you interested in them?" My mom appreciates trees and animals that call the woods home, but generally from a distance. Or at least no closer than the well-kept hiking path that starts near the parking lot.

"Because the land is for sale. But forget bidding. Unless you know a generous billionaire."

"No, but why would you be interested?"

"A big corporate developer wants to put a mall and apartment buildings there," she said, now scrolling over photos taken close up, showing big trees, a brook, deer, and birds. "It will mean environmental destruction on a grand scale."

"Isn't there some way to stop it?" I asked. That is the sort of thing she does, working in environmental law. "Get the court to order an impact study? Have it declared a landmark? Find a rare bird species that nests there?" Being an attorney's kid, I had learned there are strings that can be pulled to slow down a disaster, if not stop it entirely.

"Sure, lots of ways, but they all cost a fortune. Especially if you need them done in a hurry. I'm too busy trying to keep toxic factory waste out of the drinking water. Not much time for this other problem. But I plan to try. Believe me."

"So why not just get someone else to buy the land? Someone who will preserve it."

"Ha. You have the name of that billionaire?"

"Me. Maybe I'll be rich before you know it."

"Very funny." She tousled my hair like she did when I was twelve and went to dress for work.

AFTER BREAKFAST, I CALLED LONNIE. I DIDN'T ASK IF SHE REMEMBERED FORgetting anything; she would tell me if she did. Otherwise, it seemed like a jinx to mention it. Not that I was superstitious. But since I had come into possession of an apparently magic box that seemed to predict the future, I guessed I should reconsider what even counted as superstition.

"Are we still going to see *Creature*?"

"When were we ever going to do that?" she asked. "I didn't even know it was playing."

"You remember, when you gave me a ride from the airport ... and we talked last night." I stopped. Obviously, she *didn't* remember. "I think we've just figured out the price of your lottery numbers. You forgot what we talked about after you picked me up."

"Picked you up?"

"At the airport. If this is a joke, like forgetting how to brush your teeth, it's still not funny."

She was quiet for a moment. "No joke. It's coming back to me now. I remember talking to you last night. But I still have no memory of that other conversation. None whatsoever. I can't even remember driving you home. We were at the airport, and then I was stopping at your house. It's like the rest never happened."

"This is getting out of hand," I said. "I guess we shouldn't use the box again. Ever. We thought the effects might be cumulative, but it looks like even one use is dangerous."

She didn't disagree.

ADVENTURES TO GO |

We decided, once more, that we were going to see the movie. "We should see if Julie can come, too," Lonnie said.

With a growing sense of deja vu – the real kind this time – I said, "You didn't already ask her?"

"No … why do you say that? Oh, wait. The other day?"

"Yep," I said. "You made the same suggestion on the way from the airport."

"Okay, I guess I'll call her again. See if she brings it up," Lonnie said. "It would be too weird to call and ask if I already asked her. And we're still not telling anyone about the box, right?"

"Right."

"Okay, I'll call you back in a minute."

A little while later, Lonnie rang back and said Julie had asked if we were still going to the movie. "So that much is okay, anyway."

"Great. See you in a few hours."

28

CHAPTER VII

Early that afternoon, I mowed grass and trimmed the hedges, jobs that had been mine since I was twelve, when Mom decided I could be trusted not to chop off my toes or fingers. Afterward, I put away the mower and hedge clippers, took a shower, dressed in clean jeans and my best blue tee-shirt, and rode my bike to Lonnie's house. Her family lived nine or eleven blocks away, depending on the route. Which depended on traffic. Weekend traffic being unpredictable, I took the long way, down side streets and alleys with minimal numbers of cars.

My bike was an old-fashioned ten-speed, a Schwinn Le Tour, one of my prize possessions. There's something special about riding a bike made years before you were born. I do have a driver's license, but we have only one car, which Mom had taken to the office. We had discussed getting a car for me, but it seemed like a waste of money. We weren't poor, but we weren't rich enough not to care how we spent money.

Lonnie was sitting on the porch steps when I got there. She wore a white tee-shirt and had an Oxford button-down over her shoulder. Her jeans had fashionable holes in the right places. I heard the sounds of a baseball game through the screen door.

ADVENTURES TO GO |

"My dad is asleep in front of the TV, but he said we could use the car," she said. "It's going to be cool in the theater. Don't you want something with sleeves?" I was wearing just my jeans and blue shirt.

"I'll be okay." I knew she was right, but if she went in the house to find a shirt or jacket for me, her dad might wake up. I didn't really want to talk to him. I didn't think he liked me, but I had no idea why. Or maybe he just made me uncomfortable. Since I was interested in architecture and he was an engineer, we should have been able to find something to talk about. His job included knocking down old buildings to make new ones, though, and I liked the old places. Like the Uptown Theatre, where Lonnie and I were headed.

"Okay. I don't mind sharing popcorn and a Coke, but you're not getting my shirt," she said.

My heart did a little dance when she mentioned sharing popcorn and a Coke. From experience, I knew it was incredible when our fingers brushed in the popcorn bag. Even better when I drank from the straw that had touched her lips. One kind of touching could so easily lead to other kinds.

"I guess we'd better get going," I said. "Especially if Julie's coming. You didn't tell her about … that thing, did you?" For all I knew, her dad might have woken up and might overhear.

"Of course not. We agreed to keep it quiet."

"I know. Just a memory check."

"It's our little secret." Lonnie smiled mischievously, standing and walking toward the car at the end of the driveway. "Not jealous, are you?"

"No, but —" I felt myself blushing. "I don't want anyone to think I'm crazy, either. And I sure as heck don't want anyone to know about the thing, and what it does. You know I'm not crazy, from experience. But if we told anyone else, they'd either think we're crazy, or they'd believe us. Which would be too dangerous."

"You know my lips are sealed. Why else did you tell me?"

"I know," I said. We got in the car and buckled up.

After Lonnie had backed out of the driveway, I said, "They announce the numbers tonight. If we both have winning numbers, people will think it's an incredible coincidence."

"Coincidences do happen. It's not like we cheated. So let people think whatever they think."

30

"Somebody would probably say using the box was cheating, if they knew, but I doubt anyone's bothered to make a law against consulting honest-to-goodness magical devices." After a minute, I added, "You still remember the way to Julie's house? I ask only because my sense of direction was the first thing I lost."

"Of course. I maybe forgot some stuff, but I'm not senile."

"What's 'senile' mean?" I asked, sounding as earnest as possible.

"It means—" Lonnie began but saw I was looking too serious. "Wasn't funny when I pretended to forget. Still not. But if being an architect doesn't work out, you can always try comedy."

IT WAS A FIVE-MINUTE DRIVE TO JULIE'S HOUSE. HER DAD WAS A TRUCK DRIVer, home maybe once a month for a day or two. She had said her mom was taking her little brother to get new shoes and a haircut, so we didn't have to choose between going in to make awkward small talk or being rude.

By way of full disclosure, Julie was my friend – and Lonnie's – the same way Lonnie was my friend. I mean, we were not possessive about each other. But we liked to have fun. We didn't need labels for each other or ourselves, but I suppose you could say I mostly liked girls, and Lonnie and Julie were more into girls. Still, they liked me, too, in a physical way. We all three liked girls, so what was to disagree about? We didn't bother with labels, which are always limiting, didn't try to put ourselves in any one sort of box. We just were who we were. We liked who we liked.

I knew they had fun – yes, that kind of fun – together sometimes when I was not around. Which was great, as far as I was concerned. It wasn't as if I couldn't appreciate a beautiful boy or man, either, at least from a distance. Not that I really wanted to have sex with anyone but girls. I once found myself staring at Richie Thomas when I saw the bulge in his underwear growing larger. We were changing for gym class at school, and my penis got, you know, excited, too. I looked long enough that he looked back, and smiled. We both looked away, a little embarrassed for reasons we could not have explained (or at least I couldn't at the time), and nothing ever came of it. When I fell asleep thinking of anyone, it was usually Lonnie or Julie. But who knew where the future might lead?

I owed my outlook on sex to my very enlightened mother. She explained the basics to me when I was nine. We had been watching *Charlie's Angels*, the movie version from 2000. My mom's influence is part of the reason I like old movies, as some of the best times of my childhood were spent watching with her. What counts as old depends on when you were born, I guess. *Charlie's Angels* probably didn't seem old to Mom. But it was made before I was born, so it was old to me.

Anyway, a lot of what Mom told me that day about sex I already knew, since I grew up in the age of the internet, but it was still good to have some clarity established by an adult I trusted. She must have noticed my erection, inspired by the scene where Cameron Diaz, playing Natalie, dances around in her underwear and greets the delivery guy at the door. It's not exactly hardcore porn. The whole scene is very PG-13, but by that age, my boy hormones were starting to do their thing. When you're nine, you can get turned on by a pretty girl dancing in her underwear and not even know exactly why. At least, that's the way I remember it.

Instead of making me feel bad or embarrassed in any way, Mom commented, "Cameron Diaz is pretty, isn't she?" and after the movie, we had an informative, guilt-free talk. A couple of days later, she gave me a copy of "Sex is a Funny Word." That was one of many lessons I got from her on how to think rationally about things and why ignorance is never an essential ingredient for being a good person.

JULIE WAS WAITING BY THE MAILBOX AT HER HOUSE. SHE WORE A WHITE DRESS and had curled her dark hair in an old-fashioned style that reminded me of Julie Adams, the star of *Creature*. As it was no doubt intended to do. I could see why Lonnie had a crush on her. I did, too, though I had a bigger crush on Lonnie.

After we picked up Julie, and Lonnie turned onto Bardstown Road, I said, "I saw a clip on YouTube of Julie Adams talking about making the movie. She said the underwater scenes were done by someone else. I read elsewhere that Ginger Stanley was the stuntwoman. I want to see if I can spot the difference."

"Ha. You just like seeing her in that white bathing suit," Julie said.

"Seeing who, Ginger or Julie?" I asked.

"Both, I'm sure."

"Well, of course he does. So do I," Lonnie said. "Who wouldn't? Her butt is spectacular. Make that their butts, I guess."

I did not disagree. I did, however, consider myself the luckiest seventeen-year-old on the planet, sandwiched between these two girls in the front seat of a Toyota on the way to the movies on a Saturday afternoon in summer. If life could get any better, I didn't know how. Then I thought, *We could win the lottery. That would be an improvement.* With all the confidence of youth, I assumed I was immune to horror stories that happen when people's lives are disrupted by what looks like good fortune. Right then, the problem of having lost some memories seemed very far away. So I told my inner voice to be quiet and enjoy this brilliant afternoon.

The Uptown Theatre was in the Schuster Building. The view from outside, complete with a small cupola on the roof peak, was as interesting in its way as the movies that played inside. To me, old buildings feel like time machines. You walk in, and something built by people who no longer exist takes you to the past. You walk out, and you're back in the future.

The auditorium still had the orchestra pit, which was actually used on rare occasions, including when a silent film was shown. It was a different experience every time the movie played, if the music changed. More like seeing a play, with live actors, where anything could happen, no matter what the script said. Which is how so-called real life goes – who knows what the script says, if one even exists?

We had gotten tickets online, though it was not as if the movie was going to be sold out. So we showed our passes on our phones, got popcorn and a Coke – one large, to share – and took our seats in the same arrangement as in the car. I held the popcorn, and hands from either side occasionally missed when reaching for the bag. The hands strayed downward sometimes, and I didn't know if I was embarrassed or excited. It would have been impossible for Lonnie or Julie to miss the bulge when Lonnie took Julie's hand and held it, lying across my zipper. I did my best not to let anything twitch, but I almost certainly did not succeed.

THE MOVIE WAS GREAT, AS ALWAYS, AND I REALLY WOULD NOT HAVE KNOWN, just by watching, that it was Ginger Stanley, not Julie Adams, being stalked

ADVENTURES TO GO |

underwater by the Gill Man. By the time we finished, dusk was settling over the city.

And yes, Lonnie took my hand and squeezed it affectionately, holding Julie's hand on her other side, as we crossed the parking lot. Everything was just as it looked in the premonition I'd had that day at the airport.

"So, what to do now?" Lonnie wondered aloud.

"I should probably get home," Julie said. "My mom gets worried if I stay out late."

"Late?" I said. "It's not even ten o'clock." I had been friends with Lonnie for years, but Julie had gone to a different middle school, so we had been friends with her only since last year. The friendship was almost inevitable, once we found out she liked old movies, too. Lonnie had noticed her watching *Casablanca* on her phone one day after school, and everything followed from there.

"She probably worries that you're making sweet, sweet love to some girl if you stay out late," Lonnie said, unlocking the car. It was hot inside, so we left the doors open and gave it a minute to cool off.

"Ha. She wouldn't mind that one bit. Girls don't get girls pregnant."

"She hasn't heard of birth control? Condoms? The pill?" Lonnie asked.

"Of course. But it's my dad I have to worry about. If he found out ..."

"So he'd rather you get pregnant than take precautions?" I asked.

"He'd rather I be frigid as a statue. He imagines I'm still a virgin, and will be until I get married. Or die an old maid, which is what he'd probably like best."

"So, what, he's living in the dark ages?" I asked.

"Pretty much."

"And your mom is okay with his attitude?"

"Not really. But what can she do?"

That question sounded too complicated for me to answer. So I just asked, "Doesn't he want grandkids?"

"Not if it means he has to admit his little girl is all grown up, I guess."

"Too bad you can't stay out later," Lonnie said. "I was going to show you the new masterpiece-in-progress. It's part of my Rothko phase. Gigantic rectangles of color, but set in the middle of landscapes. Influenced by Van Gogh. A 'Starry Nights' feel to it all. At least, that's what I'm hoping for."

"We have next week. It will be summer all summer," I said.

34

Little did I know just how much stranger that summer was going to be, how many more distractions were headed our way.

"What if you had the colorful rectangles draped over dead tree branches, like in a Dali painting?" I wondered.

"I think that would look like somebody ran out of places to hang their laundry," Julie said.

Lonnie parked on the street in front of Julie's house. I was still sitting in the middle. Lonnie glanced at the house, curtains drawn but windows lit, and leaned across to kiss Julie goodnight. Julie leaned into the kiss, and for a moment their lips parted and tongues touched.

"I would say I'm feeling left out, but that's impossible when we're all so close," I said. They both kissed me next, Julie first and then Lonnie. The movie was great, but the kisses were better. I can never see or think of *Creature from the Black Lagoon* without being reminded of that summer night.

After Julie said goodnight, we didn't talk much on the way back to Lonnie's house, where I had left my bike. It was the comfortable silence that can exist only between friends.

Before I left, Lonnie and I agreed to watch the lottery drawing at eleven that night, which would probably be on just a few minutes after I got home, and text or call when we saw the results. Win or lose, they would surely be interesting.

CHAPTER VIII

Mom's car was in the driveway, but her downstairs work spot was empty and her bedroom was dark. I guessed she was asleep, so I went upstairs quietly.

I had a slip of paper with lottery numbers – Lonnie's and mine – written on it. The winning numbers would be posted online, but I turned on the small TV in my room instead. I muted the volume and listened to the quiet sounds of the house, the air conditioning clicking off as the night cooled outside, the mini-refrigerator by my desk turning on. I was too full of nervous energy to look at my phone. Between feelings of wonder and euphoria from being with Lonnie and Julie and the bizarre circumstance of having a machine that seemed to predict the future, I didn't think I could absorb any more excitement. But it turned out I could.

When the numbers showed up on the screen, I had to read them three times to begin believing our numbers had won the multi-million-dollar prize. I pushed the wrong contact on my phone twice with trembling fingers before I got it right.

"They won," I said when she answered. "Our numbers won."

"I know. Mine did. But yours didn't."

| THE ARTIFACT

In the excitement and disbelief of comparing what was on the paper to what was on TV, I had forgotten to note which numbers had won. I looked again, but the channel had moved on to celebrities mutely chatting with a talk-show host. "They didn't?"

"No. I have the winners here on my computer. But don't worry – I'll split the prize with you. Fifty-fifty."

"You don't have to do that," I said. "Your ticket, your numbers, your prize."

"Yeah, but I wouldn't have them except for your ... you know. The thing."

"We wouldn't even have thought of buying tickets if not for the thing." We had no real name for the device that shouldn't exist but did, and it seemed wrong to talk much about it out loud, especially on the phone. Probably we'd just seen too many classic James Bond movies. How long until I started pasting a hair on the door frame or windowsill to see if anyone had been in my room, like Bond in *Dr. No*? Or carrying a taser, like Morgan in *The Spy Who Dumped Me*?

"That's true," Lonnie said. "I've never bought a lottery ticket before in my life. So what does this mean?"

"What do you mean, 'what does it mean'? It means you're rich! Or at least comfortably well-off. It means you can go to college wherever you want. Whenever you want. And you don't have to work at the museum anymore."

"Well, it means the same for you," she said. "Did you count how many zeroes are in that jackpot? But I like the museum. Not quitting that job."

"A lot of zeroes."

"No kidding, it's a lot. So if you want to go to school in Detroit, you can. But I don't understand why the numbers you saw the other day were not winners. Did I just get lucky? If the thing tells the future, why did we have different numbers?"

"I have no idea." Lately, I'd had plenty of occasions to reflect on the known and the unknown. "But it seems the predictions are not infallible."

"Maybe they have to leave room for free will. Or the butterfly effect. The unpredictable. Chaos. Results of random chance."

"Probably," I said. "But what about your parents? Especially your dad? Won't he want to tell you what you can do with the money?"

37

ADVENTURES TO GO |

"What he doesn't know won't hurt him. Or us."

I didn't ask exactly who *us* was, where Julie fit into all these sudden new possibilities. Instead, I said, "Wonder how long you have to cash in a ticket. Does it expire?" I put the phone on speaker so I could look up the answer while we talked.

Lonnie was faster on the keys. "Six months. Or almost six months. You can collect on a winning ticket up to one hundred eighty days after it won. I'll be eighteen in five months, and then my parents' opinions won't matter a bit."

I felt relieved – we didn't have to make any big decisions right away. "So I guess we should just wait and think about things for a while," I said.

"I guess that's right," she said, "What are you doing tomorrow?"

"I have no idea. Maybe start looking for a summer job." Mom could always help me get a job at her office, as she had done before, but I was a teenager. I wanted to stretch my wings. Which Mom understood.

"It's Sunday. Nothing's open. Well, not most places where you'd want to work, anyway. "

"My computer is always open. I'll just start looking for possibilities."

"Besides, you don't need the money. We're sharing, remember?"

"Experience still looks good on my college applications. Proves I'm a real go-getter. I don't just sit around twiddling my thumbs. What are you doing tomorrow?"

"Working. The museum is open on Sundays. Which gives me an idea – you could get a job there. The pay's not that great, but, hey, who cares, now that we're rich? And like you said, the museum experience would look good on your applications."

"No offense, but the Speed is ugly," I said. "The expansion, anyway. It looks like somebody's idea of what to do with used gutters from an old house." The add-on to the museum had been finished a few years before, with a lot of metal and glass and concrete. Some people saw the design as a bold effect, but to me it felt cold and industrial.

"Who cares? From inside, you won't be looking at it anyway. Some day when you are king of the architects, you can redesign it. Meanwhile, working there would give your resume that boost you want."

"Probably so. What would I do there, anyway?"

38

| THE ARTIFACT

"I don't know. Depends, I guess," she said. "Just don't start by criticizing the architecture."

We said goodnight, and I fell asleep to memories of two very different but very attractive girls leaning over to kiss each other. Well, after a few minutes, I fell asleep. You know what I mean.

CHAPTER IX

CHAPTER IX

The next morning, I looked at online job listings and quickly remembered there were lots of reasons to go to college. Serving burgers and fries or mopping floors were jobs for people with no degree or special training or no relevant experience. That was not how I wanted to spend my life. Of course, if I worked at the Speed Museum, that might be what I ended up doing there until fall. Mopping up, that is. Then I remembered the museum even had a cafe. I had never eaten there, so I looked up the menu. Sure enough, burgers, some of which I might get to flip. I was now feeling rather glad Lonnie was the kind of girl who shares.

It felt like time for a bike ride.

I RODE ALONG THE RIVER ON A MOSTLY DESERTED TRAIL, FARTHER FROM PARKing lots than most walkers or riders had ventured that day. Maybe the fifty percent chance of rain in the forecast kept people away. If I got wet, it would not be my first ride in the rain. Up ahead, though, I saw a woman in khaki pants and a blue blazer. She walked at a leisurely pace. Her clothes seemed a little formal for just getting exercise, but it was Sunday. Maybe she had gone to church or brunch.

| THE ARTIFACT

Not until I was a few feet behind her and offered a polite, "On your left," preparatory to riding past, did I recognize her. Miss Blue Eyes.

"We need to talk," she said.

I could hardly disagree, so I stopped a few feet ahead and turned back.

"You used it, didn't you?" she said, looking closely at me. The unblinking pale blue eyes gave me the feeling she could see more than she should.

"Used what?" I said reflexively. The box was tucked away in the back of my closet, and I was already used to thinking of it as a secret. Denial came automatically.

"Don't bother with that line," she said. "I'm here to help. And you do need help. More than you could possibly know yet, I expect." The unnerving stare made me remember the feeling of disorientation I'd had at the airport.

"I don't remember asking for help. But I do have some questions, now that you mention it. What's the idea of tricking me into carrying your … whatever it is?" I wasn't going to admit I had any idea what the magic box did. Nor was I going to volunteer to give it back, as I assumed she wanted. I had thought someone would sooner or later ask questions, but it was surprising she had found me this soon.

"I said I'm here to help, not answer every question you can think of. And whatever you do, don't use it again. It's dangerous."

"Gee, thanks for the warning. Anyway, what is that box? What's it for?"

"You know that. What it's for, anyway."

"What makes you think I know anything? And how did you even find me? What makes you think I used it for … whatever it does?"

"How I found you should be obvious enough. I knew you were getting on a plane to Louisville."

"It's a big town."

"True, but only one person's girlfriend in Louisville won a gigantic stack of money in the last lottery drawing. Most people don't under-react as strongly as you two – unless they have something to hide."

"Wait, how would you even know about that?" *Or who my friends are, or what I was doing today, and a hundred other questions*, I thought.

She smiled and did not answer, so I went on. "You're saying that by not acting suspiciously, we are acting suspiciously?"

41

ADVENTURES TO GO |

"People who win the lottery are usually pretty quick to collect. And celebrate, even before they get the big check."

"How did you know we bought tickets? And how did you know we won?"

"Nobody else has tried to claim the prize," she said, as if that were an obvious answer to my question. "It's a big one. The kind everybody talks about. But you would have been found, anyway, lottery tickets or no lottery tickets."

"So you have spies everywhere? Who are you, anyway? Whom do you work for?"

"Again, too many questions. Just understand, you need to give me the box. And don't use it again. It's dangerous. As you probably already know."

"Why did you drop it on me in the first place, then?"

"I told you that in Detroit: I had to get it out of there. Couldn't carry it myself."

"Why not?"

"You don't need to know. Or perhaps you do. Let me ask *you* a question – why do you think I met you here and not at your house?"

I shook my head. "No idea." I would have liked to say, *Because you don't know where I live*, but that would have been wildly optimistic.

"I'm not the only one looking for the box. The others may not know where you live. Yet. But they will almost certainly find out eventually. They are not nearly as polite as I am."

"Others? What others?"

"That's not your concern," she said. "Not if you're smart."

"So what's your point?"

"I told you. You need to give me the box. The sooner the better, for everybody."

I can be determined. Or stubborn. The difference lies in the connotations.

"You drag me into this, tell me nothing, and expect me to trust you? Not gonna happen." I started to pedal away.

"I'll be seeing you again. Don't use it!" she called after me.

I kept going.

42

CHAPTER X

Mom looked gloomy when I got home. She was sipping a cup of coffee and scrolling through more aerial views of the land slated for suburban hell, otherwise known as development.

"What's wrong?" I asked. I could guess, but it was a conversation starter.

"The last chance to save this land is looking dubious. We were hoping to use the endangered species argument, but we can't find enough evidence of habitat. The case is unlikely to hold up in court."

The crazy idea I'd had before came back, along with the question, *How many memories can you afford to lose this time?* "How much does it cost?"

"To make the case? That's not the big problem. It just probably won't work."

"No, I mean the land. What would it cost to buy it?"

"Ha. More than I make in ten years."

"And nobody like the Sierra Club or some other private conservation group can buy it?"

"No group can afford to buy or protect every place slated to be paved over and polluted. Everybody has to make tough decisions."

"So, what's the number? The actual amount of money?"

Mom looked at me curiously. "Why do you ask?"

"Just wondering."

She told me.

"That's enough for a lot of popcorn and movie tickets," I said.

"Sure is," she said. "Now you see the problem."

I did, but not exactly the same way she did. I went upstairs to call Lonnie.

"You're not thinking of using the box again, are you?" Lonnie said. "What if you forget something even more important than which street to go down or the name of a goldfish you once had? Like your own name? Or maybe you'll forget who your friends are. You don't even get to choose what you would lose. You'd have to be crazy to use the ... artifact, again."

I had told her I wanted to raise the money for the land Mom was trying to preserve, which was even more than the total Lonnie had won.

"It would be a small sacrifice for the greater good. Besides, the memories came back. The big ones, anyway. I don't have any trouble remembering where I live, and you didn't forget anything super important."

"Or it might be a big sacrifice. A huge sacrifice, maybe. What if you forget how to speak? Or walk? Maybe you get a brain hemorrhage. We don't know anything about what it does. Especially if the effects are cumulative. I repeat, you'd have to be nuts to use the artifact again."

"You sound like the woman from the airport. She was down by the river when I went for a bike ride. Must have been waiting for me."

"*The* woman? Miss Blue Eyes?"

"The very same. And somehow, she knows you won the lottery. Don't ask me how."

"Oh, my gods," Lonnie said. "What did she say?" Even though I couldn't see her, I knew she was tucking her hair behind her ear. Not a magical vision, just the kind of image you get when you know someone really well. Or maybe that is a kind of magic, too, now that I think about it.

"Mainly she was just all, 'Don't use the box – it's dangerous, so give it back.' "

"What did you tell her?

"Nothing. Nothing at all. I mean, I said no, of course. No box for her. She didn't give me any useful info, so why should I tell her anything? But she found me awfully fast. It seemed like she expected me to be there. It must mean we are being spied on." A little voice told me I should tell Lonnie about Miss Blue Eyes saying she was there to help. Also, her warning that *others* would be looking for the box. But one thing at a time.

"You told her you wouldn't give her the box?" Lonnie asked.

"Of course."

"Maybe you should."

"No way," I said. "Not until I know more about what's going on."

"Some things ... maybe it's better not to know."

"Like winning lottery numbers? If you asked before she dropped the box on me, you could maybe have persuaded me that certain kinds of ignorance really are bliss. But now? Now I'm too curious."

"Do I need to quote the cliché about curiosity and the cat?" Lonnie asked.

"We don't even know what she wants to do with the box. She might use it to start World War III or something equally terrible."

"You think you can find out what she wants it for? Or prevent her from doing random bad stuff, with or without the box?"

"No, of course not," I said. "But I'm still in no hurry to give it back."

We discussed the safest place to keep the box. At first, we could think of nowhere better than the back of my closet, now that someone might be following or watching me. My mom's safe deposit box at the bank would be secure, but it would involve too many explanations I wasn't prepared to give, or questions I wasn't able to answer. Like, *What is this thing? Where did you get it? How does it work?*

The best idea we came up with was for me to stash the box in the basement instead of my closet. I promised I wouldn't use it before we talked again. Then I told Lonnie about the uninspiring job openings I had seen and asked if she would put in a good word for me at the museum. She seemed delighted with the idea.

NOTHING MUCH HAPPENED FOR A COUPLE OF DAYS. I SLEPT, READ, RODE MY bike, caught up on Netflix, watched for strangers lurking behind bushes.

ADVENTURES TO GO |

On Tuesday night, Lonnie called. She had spoken to her supervisor at the museum, and they had a job, one that paid actual money, that I should apply for. Joy of joys, it involved neither mops nor spatulas. The job would mainly consist of sorting through materials for the archives. A cache of old newspapers had recently been donated – actual ink-on-paper newspapers, some going as far back as the 1960s and '70s. Also, some audio recordings – cassettes and even a few reel-to-reel tapes – needed to be cataloged. My job would be to read, listen, and make notes, so the archivists had a starting point in deciding what to do with the materials.

On Wednesday, I went to the museum, talked to one Miss Anderson, and was told to report back the next day for my temporary job in the archives. "Nine a.m. sharp. Don't be late," she said.

CHAPTER XI

I didn't sleep much that night. Nevertheless, I made it to work on time. Most of the old newspapers someone had donated were an unremarkable assortment of the *Courier-Journal* and *Lexington Herald-Leader*, along with a few others from Tennessee, Virginia, and Indiana. "We're not really the kind of archive that can collect just anything and everything," Miss Anderson explained as she led me down to the basement where I'd be working. "But we need to at least have a look and see what's there before we decide what to do with the materials." My job would be to take notes; make a list of titles, dates, and headlines; and eventually scan at least some of the papers into the computer.

The job was fun. For me, anyway. I had an interest in history and a sentimental streak of nostalgia for all the things people used to think were important, yet nobody much cares about now. Except, you know, archivists and academics and such. Maybe that was why I wanted to be an architect – you can forget this morning's news by this afternoon, but buildings are there for years or decades. Maybe for centuries.

Nobody seemed to mind if I took my time with the job, unsurprisingly. The newspapers where I started were literally old news. One story that caught my attention was about the MK-Ultra project. I had heard that

47

ADVENTURES TO GO |

phrase many times in movies and TV shows but had never thought about whether it referred to anything real. Before I saw the news article, in a March 1976 edition of the *Progress-Index* of Petersburg, Virgina, I might have guessed the whole notion was fiction, as it involved brainwashing and mind control and so on. It sounded like the plot of those old movies like *The Manchurian Candidate* or *American Ultra*.

The Progress-Index article's byline was Jack Anderson, a name that sounded vaguely familiar, and Les Whitten, which meant nothing to me. A quick search on my phone showed that Anderson was well known as an investigative reporter in the 1970s. He had been privileged to make the disgraced President Richard Nixon's list of enemies.

Les Whitten had been a frequent collaborator with Anderson, as well as the author of a novel called *The Alchemist* (which sounded like a good weird tale, so I put it on my to-read list). Whitten also wrote a novel called *Moon of the Wolf*, which had inspired a TV movie of the same name. I bookmarked it so I could give it a watch, too. I didn't necessarily expect it to be good (whatever the official definition of 'good' might be), but it should at least be fun.

Anyway, the newspaper in front of me referred to a project called MK-Ultra-Delta, and it said the MK project was very real, and very illegal, even though it was created and carried out by a branch of the U.S. government – the CIA. Fascinated, I did some more quick searching on my phone. Incredibly, I learned, the CIA and some people who worked with that agency had hoped to use LSD as a mind-control drug. Which sounded completely crazy. I had been born and grew up in the age of the so-called war on drugs and its aftermath, the opioid crisis. I knew drugs could cause as many problems as they fixed.

I also knew problems caused by the war on drugs included people being sentenced to long prison terms for what seemed now like pretty insignificant behaviors, such as smoking a little weed. Nevertheless, stoned people tend to be harder to control, not easier. Using drugs for mind-control just sounded silly.

But the war on drugs, when the phrase first appeared in the 1970s, based on what I now read, was mostly intended to be a tool for busting hippies, civil rights activists, anti-war protesters, jazz musicians, and rap artists. In contrast, I'd heard enough news stories to know the opioid

| THE ARTIFACT

problems started with prescription drugs, prescribed by doctors, and the drugs were sold by pharmaceutical companies. All nice and legal and highly profitable, or so it seemed, at least until the lawsuits against the pharmaceutical companies began. But drugs, any of them, being expected to lead to mind control – that sounded like nonsense.

The problems seemed to start too often with the government's stamp of approval, if not its active participation. Yet people wondered why kids like me didn't trust political leaders to save the world any more than the hippies did. We might not wear beads and put flowers in our hair or go to Woodstock, but that didn't mean we were stupid.

As it turned out, according to my phone, mind control never worked in real life the way it did in the movies. (*Why should that surprise anyone?* I kept wondering.) The closest the CIA had come to controlling minds with drug use was to drive people over the edge. Literally, in some cases, like the story of a man named Frank Olson who, the newspaper said, had allegedly committed suicide. But another quick search showed a lot of people thought Olson had been murdered. After being given experimental drugs, Olson died, in a hotel in Manhattan – or was maybe pushed from the tenth floor.

If you're wondering what all this has to do with the story of me and my friends and the weird artifact tucked away in the back of my closet, well, the best I can do now is ask you to trust me. It has a lot to do with what happened that summer and fall. Way more than just what I learned at my temp job, and more than I suspected at the time.

I realized I had better get back to work. It would be bad to look like a slacker on my first day, so I made some notes about the newspaper and got on with the rest of the stack Miss Anderson had told me to sort through. But first I took pictures of the MK-Ultra article, feeling a little like a secret agent in an old-fashioned spy movie. Except the spy would use a super-tiny camera with actual film to take photos of the secret documents. The spy always seemed to snap the last photo and hide under the desk, right before the bad guys could catch them in the act. The suspense was too predictable, but still fun to watch.

I spent the rest of the morning making notes about headlines of all sorts, from the Watergate scandal to the attempted assassination of Ronald Reagan. By lunchtime, dust and moldy paper were making my nose run.

49

ADVENTURES TO GO |

The white cotton archivist gloves Miss Anderson had given me to wear had turned black on the fingertips.

I went upstairs to find Lonnie. She worked in the gift shop – aka the Museum Store, I guess because "gift shop" sounded too much like what they have in hospitals. Anyway, she ran the register where people paid for T-shirts and keychains that proved they'd been to the museum.

"Lunch?" I asked when she finished checking out a group of kids who appeared to be supervised by a single exhausted daycare worker.

Lonnie glanced at the clock. "Ten minutes to go. Meanwhile, can I interest you in any of our fine merchandise?"

"Not if you want me to buy lunch. Which I was going to do, since you got me the job. But I can't splurge. At least not until I get paid."

"Actually, I brought a sandwich," she said. "We could eat outside. You know, get some fresh air."

"Or some fresh industrial pollution and car exhaust. But at least it's sunny out there."

I had brought nothing for lunch, but in addition to her sandwich, Lonnie had an apple and a pear, so we got a couple of bags of chips from the vending machine and went across the broad concrete pedestrian walk in front of the building. Some picnic benches with a roof provided welcome shade. June gets pretty warm in Louisville, Kentucky.

I started telling Lonnie what I'd read about MK-Ultra-Delta when I noticed her looking over my shoulder.

"Do you know that woman?" she asked.

I turned and saw Miss Blue Eyes.

"I heard you mentioning the MK-Ultra-Delta affair to your friend," she said, walking around the end of the table and taking a seat, uninvited, at the end of the bench where Lonnie sat. "Did that story strike a nerve for you?"

"Lonnie, meet my stalker." To the woman, I said, "Stalker, do you have a name, or should I just keep thinking of you as Miss Blue Eyes?"

"You don't need to know my name. But as I tried to tell you before, you do need my help. You have … something that doesn't belong to you, and it will draw the wrong sort of attention from people you don't want to meet."

50

| THE ARTIFACT

"Right. I guess I'll go with Miss B, for short. As *I* told *you* before, I have no reason to trust you, since you give me no real information. All you did was volunteer me to be your courier."

"We've been over all that," Miss B said. Her eyes, as before, almost never blinked. "I also gave you the chance to win the lottery, but never mind. Let's look at things a different way, now that you know about the MK business. That project happened a long time ago. What do you suppose happened to that program, to the people involved?"

"No idea. I assume somebody went to jail, but–" A thought nagged at the back of my head.

Miss B smiled sardonically. "The kinds of people who run those projects don't go to jail. Nor do they go away." In what I thought was a non sequitur, she asked, "Do you know how much the federal budget is for this year? Or last year?"

"Trillions, I assume." The nagging thought came into focus. "Did you have that newspaper planted in the stack? Or have the whole thing donated, just so I would see it?"

"Excuse me, but what does the federal budget have to do with that box? And what is MK supposed to stand for, anyway? Mind Kontrol?" Lonnie asked. She had been quiet, just listening and watching, since Miss B sat down.

"Shh. The grass may have ears," Miss B said. "I'm making a point. MK may be history, but the mindset that allowed it to thrive – and allowed its perpetrators to go unpunished – is alive and well. Incredible amounts of money go to fund the Pentagon and CIA, the NSA, all the top-secret operations the Department of Defense is involved in. Plausible arguments are made as to why very few people should know what the money is used for. Congress gets little or no information about what actually happens to funding it approves for these agencies. So after MK and the drug experiments fizzled, the energy – and money – moved on to other areas. Government is about power, the power to control people and events. If you cannot control minds, or can assert control only through the usual means like laws, guns, and propaganda, you look for other ways to assert power."

Miss B paused, her eyes shifting nervously. "Do you see anyone behind me?"

ADVENTURES TO GO |

"No one," I said, and Lonnie calmly looked around.

"Other areas of investigation in those days included research into ESP – extra-sensory perception, or remote viewing, as it was sometimes called," Miss B went on. "The hope was to find a way to know what the Soviet Union was up to during the Cold War. Supposedly, a remote viewer – a psychic, in other words – could sit in a room in Maryland and somehow know what was happening somewhere in China or Yugoslavia. A great many other uses and abuses for such abilities would no doubt have been found if remote viewing had yielded consistent, reliable results. Instead, the whole idea that the unaided human mind could do such things turned out to be mostly based on fantasy, wishful thinking, and faked test results. But it's an old story – when there's easy money to be had, charlatans come running. Some of the charlatans are clever and keep everyone fooled, for a while."

"How do you know all this?" Lonnie asked.

"As the old joke goes, if I told you ..." Miss B said.

"Not funny," Lonnie replied.

"Not really supposed to be."

"You did not answer my question," I said. "It seems like too much of a coincidence that you're here to discuss MK-Ultra right after I read about it. Or do you have hidden cameras in the basement of the museum? Did you plant that newspaper in the materials I was supposed to work on?" I asked again, not expecting a straight answer. "Maybe you had someone donate the whole stash?"

"I don't have any cameras there. Doesn't mean there aren't any. But if seeing the future is possible, why should a little synchronicity surprise you?" Miss B said.

"I think you're trying to make me paranoid. And you answered only one of the questions I just asked."

"Good. You should be paranoid. It might keep you alive. As I told you before, I'm not here just to satisfy your curiosity."

The air was warm, but I felt a chill.

Miss B kept talking. "The results of remote viewing were as disappointing as you might expect, just as mind control had been. When the 1990s rolled around, complete with the tech boom, some people were prepared to spend billions on the new magic, which included anything

| THE ARTIFACT

with a digital chip in it. One such person, whose name you won't hear from me – call him Bob – learned of a certain artifact. The item had been found by Howard Carter in November 1922 in the tomb of the ancient Egyptian Pharaoh Tutankhamen, more popularly known as King Tut."

Lonnie rolled her eyes. "I saw that movie. You're going to tell us Linc will suffer from the 'Curse of the Pharaohs' if he doesn't give back the box? Or the ancient Egyptians had electronics donated by aliens, and the digital toys somehow meshed seamlessly with Bronze Age tech?"

"Hardly," said Miss B. "It's true that George Herbert, also known as Lord Carnarvon or the Earl of Carnarvon, who funded Howard Carter's work, died a few weeks after the discovery. However, most of those involved in raiding the tomb of King Tut lived on for years and died the sort of ordinary deaths common to humans. As for ancient Egyptians' technological sophistication, well, you don't have to know how to make a tool in order to use it, do you? Or where it came from, or who did make it? Can you explain every element of that phone in your hand? Such questions aside, my point is this: of all the gold and other valuables taken from the tomb, one artifact was never cataloged in public records or displayed in any museum exhibit. A box, made of cedar and inscribed with certain hieroglyphs, the correct translation of which remains controversial, was found and mostly overlooked. At least publicly. The box was not decorated with gold or encrusted with jewels. Its apparent plainness might have contributed to its being forgotten. People would have assumed a relatively plain cedar box couldn't be worth much, at least not in monetary value, unless it was full of treasure or unless it contained some other interesting artifact."

"So what was in the box, if not gold?" Lonnie asked.

"A jar," Miss B said. "A canopic jar, to be specific. Or at least that's what it looked like in the X-rays taken later. The box itself was impenetrable, seamlessly constructed out of a single piece of wood. Or so it seemed. As the story goes, no one could find a way to open it without applying destructive force."

"What was in the jar, then?" I asked. "Did X-rays answer that?"

"Probably not what you'd expect, given the standard purpose of such vessels, which was to store body parts removed during mummification. But no one knew for sure, because, as I said, the jar was tightly sealed in the

ADVENTURES TO GO |

box, and there is no record of Carter ever opening it. The jar was not X-rayed until after he went to the great archeological dig in the sky.

"We know of the box only because it caught Carter's eye for some reason, and he noted it in his personal journal – the one nobody has been allowed to publish. No record exists as to the box's whereabouts until an associate of Bob's came across the box, jar still inside, at a street market in Cairo, sometime in the early 1990s. He thought it looked old, and it matched the descriptions Carter gave, down to the hieroglyphs carved into the wood. The associate bought the box for a few dollars and brought it back to Washington, where it sat on a shelf in a warehouse for nearly a decade."

"Oh, I get it," I said. "This story is not about the curse of the mummies – it's an Indiana Jones knockoff. The Ark of the Covenant stashed in a government vault instead of being studied by experts. Or are you coming soon to the part about a Crystal Skull?"

Miss B looked at me impatiently. "The box you have hidden under your bed is not a skull, and it's not in a government vault, is it?"

"No. For the record, it's not under my bed, either."

"Of course not," Miss B said. "However, Bob is a fan of the sort of stories you mention – myths and legends of ancient religion, technology, and magic. When Bob heard the box was gathering dust in the National Archives' warehouse in Maryland, he thought it might be important, so he brought it back to the lab for study."

"The National Archives just let him walk off with it?"

"Bob has connections. I'm sure the person working the desk that day got a phone call that said Bob could take what he needed."

"So what was in the jar?" I asked.

"I doubt anybody knows, exactly, even today. Except Bob. Maybe Bob doesn't know. I'm not going to ask him. In fact, I fervently hope never to meet him again. But the way the story was told to me, Howard Carter must have figured out how to open the box, according to notes left in his journal about the jar inside. However, he failed to record the method used to open it. Maybe it required a prayer or spell from *The Book of the Dead*. Whatever the case, Bob found it impossible to open the box without cutting, drilling, or breaking it. Which Bob was unwilling to do. So he ran it through a CAT scanner and an MRI machine. Medical imaging has come a long way

| THE ARTIFACT

since the 1920s, and it occasionally turns out to be very useful for other purposes." Miss B paused dramatically.

"So? You do know we have to go back to work, don't you?" Lonnie said.

"Long story short, Bob found the box contained a canopic jar," Miss B said. "But the jar's contents, well, that information proved impervious to ordinary imaging methods. Nevertheless, the box and its mystery jar were intriguing, not just for whatever they contained but for what they did. And he set about reproducing it. 'Reverse-engineering' it, as the fashionable conspiracy aficionados like to say. He produced not a cedar box or jar with hieroglyphic inscriptions, but a stainless steel box with lights and a switch. One that runs on digital technology, not ancient magic. Or maybe the ancient magic was also digital technology, translated into the mythic language of its time. Nobody seems to know exactly how the box works – either of them, the new or the ancient one, for that matter – except maybe Bob and one or two of his closest associates.

"The point is, you have Bob's box. He wants it back."

"Right," I said, when she came up for air. "So you want me to give you the box so you can give it back to him?"

"No. I want you to give it to me so I can keep it safe. Put it where it can do no more harm. I need to do it before Bob catches up with me."

"This is interesting, but we really do have to get back to work soon," I said. "So if all you're doing is giving us a history lesson, fascinating as it is, in hopes of persuading me to do what you want, I have to say it's no-go."

"I'm trying to let you know what you've gotten yourself into."

"You mean what *you* got me into, don't you?"

"The question of who's responsible is irrelevant at this point. Anyway, I've reached the part in the story where you come in. I will sum the situation up as succinctly as I can. The thing you have was developed by a group so secret you never heard of them, though maybe someday, if their plans go completely off the rails, they'll make headlines the way MK-Ultra did. The ability to see the future, even little bits of it, could mean huge advantages in defense and intelligence. The device you have is the only working prototype of the design they came up with. Essentially, what it does is to stimulate certain parts of the brain, ones that are not at all well understood, to create premonitions. Probably every human being, or nearly every human being, has the ability to spy glimpses of the future.

ADVENTURES TO GO |

Such phenomena may be nothing more than an extension of our ability to make simple predictions, like knowing that if you drop something, it will fall down. What are called premonitions might just be sophisticated unconscious analyses of cause and effect."

"Cause and effect. Like being late to work causes awkward questions to be asked," Lonnie said.

"But as you know already," Miss B continued, undeterred, "the premonitions come at a heavy price. Seeing the future once or twice costs you a few memories. Repeated exposure to the machine, for most users, causes its harmful effects to grow progressively worse, while glimpses of the future remain pretty much the same. Nevertheless, there are people in our government who are happy to go on using it. And happy to go on destroying the minds of those they use.

"I couldn't allow that. So I took the machine. Obviously, that pissed off some people who will now do anything to get it back."

"What do you mean, 'anything'?" Lonnie asked, taking out her phone.

"It's a simple word."

Nobody spoke for a few seconds.

"Smile," Lonnie said, and the light on her phone flashed briefly. She flicked her finger across the screen, looked briefly, and held the picture up for me and Miss B. "It's good enough for an image search on the interwebz," she said.

"You won't find anything of interest," Miss B said.

"We'll see, won't we?"

"You claim you want to help," I said. "How do you propose to do that? Because scary history lessons are interesting, but they don't really change the present."

"Another simple answer. It's possible, even likely, that no one but me knows you have the box. Give it to me, and you can go back to being a regular kid whose biggest problem is deciding where to go to college. You even get to keep your lottery winnings."

"Sorry, but that's not good enough. For all we know, you could be one of the bad guys here. You're right, the device is dangerous. But we're supposed to think the top-secret government lab, or wherever the thing was made, just let you walk off with it? Seems unlikely. How do I know I'm

56

| THE ARTIFACT

not just a guinea pig? 'Let's run an experiment – give the box to this kid, see what he does with it and what it does to him.'"

"What would count as proof that I am not helping anyone use the device to experiment on you? How could I prove the opposite, that I know what the box does to people and want it to stop?"

She had me there. I did not know how she could prove she had my interests at heart.

"Your only options seem to be to trust me, or let the real bad guys track you down," she said.

"In that case, I should probably just throw the box in the river."

"You won't do that, though."

"Why not?" I asked.

"Two reasons. First, you're too interested. Too invested. You know you are in possession of a unique and priceless artifact. One of a kind. Well, two of a kind, counting the original, but the one you have is obviously not an exact copy. Second, you're smart enough to know it gives you leverage. As long as you have it, you have the option of giving it back. You can't give something back if you no longer possess it."

"Actually, we have no way of knowing it's the only one," Lonnie said. "The only modern reproduction, I mean."

"You know you can't buy one on Amazon, though. Or anything like it."

I looked at my watch. "Nice talking to you, but we have to get back to work. It's my first day, so I don't want to be late."

"You won't see me again," Miss B said as we got up and walked back to the museum.

"She knows a lot about us," Lonnie said, working on her phone as we walked. "Like, where to find us at lunchtime, and we're deciding where to go to college. That by itself is scary enough."

"I don't know if she's one of the good guys, like she says, but she had the box, so she must have some scary connections. People who can find out anything about anybody. The probably know all about your lesbian erotica searches."

"Yours, too. But she was right about one thing – I get nothing when I search for her image. Well, not nothing, but a lot of images that are not her."

I glanced over my shoulder, an action I was getting used to. Miss B was still sitting at the picnic bench. She smiled and waved. We went inside and got back to work.

CHAPTER XII

I had ridden my bike to the museum, but Lonnie offered to give me a ride home. With the front wheel removed, my bike fit in the back of her dad's car, which was really her mom's car, since she and Lonnie were the only ones who ever drove it. Or almost ever. "Just don't get chain grease on the seat. My dad will pitch a tantrum if he sees it."

"Doesn't he always drive his pickup truck?" I asked.

"Yeah, but he would still be royally pissed if he found a spot on *his* car seat. Besides, I have this incredible pair of white pants and shirt to wear next time we go to the movies, and you wouldn't want me to get them greasy."

"Certainly not," I said. "Though if they get dirty, you might take them off, which would be nice."

"Don't get ahead of yourself, Linc," she said, but she smiled.

"Have you talked to Julie lately?" I asked.

"Not in a couple of days. Why, are you jealous?"

"No. Yes. Only a little," I said. "I know Julie can keep a secret, but do you think her parents know about us?"

"Of course they do. They've met us."

"No, I mean *know about* us."

59

ADVENTURES TO GO |

"Doubt it," Lonnie said. "Or maybe her mom. Probably her mom. She's pretty open-minded. Like Lonnie said, if she doesn't get pregnant or hurt, her mom's okay with whatever makes Julie happy. Her dad, though – he'd meet us at the door with a shotgun if he suspected."

"That makes sense. Her dad seems super-religious, and not in a good way. He'd at least ground Julie for life if he knew. Or try to. Anyway, I also feel guilty for keeping secrets from her."

"Secrets?"

"Well, one secret. The box. The lottery is another. Secrets, plural."

"Me, too," Lonnie said. "Maybe we should tell her."

"I guess it couldn't hurt."

"Then again, maybe it could hurt. If scary people are looking for the box, it might be safer to know nothing about it."

"The scary people, or at least Miss B, would assume we told her, anyway," I said.

"You think she, or they, or whoever, are really keeping close watch on us?"

"She knows we got the winning lottery numbers. I didn't tell anyone. And like you said at lunch, she knows we're looking at colleges, and where to find us at work. It would be too big a coincidence if she just happened to be walking down the street and spotted us there by accident."

"Right. She has too much information," Lonnie said.

"So how would she know? She must have spies, or hidden cameras."

"Or access to the ones you see all over, like security cameras. I expect they have one at the store where we bought lottery tickets."

"Maybe our phones were hacked," I said.

"Maybe." We were almost to my house, and Lonnie's attention was on the other cars at a four-way stop.

"*Close Encounters* is on at the Uptown this weekend. We should go," she said before I got out.

"Agreed." On impulse, I added, "I'm definitely going to go to school at U of L this fall. I would miss you too much if I went to Detroit."

"Same here," she said and kissed me. Just a peck on the cheek, but believe me, I floated on a cloud the rest of the afternoon.

"Don't forget your bike," she said through the open window as I closed the door.

60

| THE ARTIFACT

I DIDN'T KNOW JULIE'S PARENTS VERY WELL, BUT I'D MET THEM A COUPLE OF times. You could tell at a glance her dad was the conservative type who would oppose everything from *Roe* v. *Wade* to Black Lives Matter. He'd pasted one of those ridiculous *Don't tread on me* stickers on the back of his giant SUV, like he was some kind of eighteenth-century American patriot. Julie kept scraping it off when he wasn't looking, which infuriated him. I sincerely hoped he never caught her. If he guessed his daughter had a thing for both me and her female best friend, well, he'd try to have her excommunicated. If excommunication was something Southern Baptists did. Neither my mom nor I were religious, at least not that way, so I didn't know.

If my mom and I had a religion, it was nature worship. Not the way Wiccans or any group with a label did things. She just loved trees and animals and rain and blue skies, and she'd passed the feeling on to me. When I asked her questions about God when I was younger, she said, "God is a metaphor."

"You mean God doesn't exist?"

"That's not exactly my point. Maybe some powerful supernatural being or beings exist, or maybe not. But people make stories about what they care about. The stories create myths, and myths create metaphors. Angry people create angry-god metaphors. Metaphorical gods of love are created by people who know and follow the ways of love."

CHAPTER XIII

That night, trying to get some factual context for Miss B's tale of the Egyptian artifact, I reread parts of the story of Howard Carter and the tomb of Tutankhamen.

If ancient Egypt and pyramids don't interest you, you can skip this chapter. Or skim it. Of course you can – who am I to tell you how to read? But they interested me (still do, in fact), so it was fun to review what I already knew and learn some things I didn't know.

I knew the basic story of King Tut from old movies and TV shows, many of which were highly fictionalized, of course. On the web I found photos of Howard Carter. He had become famous in the early twentieth century for excavating Tutankhamen's tomb. I saw pictures of him striding purposefully, arrogantly, across Egyptian sands, while natives bore the burdens of equipment he needed to plunder their country's heritage. A perfect specimen of the highly respected, socially acceptable grave robber. But as Taylor Swift and my favorite dead writer – Kurt Vonnegut – said, "So it goes."

I also knew something about ancient Egyptian mythology and religion. I had found videos about the pyramids on YouTube when I was eight or nine. How and why they were built had fascinated me for a long

62

| THE ARTIFACT

time. (When you're seventeen, almost ten years seems like forever.) That interest was a big part of why I wanted to be an architect. The buildings any civilization makes reflect their beliefs and myths. The pyramids were no exception.

The Great Pyramid was the tallest building in the world for centuries, until modern engineers started trying to make the tallest everything. The pyramids were built without computers to design them and with no machines powered by steam, coal, gas, diesel fuel, or electricity. And, I was sure, without the help of aliens. It seemed way more likely that ancient Egyptians were just as clever, if not more clever, than modern engineers, given the scope of their accomplishments and the limited tools and technology they had to use.

Until Miss B came along, I had been more interested in the engineering and architecture, though, than exploits of the modern European plunderers who called what they did archeology. Sure enough, various websites displayed records of Carter's journals and diaries, including images of the original handwritten notes and drawings. Not that I found any mention of the artifact Miss B had described, or expected to. If Carter kept the cedar box and its contents a secret, before he died he would likely have burned the pages of his journal that mentioned it. If he wrote about it at all. Or maybe Miss B and her cronies had the secret journal. I had no way to know.

Images of mummies dragged from their eternal rest by European or British archeologists also popped up. My emotional reaction to those images was to feel embarrassed. *Embarrassment for whom or what?* I asked myself. I felt bad for the mummies, I realized. Not that I was superstitious enough to believe the dead, or souls of the dead, if they really existed, knew or cared what happened to their biological remains. When I die, if I find myself still alive and conscious, yet freed of the constraints of flesh and blood as we know them, I think I will be mainly interested in the new form of existence and its possibilities. I doubt I'll worry much about the past, at least for a long time. Or would the dead even experience past and future time as we do? Anyway, it still seemed wrong to treat human remains and their resting places as mere property.

I also felt embarrassed for humanity. It seemed outrageous that Howard Carter and others felt it was okay to desecrate the tomb of an ancient king (or anyone else, for that matter). If anyone did the same in, say, Westminster Abbey or Arlington National Cemetery, they would be arrested in a heartbeat, if only because their living relatives would object. But those places are symbols of patriotism or national heritage, and I guess the British had a different view of ancient Egyptian national heritage. We do a bad job of respecting the living, who at least might fight back if they feel disrespected. The dead are soon on their own. So it goes.

One search result mentioned the *Book of the Dead*. I already knew that text was important in some way to ancient Egyptian mythology. Now I learned, reading an online copy of an old version, translated by one E. A. Wallis Budge, that there were many "books of the dead" inscribed by different human authors in various times and places. I wondered who Budge was, so I read a couple of articles that put him in the group of early twentieth century British artifact pirates like Howard Carter. For his efforts, Budge was knighted and became Sir Ernest in 1920, two years before Carter burglarized King Tut's tomb. Anyway, from what Budge wrote, I gathered it was fashionable for ancient Egyptians to claim the texts were divinely inspired by Thoth, or the Voice of Ra. Drawing some very inexact parallels, I thought Thoth sounded like the voice of Yahweh in the Old Testament. Or the Holy Spirit in the New Testament, or the Angel Moroni, who was said to have delivered the Book of Mormon to Joseph Smith. Having been raised by a parent who was not religious in any conventional or formal way, I thought of such claims of inspiration as metaphors or symbols at best. A way for writers to say, *Hey, this text is about something really important, so pay attention.* More than that would be fiction, I guessed.

And yet ... I had seen a vision of the future. It occurred to me that if an ancient Egyptian had a vision of the future like I did, they might well have decided it came from Thoth. Was the mechanism that caused visions powered only by the human mind and human technology? Could I rule out a supernatural element with complete confidence? Could I say, with absolute certainty, that Thoth – or whatever name anyone cared to use for unknowable forces – had not used my eyes and hands and mouth to foretell the future? I didn't have any easy, obvious answers to those questions.

CHAPTER XIV

I awoke to sirens and flashing lights. It was dark outside, but I heard voices downstairs. The clock said three-thirteen a.m.

I got up and went to see what was happening.

From the top of the stairs, I saw two police officers, a man and a woman, talking to my mom. Patches on their uniform shirts displayed the insignia of the LMPD – Louisville Metro Police. I went down to hear more.

"This is my son, Linc," Mom said. The officers nodded.

"We've had reports of a suspicious person prowling around the neighborhood," the female officer was saying. The shiny nameplate on her uniform said she was J. Morgan. "Someone reported the suspect crawling into a basement, through a window or vent around the foundation. Do you mind if Evan takes a look downstairs?"

"It's just for your safety," the male officer said. The name on his uniform said he was E. Benton. *E* for *Evan*, apparently.

I had hidden the box in the basement, so alarm bells began to ring in my head. First, I had planned to put it in the gun safe. My mom said the safe was a relic of my deceased dad's obsession with firearms, only one of which she had kept, an old revolver with no ammunition. When I asked once why she kept it, she said, "Just sentimental, I suppose." She

65

ADVENTURES TO GO |

didn't even remember the combination to the safe, though I did. But what screams "Here are the valuables" like a safe? Which is why nothing anyone would want to steal was stored there. Granted, the safe was locked, it was in the basement, and it was heavy, but a clever and determined thief might find a way. Conversely, you can't steal what you can't find.

So I had put the box in the cubbyhole under the third step from the bottom of the basement stairs. The step wasn't really loose. But if you knew how to slide it to the right, inch it forward, and then to the left, it would lift up easily and reveal a snug little hiding spot. I had discovered it when I was seven or eight, playing hide and seek with Jimmy Fisher and his sister Kim, who lived next door to us until they moved, when I was ten. Hiding under the stairs, when I was small enough to do that, I had noticed the third step had a support beam that made a little shelf, the perfect spot for juvenile contraband like candy or, later, during a brief rebellious phase, cigarettes that Lonnie snatched from her dad's packs. Once, half a pint of vodka was stashed there, though trying booze and smoking had been nauseating experiences neither of us were in a hurry to repeat. Later, it was a good place to stash condoms, until my mom found one (unused) in my pants pocket. She had just looked thoughtfully at me and patted my shoulder and said, "I'm glad you're being careful."

Anyway, Mom nodded to Officer Benton, who wanted to look in the basement. "Please, check it out."

"Which door?" Benton asked, looking around.

"I'll show you," I said. I wasn't about to let him go down there and poke around alone, prowler or no prowler.

Benton went first down the basement stairs, beaming his baton-sized, laser-intensity cop flashlight every which way as we descended. The basement light switch was at the bottom of the steps, for some odd reason, so normally I just depended on light from the open door to see the way down.

When Benton was almost at the bottom, right over the spot where the box was hidden, the step squeaked. He said, "You should check that. If it comes loose, somebody could take a nasty fall."

My adrenaline gland must have been in overdrive. "Yes, sir, Officer," I said, a little louder and more quickly than I normally would.

66

| THE ARTIFACT

He glanced sharply at me. Maybe he thought I was being sarcastic. He must have decided no sarcasm was intended, or else to just let it go, because the next thing he said was, "What's in the safe?" He pointed the light at it.

"Nothing, as far as I know," I fibbed. The last time I checked, there were old and useless boxes of my dad's military records, that unloaded antique revolver, some letters he'd written to Mom, that sort of thing. But I figured none of those contents were any of Officer Benton's business, not unless he had a warrant.

He stared at it for a minute. "Looks just big enough for a burglar to be hiding in. You mind opening it?"

"I don't know the combination," I said, fibbing again, and not adding my question: *You're the cop, so shouldn't you be taking the risks like that?*

"It's locked?"

I nodded, then remembered he probably couldn't see me in the dark, and said. "Yes. That's what safes are for." *Ask a stupid question. …*

Benton had no doubt about the sarcasm that time. He pointed his blinding light in my face long enough to make it obvious why he was doing it. I put my hand up to shield my eyes.

Benton said nothing. He flashed his light briefly around the safe and went on poking around other corners of the basement. Nooks, crannies, and shelves were cluttered with old dishes, canned food, and other kitchen overflow. Garden tools and boxes of old clothes were stacked here and there.

I knew there was no hiding place big enough for a burglar, because it was our basement. Benton couldn't very well know what might lurk behind shelves and in dark corners, yet his concern about any hidden prowler seemed casual at best.

"Looks like we're all clear here," he concluded and started back upstairs.

The two officers asked to walk through other rooms in the house, then around the yard, which of course Mom allowed them to do. They found no one and nothing out of order. Shortly afterward, they advised us, "Call if you see anything suspicious," and departed.

"That'll give the neighbors something to gossip about," Mom said after the police left. "At least they didn't come in with guns blazing like

ADVENTURES TO GO |

they were on the set of a cop show." We sat in the living room, too wide awake to go back to bed just yet.

As an attorney, my mom had too much respect for law and order to be a cop-hater, though she was well aware of abuses and crimes sometimes committed by people in uniform. She supported Black Lives Matter. She had a rainbow LGBTQ bumper sticker on her car, too, and she meant it – any candidate for local, state, or national political office had to support freedom, respect, and equality for everyone to earn her vote or the small donations she could afford to make. Most of her energy went toward environmental justice, but that didn't mean she was unconcerned about other problems. "You can't fix everything all by yourself, Linc," she had said many times. "Pick a cause and stick with it. There are lots of good people in the world to work on other problems. And all of us need clean air and water, no matter who we love or what we look like or what language we speak."

Nevertheless, this visit from the police happened after Breonna Taylor was killed by the police in a botched nighttime raid on her apartment, right in our hometown. So, like I said, Mom didn't hate cops on principle, but she didn't exactly trust them, either. To gain her confidence, a person had to do more than wear a uniform. "This might all have gone down very differently if we lived in a different part of town," she said, nervous energy making her talkative and forcing her to get up and close curtains and make sure doors and windows were locked.

"There will always be people who cause trouble, unfortunately," she added. "Sometimes you need police officers to deal with the situation. But cops are people, too, and sometimes they cause the problem. You have to see them as individuals like everybody else. Some you can trust, and some are very dangerous."

She didn't know the half of it, I thought, and wondered, not for the first or last time, if I should tell her about the box. I decided there was no point in worrying her just now.

But she was already worried. Of course she was. I could see concern in her eyes, hear it in her voice, when she asked, "Linc, is there something you need to tell me?"

"Like what?"

"Like anything. You seem distracted lately."

68

| THE ARTIFACT

"Just working hard, and wondering where to go to school this fall."

"Well, when you want to talk, you know I will always listen."

That was her way of telling me she trusted me to ask for help if I needed it. "Okay, Mom. Thanks." I went back upstairs and got back in bed and eventually fell asleep, hoping to prove Mom's faith in me was not misplaced.

CHAPTER XV

I was groggy the next morning, so I had two cups of coffee, which woke me up but also made me jittery. The bike ride to the museum smoothed off the coffee nerves some, but I must have still looked a little spacey.

"Nightmares about Gort keep you awake last night?" Lonnie asked, when I stopped for a moment at the gift shop to say hi. In case anyone doesn't know, Gort was the robot in *The Day the Earth Stood Still*. I did, in fact, sometimes have nightmares about Gort. Who knows why. What you find super-scary is as subjective as what you think is funny.

"I just need more coffee," I said. Of course, food and drink were out of the question while I was working on archive materials, so coffee would have to wait. "We had a little excitement at our house last night."

"What happened?"

"The police came. Said they were looking for a prowler somebody had reported, but I don't think that's really why they were there."

"So, why?"

"I'll tell you the whole story at lunch," I said, pointing to the clock and heading for the basement. "Don't worry, everything's good. For now anyway."

WE ATE AT THE SAME PICNIC BENCH WHERE MISS B HAD FOUND US. I TOLD Lonnie about the two cops and how I thought Officer Benton had seemed more interested in snooping than looking for prowlers.

"You think he was hoping to find the box?"

"The thought crossed my mind," I said. "It seems likely, in fact. The prowler story – I guess somebody could have called and reported something. People are paranoid these days. Some people, anyway. But it reminded me of the 'anonymous tip' ruse in cop shows. The cops themselves can make a phone call if they want an excuse to interrogate someone."

"What about the other officer, the woman? What was her name?"

"J. Morgan. She seemed okay. She mainly stayed in the living room and talked to Mom while Benton looked around."

"That seems odd, though, doesn't it?" Lonnie asked. "I mean, if the cops are really looking for someone, wouldn't they stick together to watch each other's backs?"

"Sounds logical to me. But I have no idea how they're trained to act in that situation. Or how closely they follow whatever training they have. But neither of them seemed to have a major sense of urgency. More like they were checking an item off their list. All in a night's work."

"But if your instinct is right, and Officer Benton was looking for the box and not for a suspicious person at all, do you know what that means?"

"Not exactly," I said. "I guess it means … something that would have sounded crazy and paranoid a few days ago. It means people in positions of power and authority are interested in me. Or interested in what I have. They know where I live. It means I have problems I didn't ask for. Maybe I should just give the box back to Miss B, if she ever turns up again, and be done with it. Or toss it in the river. Right now, I just want my simple life back, where the hardest choice I have to make is where to go to college."

"But you can't toss it. Or give it back, at least without getting something in return. The box is dangerous. Even if Miss B has good intentions – and we don't know if she does – we don't know how she can keep it safe, either. It's your leverage. As long as you have it, you have a bargaining chip."

"Bargaining for what, though?"

Lonnie shrugged. "A promise of peace and quiet, no more visits from cops in the wee hours. She did stash it in your bag without your permission or knowledge, after all. She owes you something for your trouble."

"That's true," I agreed. "But her promise would mean nothing. She cannot be trusted."

Lonnie nodded and didn't say anything.

"You're right," I went on. "I can't give it back. Keeping it is also dangerous. But it seems like I should do something. Something besides waiting for Miss B, or Officer Benton's boss, or whoever, to send somebody scarier to look for the box. But if that happens, and I don't even have the box to give back. ..."

"I believe it's called a catch-22," Lonnie said. "There's nothing you can do that will necessarily fix the problem."

By the time lunch was over, we both knew we didn't know what else I should do, except let the box stay right where it was. Perhaps I was just being paranoid. Maybe the cops really were looking for a reported prowler who had nothing to do with me.

Maybe. But I didn't believe it.

I SPENT THE AFTERNOON MAKING NOTES ABOUT RECORDINGS ON OLD REELS OF magnetic tape. Some of the tapes had become so brittle they cracked when I tried to unwind them and put them on the player. A couple sounded like kids' birthday parties. I guess that's how parents made records of their kids' memorable events before they had phones to take video. At least, parents did if they had money to burn. A tape recorder in the 1950s or '60s probably cost a lot more than a decent phone does now, when you consider inflation.

One recording included John F. Kennedy's inaugural address. Bursts of static interrupted occasionally, like someone had set a microphone in front of a TV or radio speaker. I had heard clips from one of his famous speeches, the one calling for people to be sent to the Moon, in history class. The Moon idea came in a later speech, after the inauguration. I had also read Kennedy's famous claim that said people should ask "what you can do for your country" instead of "what your country can do for you." I had never heard a recording of him saying it, though, until now. The idea sounded like it was at least on the right track. But why don't we ask how everybody can work together for everybody's benefit, instead of asking people to sacrifice their lives for no return, or just look out for number one? Kennedy's advice also seemed very contrary to basic human nature. Most people seem to look out for themselves and their family and friends first. Like my mom said, one person can't solve every problem by themselves.

Still, it gave me chills, there in the dark basement, over half a century later, to be hearing the voices of the dead. A dead president, or the voices of a birthday party from 1951 – a lot of those people, maybe all of them, were surely dead, too. A few feet of magnetic tape or perhaps some YouTube videos, if anybody cared enough to copy tapes and put them out, were all that was left of their voices.

Such thoughts were a good distraction from wondering what to do with an even older reminder of the past for which I had been volunteered to act as caretaker.

THE NEXT FEW DAYS WERE QUIET. DECEPTIVELY SO, IN LIGHT OF WHAT FOL-lowed. The next weekend, we went to the movies: Lonnie, Julie, and me. We saw Roy Neary, the husband and father whose family can't understand why he starts being so weird after he sees a UFO, in *Close Encounters*. Being a character in a movie, Roy opts to get on a spaceship and leave all his problems behind. No apologies for the so-called spoiler – the movie's been out awhile, so what are you waiting for? Anyway, that's just the beginning and ending of the movie, and like any good story, the middle's important, too.

Afterward, we went back to Lonnie's house, where a good time was had by all. Her mom had gone to a church meeting after doing her best to make Lonnie feel guilty for not coming along. Her dad was out of town for some construction project he was helping to plan, somewhere in Indiana, so we had the house all to ourselves. We had a lot of fun. I won't kiss and tell, though. At least not any of the titillating details. This is not that kind of story.

So it was tempting, in the midst of teenage fun and no recent encounters, close or otherwise, with ominous strangers or police, to hope Officer Benton had reported no sign of the artifact in my possession and that the trail had been marked cold. Maybe I was just being paranoid

ADVENTURES TO GO |

in mistaking Benton's casual curiosity about the gun safe for something sinister. Or at least, maybe Miss B and the secret agent/cloak-and-dagger types were looking elsewhere for the box.

Go ahead, say I was being naively optimistic. I won't deny it.

CHAPTER XVI

The next Sunday night, things took a turn. Around eight, I was watching *The Big Bang Theory* and reading a book from 1923 called *Tutankhamen and the Discovery of His Tomb*, by G. Elliot Smith, during commercials. Mom was working downstairs, getting ready for a big day tomorrow. I still hadn't told her about the winning lottery ticket, because I knew, once I started, I would end up telling the whole tale, including how I got the mystery box and what Miss B said about it. Which would only cause her to worry. Unnecessarily, I wanted to believe.

I drifted off to sleep and woke to the sound of breaking glass. *The Big Bang Theory* had given way to some animated comedy show. My phone lay dark on the bed beside me. I muted the TV and listened. Had the sound of breaking glass been a dream? Or on TV?

Downstairs, the door to the basement squeaked. I recognized its distinctive sound. I looked at the clock. 12:17. Mom was unlikely to be up at that hour, especially in the basement, unless something was wrong. I tiptoed out to the hall. No light showed under the door to her room, so I guessed she was still asleep. I went back and got my phone, turned off the reading lamp, and tiptoed toward the stairs.

75

ADVENTURES TO GO |

It occurred to me I had jumped to conclusions about Officer Benton. Maybe he did not report failure to his boss – maybe he was just the advance scouting party, sent to spot likely hiding places. I realized, in a terrifying rush, how dangerously complacent I'd been in the past few days.

You never think about how many noisy floorboards and creaky steps on the stairs a house has until you try to walk silently, in the dead of night. Halfway down to the living room, I also realized I should not have brought my phone. Was it on silent? I didn't know. Anyway, what was I going to do-- call the cops? Well, maybe later, but I was not sure they could be trusted, at least not all of them, and who knew how many connections Officer Benton had in the Metro Police Department? But I might need light, or just want to take a picture. Regardless, I and my phone were past the squeaky step, and I was not going to turn back.

Light from the street filtered through drawn curtains and showed the door to the basement standing open. All I could see was the door itself. It opened to the right and was on the right side of the hall from where I came down the stairs. I stood still and strained my ears.

Nothing.

More nothing.

Then a clatter that sounded like metal cans or pans, followed by a man's voice muttering, "Damn!" Hurried footsteps came up the basement stairs.

I stood transfixed for a moment, and suddenly realized what I should do. I leapt forward, slammed the door closed, and locked it.

Something--an arm, I guessed, or maybe a forehead--banged against the wood, which made a splintery screech, followed by the dull thump of a body tumbling down the steps. More cursing, and steps coming back up the stairs. This time, the climber threw his weight more carefully against the door, which flew open and smashed into my nose. The burglar pushed me roughly aside.

I fell down and managed to get back up just in time to see him escape through the broken window over the kitchen sink.

"What the hell is going on?" Mom said, turning on the light. "My god, Linc, you're bleeding!"

"It's just my nose," I said. My lips were wet and tasted salty. I barely avoided poking my eye out when I raised a hand to wipe away blood.

76

| THE ARTIFACT

A jagged splinter from the door frame was sticking through the palm of my hand.

Of course, Mom called 911. Of course, the police came--several officers--and found no sign of the burglar around the house or anywhere in the neighborhood.

The police also called for paramedics when they saw my hand. One of the officers was J. Morgan, the same one who had come before with E. Benton. I didn't see him this time.

Mom wanted to take me to the emergency room, but Morgan suggested I should stay. She pointed out I was the only one who had actually seen the man who broke in, and told me to hold my hand up by my head to reduce bleeding. "The paramedics will fix you right up, even quicker than if you went to the ER," she assured me.

When they arrived a few minutes later, one of the paramedics pulled the splinter out of my hand, a procedure that naturally induced a fresh round of bleeding and hurt like H-E-double-toothpicks. A bandage was applied, and I was told I should go to the hospital the next day to have my hand X-rayed or scanned. There might be small splinters left that would need to be removed surgically before the wound healed. I would also need to watch for signs of infection.

"Tell me about the burglar," Officer Morgan said, while a paramedic put disinfectant and a bandage on my hand. We sat on the front porch, where the blood would be easy to hose off.

"I think it was a man. I didn't actually get a good look," I said. "It was dark, and I was too busy falling down."

"You're pretty sure he was a he?" Morgan was writing in a little notebook.

"Sure? No, like I said, I think so. But that was just my impression. We Gen Z kids don't make assumptions about gender."

Morgan squinted at me, checking for sarcasm, I guess. Cops must get a lot of that, so they're on alert. I was too busy watching blood drip down my forearm to bother being sarcastic, though. More notes on her pad. "Caucasian?"

"I think so."

"How tall was he? Or she?" Morgan asked.

"I don't know. About average, I guess. About my height."

77

"Which is?"

"Five feet, eleven inches."

She had a few more questions: How long did I hear the intruder before I went downstairs? Why didn't I call 911 as soon as I realized someone had broken in? And so on. I gave vague answers she must have considered unhelpful. Turning to my mom, she asked if anything was stolen. Mom said no, probably not, but pointed out she hadn't exactly had a chance to take a thorough inventory. One of the other cops had found some boxes and old cans of paint scattered on the basement floor. Not surprising news, since the crash I heard came from there. "There's nothing very valuable down there, though," Mom said.

"Can you think of any reason why your house would have been targeted?" Morgan asked.

"No, none," Mom said. I also shook my head *no*.

I wanted to ask where E. Benton was tonight but couldn't think of a way to frame the question that wouldn't lead to other questions I couldn't or didn't want to answer. At least not until I talked to my mom.

Morgan told us to call if we could add anything helpful. She went back to the police car and talked on the radio. Meanwhile, another officer, whose name I never got, was inspecting damages and making notes about the broken window and door.

When the police and paramedics were gone, I went directly to the basement to check on the box. It was undisturbed, still in the cubbyhole under the third step. My hand throbbed with the effort of going back up the steps, but it did not bleed through the bandage.

Mom and I sat on the porch a while longer, watching lights in other houses go out and surreptitiously opened gaps in curtains being closed.

"Mom, I have to tell you something."

"I know."

So I told the whole story, the encounter with Miss Blue Eyes in Detroit, how she turned up in Louisville, the visions the box gave me, the lottery numbers, my vague suspicions about Officer Benton, and Miss B's ominous warnings about the box's origins and whoever wanted it back.

Mom took a minute to process everything. "So, where is it now?"

| THE ARTIFACT

I told her.

She was quietly thoughtful for a minute. "I'm glad you told me. I can also see why you didn't. It's an unprecedented situation. There's no obvious best thing to do, is there?"

"Not that I can see."

"It seems like at least one unsuccessful attempt to steal the box has been made by somebody. Probably two, assuming your suspicions about Officer Benton are true. I'll see what I can learn about him."

That was about the only thing Mom could possibly do to help. She did not practice criminal law and thus did not have much professional contact with the police, but she had friends who did. Maybe one of them could tell her something.

We talked a few more minutes before going back inside. Mom said she would take me to the hospital for a scan of my hand in the morning, but I said I would check with Lonnie and see if she could take me. I knew Mom really needed to be at the office all day. I took two ibuprofen tablets and climbed the steps to my room.

What I found there gave me chills. Laying on my pillow was a note with five words written in blue ink on an otherwise blank, blue-lined piece of paper torn from a pocket-sized notebook: *We'll be seeing you again.*

The note was almost scarier than the burglary. It had to have been left there after I went downstairs to see what was happening in the basement. Did that mean there were two (or more) burglars, one upstairs and one down in the basement?

Or, even more disturbing, did one of the cops leave the note? Granted, my suspicions about Officer Benton were only that – suspicions. But if he were not just an honest cop, how many others might be like him?

My first rational thought after finding the note was that I should move the box to a better hiding place. The second rational thought came just as quickly: *No, maybe that's what they want. They'll be watching for me to leave the house with a package.*

I looked around the room. A couple of drawers and the closet door were open. I knew I hadn't left them that way. Items in the drawer were disordered. Shoeboxes off the top shelf of the closet lay open on the floor.

Sleep didn't come until just before dawn.

79

CHAPTER XVII

In the morning, I was preparing to go to work, struggling to butter a piece of toast with one hand, when Mom came into the kitchen. "You're up early," she said.

"No earlier than usual."

"Today is not usual," she said, surveying my khaki pants and shirt with buttons, which were both less casual than my preferred jeans and T-shirt. "You don't think you're going to work, I hope?"

"Why not? It's only my left hand. I'm right-handed, so I can still sort through papers and listen to tapes and make notes."

"And bleed all over the archives? You are going to stay right here, call Lonnie and see if she can give you that ride, and get your hand scanned. If she's busy, what about your friend Julie? Could she take you? Or I will, if they can't."

"Maybe. I know Lonnie or Julie will if they can. Though Julie's parents are kind of weird about … you know, stuff. If her dad is home, he won't want her to come. Plus, she doesn't know about the box."

"That's just as well. Julie doesn't need to know. You fell and hurt your hand. Nothing implausible about that. Anyway, if Lonnie can't take you to

80

the hospital, I'll take the afternoon off and do it myself. And then I'll call someone to fix the broken window and basement door."

AS IT TURNED OUT, LONNIE WAS HAPPY TO HAVE AN EXCUSE TO TAKE A MORN-ing off, and the gift shop was not expected to be very busy. I told her the story in detail as we drove to the hospital.

"Why would they warn you if they're coming back?" Lonnie wondered.

"So I don't get rid of the box, I guess. Or so I do try to take it somewhere else, to a better hiding spot. Whereupon they grab it."

"So it's still in your house?"

"Of course."

AT THE HOSPITAL, WE WAITED FORTY-FIVE MINUTES BEFORE SEEING A NURSE, then a doctor, both of whom heard the story of how clumsy I was, falling over the living room carpet and jamming my hand into a piece of kindling by the fireplace. I wasn't sure why I made that story up. After all, there was already the police report and whatever sort of records the paramedics kept. I guess I was getting used to keeping secrets. Which, I admit, was kind of fun, in a scary way. But mostly a habit I didn't want to keep.

The scan showed my hand was wood-free. I left with a warning to look out for signs of infection, and assurance that the wound should heal nicely as long as I kept it clean and dry and changed the bandages once a day.

CHAPTER XVIII

"You remember the Valerie Plame scandal?" Mom asked when she came home from the office a couple of days after our visit from the burglar. "Probably not. You're too young."

The name sounded vaguely familiar, but I had no details.

"No matter," Mom said. "She's just an example, but relevant to this situation, I think. Plame was a CIA agent. Nobody outside the CIA was supposed to know what her real job was, until a journalist told the world. The whole affair may have been a revenge outing. Anyway, it caused an uproar at the time. There were a lot of headlines and finger-pointing at important and powerful people, various attempts to place blame.

"But most of the secret CIA agents have such good cover, nobody ever knows what they really do. Or who they work for, or how they are funded, or who supervises them. At least, the people who do know don't tell. What Miss Blue Eyes told you about money and power, and how they are often not answerable to Congress or public opinion – it may sound paranoid, but it's pretty much true."

I nodded, unsure where Mom was going with this story but convinced it was going to be interesting.

| THE ARTIFACT

"I asked Jim Weber, a friend who's been a public defender for over a decade, what he knew about Evan Benton," she continued. "Jim had never heard of him but promised to see what he could find out.

"Turns out, there was a good reason Jim had never come across Officer Benton before. He was hired at LMPD just a few days before he showed up at our house. Trying to find records or get any sort of info on his previous jobs and law enforcement credentials proved strangely tricky."

"So maybe he's not even a real cop?" I wondered.

"Oh, he's real enough, if by 'real cop' you mean officially employed by the LMPD to do police work. The questions are about his background and why he was hired.

"Jim told me he had once tried to investigate an officer, one he suspected of planting methamphetamine on a client, and had run into similar roadblocks. A couple of days later, some no-nonsense, all-business types from the CIA – or at least they claimed to be from the CIA – showed up at Jim's office and told him in no uncertain terms to cease and desist. If he kept asking inconvenient questions, he might be charged with half a dozen federal crimes, all felonies related to violating national security laws. Or so they threatened.

"Like I said, Jim has been a public defender for a long time. He knows bluff and bluster when he hears them. But he also knows the signs when very powerful, very sensitive toes are being stepped on. So his conclusion is that Evan Benton is likely a temporary LMPD officer, really doing undercover work, maybe for the CIA or NSA, or maybe some group whose name or existence is not even common knowledge. More than that he couldn't find out, not without stirring up a real hornet's nest."

"I think it's already stirred up," I said.

"Yes, but of course I didn't tell Jim about the box, just that I had my suspicions about this particular cop. I did ask why a former – and maybe current – agent of the CIA, or whatever dark group, would be working local law enforcement. He didn't have any specifics, but pointed out the obvious: Something must be happening in the city that interests the CIA. Or NSA, or whoever."

"How does any of that help?" I asked.

ADVENTURES TO GO |

"It doesn't, not much, except to confirm you're not being paranoid. Maybe if we just sit tight, and you do nothing with the box, this will all go away."

"Do you really think so?"

"No. Of course not. Not before somebody else comes looking for it. Somebody has looked in the house, twice now, it seems, and found nothing. We can still hope maybe they will suspect you don't have what they want. If they persist, maybe you can give them the box and hope they are satisfied."

"Sounds too good to be true," I said. I hadn't told her about the *We'll be back* note I found on my pillow. She had enough cause for worry. "Isn't there some kind of law that applies here? The No Harassment of Innocent Civilians Act or something?" I was suddenly feeling frustrated, overwhelmed, and downright put-upon to have this mess dumped on me when all I had been doing, that day at the airport, was minding my own business and being a normal seventeen-year-old.

"A dozen, or more, laws apply. But just for starters, to even try to invoke them would require mountains of evidence and explanation – and generate the kind of attention you don't really want."

She was right, of course. Mom usually was.

"Now tell me more about these lottery tickets. You still have them, I assume?" Mom said.

"Of course."

"How much did Lonnie win?"

I told her. She got a faraway look in her eyes for a moment.

"That's why you were interested in the land near Hiawatha Creek that's slated for development, isn't it? Asking how much it cost?"

I nodded.

"You're not thinking of using the box again, I hope?" she said. I had told her what Miss B said about the box scrambling the brains of repeat users instead of just knocking out a few memories.

"No, of course not," I fibbed. My memories had all come back before, so maybe they would again. Or maybe not. Still, it was something to think about.

"Good. No land or money is worth damaging that wonderful brain of yours." She tousled my hair, the way she used to do a lot more often when

84

I was younger and shorter and my hair was easier to reach. "Just stay calm, and we'll see this through somehow."

CHAPTER IXX

I was just a kid who was out of his depth, but I wasn't completely naive. I was familiar with the ancient wisdom, often attributed to Lao Tzu, that says if you do nothing, everything is accomplished. Nobody has to change the world, all on their own. But I also had a choice to make – keep the box, or get rid of it. And I knew refusing to choose was also a kind of choice.

I texted Lonnie that night and asked if she had seen Miss B lately. I didn't expect she had. But I was planning to ask Lonnie, if she did see Miss B again, to tell her she could have the box. Just take it, go away, and leave us alone. Before someone got hurt. Someone besides me, that was, or before I got more than a splinter of wood in my hand.

No, Lonnie texted back. *Haven't seen her. Why do you ask?*

Just checking, I thumb-typed. *More tomorrow.*

Ride to work? she asked. *Might rain.*

Sure. Great, thanks, I replied.

"How's the hand?" Lonnie asked when I got in the car the next morning.

"Barely hurts. Few more days, and maybe I can ditch the bandages. I feel like I'm wearing a miniature mummy on my hand."

"A mummy hand puppet," she said with a laugh. "We should sell those in the gift shop. People will buy anything."

"You could do some ancient-Egyptian-themed artwork to decorate them."

"Then again," Lonnie said, "the whole project might seem disrespectful." Stopping at a red light, she asked, "Don't you think it's odd how Miss B just disappeared and didn't even give us a clue how to get in touch with her?"

"She did kind of act like someone on the run. Or, if not on the run, at least someone who has enemies. Worried about who might be behind her, that day outside the museum. And she claimed to be one of the good guys. Or, at least, not one of the bad guys."

"You believe her now?"

"No," I said. "No more reason to trust her now than before. But you're right – it would be strange for her to really go away without so much as a phone number or email address to let her know if I change my mind."

"Right. She wants the box, and she knows you have it, so she would want to be able to connect. Even if she is hiding from Bob. Whoever he is. If he even exists. So maybe she's still in the city," Lonnie concluded. "Maybe she isn't worried about you calling her because she and Officer Benton, or whoever, know just what you're doing, all the time."

"Could be. Let's keep watch."

"You're considering giving the box to her if you see her again?"

"How can I not? I mean, people breaking into the house in the middle of the night is pretty scary. Who knows what comes next?"

"I see your point."

ALL MORNING, I COULD BARELY CONCENTRATE ON THE MATERIALS I WAS SORTing. As often as I could, without the risk of arousing suspicions, I went upstairs and looked out at the picnic area. No Miss B. Not that I expected to see her. It was just a way to dispel some nervous energy.

That night, around ten-thirty, my phone buzzed. The screen said there was a new message from Lonnie. I opened it and read: *Meet at Willow Park. Bring artifact.*

When? I typed back.

Now. ASAP.

Why?

We need to talk.

About?

I know what to do with it.

Something seemed wrong. Actually, several things, when I thought about the messages. Lonnie was not usually that vague, almost cryptic, even in text messages. On the other hand, maybe I was just being paranoid. Not that I didn't have just cause for paranoia.

I read the messages again. The word *artifact* bothered me. It sounded too formal, too technical or academic. Lonnie would say *the thing*, or *the box*, or just *IT*.

I thumbed the icon to call her number. It rang. And rang. And rang some more.

The suspicious voice in my head was now louder than the voice that said I was being paranoid. Much louder. If Lonnie were on her phone, she would answer my call. So, if someone were spoofing, sending messages that looked like they were from Lonnie but were not, what should I do?

Still no answer from Lonnie. She must have turned her phone off, but I let my phone keep dialing, and meanwhile considered calling the landline her mom still used. Assuming anyone answered, though, and was not too pissed off to talk much, given the late hour, what would I say? "Hello, I would like to talk to your daughter about the weird, dangerous, and probably somehow illegal business I've gotten her involved in. Do you mind awfully seeing if she's awake?"

I ended the attempt to call. One possibility seemed obvious, on the assumption the message was not from Lonnie. Someone – Miss B, Officer Benton, the anonymous burglar, or one of their associates – wanted me to bring the box somewhere they could easily grab it. If that were the case, I saw two options: play along and go to the park with an empty coffee can

| THE ARTIFACT

in my backpack, or the sensible choice, keep my butt safe at home and see what happened next.

But what if Lonnie had gotten similar messages, sent by someone pretending to be me? What if she were on her way to the park, expecting to find me there? That didn't explain why she wasn't answering her phone. But maybe the battery died. Or she forgot, or it was on mute.

One of the privileges of being seventeen is the ability to boldly avoid doing the sensible thing. I pulled on some jeans and shoes, and found my old backpack, the one I never used anymore. I also took my little binoculars off the shelf and stuck them in my pocket. Downstairs, I quietly checked the trash can for something worthless to put inside, meanwhile assuming, hoping, Mom was asleep and would stay that way. An empty mixed nuts jar and an empty almond milk carton would have to do. I zipped them in the pack, took the carton back out and filled it halfway with water, and put it back. It was a long shot, but I wanted the pack to feel about as heavy as the box would. If someone grabbed it and the weight felt right, they might not look inside until later.

I went out the back door, closing it softly, and headed for Willow Park.

This was my first secret-agent-style recon mission, so maybe I can be forgiven for not knowing what I was doing. I did stop to look and listen often, especially when I got close to the park. The walk took awhile, but the bike would have been too conspicuous. All I heard were the city's night sounds – light traffic, a dog barking somewhere, a siren blocks away and receding. The park looked empty.

But when I came in sight of the benches where we usually met, I was surprised to see Lonnie sitting on one of them, in her red hoodie and Cardinals baseball cap. Then I remembered the binoculars. I stood in the shadows of a couple of trees. It took a few seconds to focus. The binoculars clearly showed the person on the bench was in fact Lonnie, not a lookalike. Congratulating myself on my cleverness and stealth, I turned cautiously to walk around the tree and was immediately staring into the faces of the two very large persons.

They both wore dark clothes and caps pulled low over their foreheads, so the faces were mostly just dark shadows. One grabbed my arms and pinned them behind my back in a practiced move. It felt like I wasn't his

ADVENTURES TO GO |

first victim. Or hers or theirs. It was impossible to tell much except that I was being mugged.

The other unzipped my pack, pulled out the decoys, and said, "Nothing here."

"Where is it?" I guessed he was talking to me. Again, I know I'm assuming. The voice sounded male, that's all.

"Where's what?" I said, struggling vainly against the grip that held my arms behind my back.

No answer, but hands ran up and down my legs and under my shirt.

"He's clean. Let's go," another voice said.

"Wait. Where is it? Did you give it to one of your girlfriends?"

"Let it go," the other voice said. "We were told to get in and get out, not to do an interrogation."

At that point, I heard Lonnie scream and blow the whistle she carried on her keychain. A moment later, cursing and cries of pain sounded from the direction of the bench.

Meanwhile, my muggers seemed to melt away in the shadows. I ran toward Lonnie and saw two other dark-clad figures staggering away from her.

I caught the tang of pepper spray in the air. "It's me, it's me," I said as I got closer to the bench, where she stood and looked all around for other assailants. The last thing I needed was to be sprayed.

"Linc! Are you okay?" Lonnie asked.

"I think so. Are you?" I checked for scrapes and scratches or other damage. I was probably going to have a nice bruise where I'd been grabbed, and my arms and shoulders would be sore from having my hands twisted behind my back, but at least my hand, still bandaged, did not seem to be bleeding.

"Just a little freaked out. Or a lot. Who were those creeps, anyway?"

"Didn't leave their cards," I said. "Which is just rude, when you think about it."

"I guess we should call the police," Lonnie said.

"In my experience, that's like closing the barn door after the horse is gone. What are the police going to do? Even if we get honest cops?"

"Not much, I suppose. So, let me guess – those text messages really weren't from you?" Lonnie said. She put her hand in mine. We both felt

90

| THE ARTIFACT

shaky. At least, I did, and I thought I could feel her hand trembling, too. The assailants appeared to have fled, though, so I felt safe. They wanted the box and were convinced I didn't have it. Not with me, anyway. Lonnie had shown them she was no easy target.

"Didn't you try to call me before you came?" I asked. "I tried to call you."

"Of course I did," she said. "But if someone can spoof your phone, maybe they can block a call, too."

"Seems even more obvious now – keeping quiet and doing nothing is not a good choice," I said. "This situation has to change."

"Why would they even want me to come here?" We walked away from the bench, avoiding shadows.

"Maybe they – whoever *they* are – think you might have the box. They've tried to steal it from my house but did not succeed, so maybe they wonder if I passed it along for safekeeping."

"That's a disturbing thought," Lonnie said. "By the way, Julie is mad at us."

"Mad? Why?"

"She feels left out. Thinks we have a secret, something we're not telling her."

"Oh. Well, we do," I said.

"If only we had a way to tell her it's something she's better off not knowing without telling her what it is."

"We'll have to put that on the to-do list for when this is all over."

Nobody said anything for a minute. We had stopped, still standing in the park, in the open grassy area across from the gazebo. It felt like we should move, go somewhere, but I didn't know where. I guess Lonnie didn't know, either.

"They wanted us to come to Willow Park. Does that mean they know it's close to where we both live, and they know we've been here before?" Lonnie wondered aloud.

"Sounds right." We started walking away from the park, along the short distance before our ways home went different directions.

"So, what else do they know? And how do they know it?"

ADVENTURES TO GO |

A disturbing thought came to me. "What if the burglar wasn't actually expecting to find the box?" I asked. "He probably would have grabbed it, if he saw it, but…"

"But what?"

"Maybe the house is bugged. Maybe the burglar wasn't there only to take the box, but to leave something."

"What, you mean like hidden cameras and microphones?"

"Why not? We're dealing with people who don't mind breaking the law, who obviously have access to sci-fi-level technology. A few tiny cameras and microphones would be no problem."

"If so, that means you'd better not even look at the … spot where you stashed the box." She looked around nervously. There were streetlights, but you don't think about how many shadowy hiding places streetlights make – not until you have a reason to wonder what's in the shadows.

"There has to be a way to find hidden microphones or cameras," I said.

"Even if you found one, how could you know you got rid of them all, though?"

"Maybe I shouldn't want to get rid of them. If you know someone is watching, you can control what they see."

"So you could use the strategy they follow in movies and TV shows. Replace the video feed of your basement with a recording of nothing happening?" Lonnie asked.

"Sounds like fun, but I don't know how to do that. I can probably solve the problem with my Swiss Army knife, if I can find the bugs. If the house really is bugged. I'm just speculating."

"I bet it is, though. Why wouldn't it be?"

The adrenaline was wearing off, and suddenly I felt exhausted. "I need sleep. Lots of sleep," I said.

We reached the street where we had to part ways. We checked to make sure our phones were working. They were, so I suggested we stay connected by phone until we were home.

We both made it home safely.

92

CHAPTER XX

I finally fell asleep while thinking I knew what I had to do. I thought the same when I woke up the next morning. I had to find a way to get rid of the box. If I didn't, someone besides me was going to get hurt. Or die. I reconsidered and decided again that I couldn't give the box back. In the wrong hands, it was too dangerous, and I was pretty sure all the hands trying to grab it were wrong. Even Miss B, who seemed like she might be only the least bad of a bad lot. She claimed she didn't want to see the box used to destroy any more minds, but she was also the one who had dumped it on me without warning. As the saying goes, the road to hell is paved with good intentions, if that's what her intentions were.

Which meant I'd better have more than good intentions, too. I needed a good plan. Absolutely foolproof. Or a plan as close to foolproof as possible. Any action I took, any choice I made, would lead down a road with no turning back. I had never been more aware of how refusing to make a choice was making a choice. We'd read that weird little short story by Jorge Luis Borges, "The Garden of Forking Paths," last fall in Junior English. I was beginning to feel like a character in that world, where every decision I made might be a matter of life and death, and I couldn't say which path was right.

Except I could, of course. I could tell – if I used the box. It would cost me nothing but a little amnesia. Hopefully temporary. But I couldn't give it back. I had a powerful tool. I would use it if I had to, but then I had a different idea.

STEP ONE OF THE PLAN INVOLVED ASSESSMENT OF THE SITUATION. DESPITE THE excitement of the night before, I was up at seven that morning, doing a search for how to find hidden cameras and microphones. It turns out there are various ways, and you don't need to be a tech genius to do the basics. In addition to putting an app on a phone to detect electromagnetic fields, the ways to find bugs varied from common-sense methods – look in the smoke detector or the potted plant for something that seems out of place – to expensive ones, like buying a special device to detect cameras or transmitters. The next simple way was to turn out the lights, close the curtains, and shine a flashlight in every direction to look for reflections. Even a tiny camera has a lens that should reflect light. I decided to try that one first, starting with the basement, since Officer Benton and the burglar had seemed most interested in it. Also because it was the easiest, as it was naturally dark.

I took a flashlight and headed downstairs. Standing in the middle of the basement, I methodically moved the light up and down, starting in the far left-hand corner and progressing clockwise. I felt simultaneously silly and exposed, like a character in a novel or spy movie. But if someone really were watching with a hidden camera, it would be very creepy, not silly.

Sure enough, halfway across the right wall, on a shelf where some old magazines were stacked, a glint of light flashed back. The magazines were issues of *National Geographic* and *Time* and *Newsweek* from days when information came on paper instead of a phone or computer. In another fifty or hundred years, they might belong in the basement of a museum like the Speed, to be sorted and maybe scanned into a computer by someone like me.

Suddenly I felt like a performer. I quickly moved the light past the spot where the reflection came from between the magazines. A toolbox sat on the shelf below and to the right of the presumed camera. I put the box on the floor near the middle of the room, in view of the camera, made a show of rummaging through it for a screwdriver, and put the toolbox back on the shelf. I hoped my performance had been sufficient to convince any spies that I had only been looking for a tool, not a hidden camera.

Mom was in the kitchen when I came back upstairs. Feeling like a character in an episode of *The X-Files* or *NCIS*, I wrote, *Don't say anything, but I think the house is bugged*, on a piece of paper and handed it to her. I tried to think of what to say to explain the paper, in case there was a camera in the kitchen, too, but I drew a blank.

Mom read the note and, after a thoughtful moment's pause, said, "You really think it will cost this much to go to college?"

"It's just an estimate," I said, catching her drift.

MOM GAVE ME A RIDE TO THE MUSEUM THAT MORNING. I DID A QUICK SEARCH of her car using the flashlight and the phone app and felt reasonably sure it wasn't bugged. On the way, she said she would talk to someone about getting a professional to check the house for bugs. I asked her to hold off on that.

"Why?" she asked.

I told her I was working on a plan. If the listeners/watchers didn't know we knew, there might be a way to use that to our advantage, to feed them disinformation.

"What sort of disinformation?"

"I'm still working on that."

AT THE MUSEUM, RIGHT BEFORE WE WENT TO WORK, I TOLD LONNIE WHAT I'D found and suggested she check her house, too. "Let's talk about it at lunch," she said.

Julie stopped by the picnic bench outside the museum, where we still ate whenever the weather was nice. "What are you planning to do about –" Lonnie was saying when she saw Julie walking our way. Lonnie was looking over my shoulder. I said, "About what?" but Lonnie did not answer.

"What's up?" Julie said.

I looked from her to Lonnie and said, "Nothing much."

"It sounded like something. Something that needed a plan to do something about it."

ADVENTURES TO GO |

"No, really, it was nothing," Lonnie said.

"Okay, tell me about it anyway," Julie said. Nobody spoke for a moment. "It must be an awfully big nothing if you can't talk about it," she added.

"We were talking about *Dr. Strangelove*," Lonnie said. She was way better than me at improvising. *Dr. Strangelove* was the last movie the three of us had seen together at the Uptown.

"I was saying Tracy Reed in that bikini looks so hot it's a crime," Lonnie continued, "but if she had a bulge in the bikini bottoms, it would be too perfect. I would have to excuse myself from the theater for a few minutes." She winked at me and Julie. Tracy Reed, I should explain, appears in an early scene in the movie, playing Miss Scott and wearing what by today's standards would be seen as a very modest bikini. But in 1963, it must have turned a lot of heads.

Julie did not smile. "Yeah, I'm not buying it. I heard what you were saying. Nobody needs a plan to deal with Tracy Reed."

"Excusing herself from the theater is a kind of plan," I tried, but it was no good.

"You guys have been keeping secrets lately. I thought we were friends."

"We are," Lonnie said. "You and Linc are my best friends in the world." I nodded.

"Friends don't keep secrets," Julie said.

"They do if someone's planning a surprise birthday party," I said, trying my hand at some ill-advised improv.

"Whose birthday?" Julie asked, looking slightly mollified, but only for a moment. I guess she could see me fumbling to do the math in my head. Nobody we knew well enough to throw a party for them had a birthday anytime soon.

"Fine," Julie said. "Enjoy your little secrets." She got up and walked away.

"Wait, I'm sorry," I said. "Don't go."

Lonnie put her hand on mine and didn't say anything. It was her way of letting me know there was nothing we could do right now that would fix things. I thought she was right. Laying the whole wild tale on Julie right then, true though it was, would be a bad idea. She would likely not believe it, so it would just make her feel worse.

96

THAT EVENING, I GOT TO WORK ON MY DECOY. WHICH WAS WHERE MY SWISS Army knife came into play. My original thought had been to just cut the power cord or pry batteries out of the cameras, if there were any, but I had since decided Lonnie was on the right track. Like I had told Mom, disinformation seemed to be required. I didn't have to patch in any fake video feeds, though, which would be complicated and above my skill level. Nevertheless, I could do something better than just hacking away at the spy equipment. I would put on a show for the cameras.

After searching my room for reflections from lenses, and also using both of the phone apps I'd downloaded that were supposed to detect hidden electronics, I felt fairly confident the room was surveillance-free. I unzipped my backpack and spread its contents on the desk: an empty coffee can, a roll of silver duct tape, a half-pint can of silver paint and a small brush, pliers and wire cutters, some cardboard, and magic markers.

An hour and a half later, after two tries, I had fashioned a reasonable facsimile of the magic box that started all this trouble. My first effort was totally unconvincing, so I saw it as a prototype. A trial run. The second just might do the job. It was a reasonable facsimile in low light, from a distance, and in what I hoped would be a grainy image from the tiny camera in the basement. I left the facsimile on the desk, on a paper towel, so paint and glue could finish drying, while I took a nap.

When I woke up half an hour later, the paint was still wet. I thought about my next step.

If there was a camera in the basement, as there appeared to be, it had to have a transmitter of some sort and maybe a power supply, unless it had a very good battery and a huge memory. But planning another burglary to retrieve the camera and download whatever it had recorded seemed way too pedestrian and low-tech for the people we were dealing with. Besides, information a week or two old might be useless to whoever was watching.

I went downstairs and looked in the hall closet, the one under the stairs to the second floor. Far in the back, in the nook where the last step met the floor, was the space right above the shelf of old magazines in the basement. I crawled on hands and knees to the back of the closet and, sure enough, spotted the wire. It ran through a small hole and was attached to a small black box with what looked like a telescoping antenna. I didn't know, but I thought I was looking at the transmitter and maybe a power supply.

The significance of this find rattled around my brain. On at least one other occasion, someone must have been in the house to install this thing, because there was no way Officer Benton had time to do it, and I didn't think the unknown burglar had, either. I wasn't sure Benton had even looked in the hall closet, much less crawled around there. Whoever installed this must have been a pro, coming and going in stealth and without breaking things. That thought lent at least some credence to Miss B's claim that more than one person or group wanted the box back. Representatives of one group came and went undetected, and those from another broke windows. Or maybe the broken window had been an accident, a slip of the hand or tool while trying to open a lock.

I hoped there were no cameras in the hall, so no one had seen me inspecting their handiwork. My plan, such as it was, depended on the bad guys not knowing I knew they were watching. I backed out of the closet without disturbing anything.

It was already ten o'clock. It seemed like a good idea to sleep on it, see how things looked tomorrow. I needed to let Mom in on the plan. I could also talk to Lonnie and see if she saw any obvious flaws. My first instinct was to text her in the morning, but since our phones had apparently been hacked, texting would never do. Unless, of course, we wanted to spread disinformation that way. Maybe we needed a code.

STAGE TWO OF MY PLAN INVOLVED MAKING WHOEVER WAS WATCHING THINK I had gotten rid of the box.

It's funny how you can live near something remarkable for decades and know little about it. How many New Yorkers have ever been to the top of the Empire State Building or the Chrysler Building? A small percentage, I'd guess. From what I'd seen, when we went to New York on a class trip, it's true what they say – only tourists gaze up at the tall buildings. As an architect-to-be, as well as a visitor, I couldn't get enough. The shorter buildings were fascinating, their styles and histories, but the tall ones – these are our pyramids. The ones that people will wonder about a thousand years from now.

| THE ARTIFACT

A pessimist might imagine nuclear war and planes falling out of the sky and New York and all the other major cities leveled. Me, I'm still young enough to be an optimist. At least sometimes, what we build outlasts us.

Anyhow, the point is, I had lived my whole life on the shores of the Ohio River yet never really thought much about it. The Ohio is as remarkable as New York's Chrysler Building, or the Eiffel Tower or the Taj Mahal, or any artificial structure. Or more so, in its way. Not that we didn't have some remarkable architecture in Louisville. Our tallest specimen, at 400 West Market, was a little over half as tall as the Chrysler Building, if you counted the antenna structure on top of the Chrysler.

Now that I had cause to investigate, I learned the Ohio River is at its deepest, between one hundred and thirty and one hundred and seventy feet, where it passes Louisville. It runs for almost a thousand miles between Pennsylvania and Illinois. People ignore it most of the time, everyone except tourists, people responsible for maintaining bridges, occasional party boats and pleasure cruises, and coal barges scudding by. Yet there it always is. A hundred and sixty feet of water, a mile wide where it passes north of downtown, over a kilometer and a half to the Indiana shore, constantly flowing past the city, day and night.

The river may not rival the Chrysler Building for inspiring immediate awe, but it has plenty of water for one small box to get lost in forever. Or seem to.

Several bridges cross the Ohio at Louisville, including a former railroad bridge converted to accommodate only pedestrians and bikes. I had ridden across it many times, always during the day, as the area had a reputation for not being entirely safe after dark. The weak spot in my plan was, how to make sure the right eyes saw me on the way to the bridge, without stopping me?

So I decided I should make my way to the river in a car, on one of the other bridges. On foot or riding my bike, it would be too easy for guys like the ones who grabbed us in the park to intercept me long before the show was complete. Stopping a car on the bridge and throwing something out was surely all kinds of illegal, but considering what was at stake, I thought I could risk it.

ADVENTURES TO GO |

Not that I intended to drop the real magic box in the water. That's what my art project was all about. The river was big enough to hope what it swallowed would never be seen again.

Best laid plans . . .

CHAPTER XXI

I talked to Lonnie at lunch and told her my plan. "So, you wanna be the getaway driver?"

"Why don't you just smash it to bits with a hammer? In front of the camera? Smash the fake, I mean."

I realized I'd been thinking of throwing the box – the real one – in the river as a final desperate gesture since the beginning. She was right, though. Doing the same with the decoy just made the plan more complicated than it needed to be. Especially now that the house was under surveillance.

"They might want the remains, though, even if I smash the box," I pointed out.

"Then set the remains on fire. The parts that will burn. All in front of the cameras, of course."

"There might be toxic chemicals, if the real thing were burned. Who knows what's inside? Maybe nothing that will burn. The outside of the real thing looks like stainless steel. Or maybe it's supposed to blow up if somebody tries to burn it. They might've booby-trapped it. For all we know, there's a stick of dynamite inside. Besides, it would set off the smoke detector. Or, my luck, I'd burn the house down."

101

ADVENTURES TO GO |

"Ha. Now he worries about the fire alarm," Lonnie said, rolling her eyes, but smiling. "If you don't want to burn it, the fake one, then just smash and smash, and smash again. Pulverize it, and drop the remains in the trash. Let them go dumpster-diving if they want the pieces back."

"But if they do recover it, they'll know it wasn't the real thing."

"The same applies to dropping it in the river. They might find it. You would have to weigh it down so it goes straight to the bottom. But then they have only a small part of the bottom to search."

"At least the fire hazard is eliminated," I said. "If they search the river bottom and find anything, they'll have to work for it."

"Or, you know, you could just do nothing, and hope the burglars or kidnappers give up."

"They'll keep coming. I have to try something before the whole situation gets any further out of control." I thought a minute and added, "You're right – the best bet is to try to leave them convinced it has been smashed beyond use. And just hide the remains in the knothole of the big tree in the back yard. No clues in the trash. Let the river flow without my contributing to pollution. I like the dramatic gesture, but it's too awkward. Pointless if they don't see us, and dangerous if they do. The last thing we need is a car chase."

"So you're planning to smash the decoy?"

"Yes."

"The real box – you're just going to keep it under your basement steps? Forever?" Lonnie asked.

"Until it seems safe to move it somewhere else, yeah, I guess so. I still don't see a better option."

"And the temptation to use it, and zap your brain, and kill who knows what memories – you can resist it indefinitely?"

"I think so."

"You don't sound too sure."

"All I know for certain is, as long as I have it, nobody else is using it, and if I decide I need to destroy it later, for real, at some future date, I can. Or if I decide I have to give it up, to whomever, I can."

"Maybe it's like the Ring, in Tolkien, and it's dangerous even to possess, because it also possesses you."

102

"Yeah. Maybe, and what if, and who knows? One step at a time."

THAT EVENING, LONNIE CAME TO MY HOUSE TO LOOK AT THE DECOY. "Not bad," she said. "It should fool them. In low light, anyway."

We went to the backyard, where I told her very quietly about the rest of my plan. The basement camera was connected to what I assumed was a transmitter in the hall closet. I would disconnect it for a couple of minutes, stash the decoy in the gun safe in the basement, and reconnect the camera. Optimistically, this could be done before anyone was dispatched to repair the camera. Then, let the show begin. The camera would see me take the decoy out of the safe, where the audience would assume it had been undiscovered all along.

"They're bound to notice when the camera sees nothing, even for a couple of minutes, though," she said.

"I'm hoping they chalk it up to a disturbance in the ether, or something like that."

"So what's the hold-up? What are you waiting for?"

"A better idea, I guess."

"I got nothin'."

"You wanna be part of the show?" I asked. "You can tell me it's totally pulverized and will never give anyone forbidden knowledge of the future again. Just to drive the point home, in case they didn't notice."

"That's what friends are for."

SO WE DID IT. IN DIM LIGHT ONLY FROM THE OPEN DOOR AT THE TOP OF THE steps, I smashed the decoy box repeatedly with a carpenter's hammer from the rarely used toolbox on the workbench. Both hammer and bench were inheritances from my departed father, like the safe.

"I think you got it," Lonnie said on cue, and held up a plastic trash bag. I scooped bits and pieces off the floor where the decoy had been.

"To the garbage?" she inquired.

"Tally ho," I said, and we made our way cautiously up the dark basement steps. But instead of leaving the bag to be found in the trash, I

ADVENTURES TO GO |

dropped it down the knothole of the big maple in our backyard, where it settled out of sight.

It all seemed a bit anticlimactic. Little did I know what the future held.

CHAPTER XXII

Next afternoon, I was walking my bike down the sidewalk by a street too busy to ride safely. It was a beautiful summer day, afternoon turning to evening. An hour you'd want to last forever. At least, you would unless you had other things on your mind.

I was hoping Miss B or whoever else might care would believe the box had been destroyed, so they would go their merry way and let me think about architecture, where to go to school, and old movies. I was tired of dwelling on secret technology and possible conspiracies. A little voice I didn't want to hear suspected it couldn't be that simple.

"Get in the car, kid. Let's go for a ride." I turned and saw an ordinary sedan. It was unremarkable enough to avoid unwanted attention. White, with tinted windows. The driver had pulled to the curb and opened the passenger's-side window. He wore dark sunglasses. I didn't recognize him.

"No, thanks." I started to walk more quickly and ran right into one of two large, solid gentlemen who had stopped in front of me and beside me. The one I bumped into was blond, with a neatly trimmed beard.

"Excuse me," I said, turning to go around him. The other, a dark-haired man, blocked the way. Both wore tennis shirts and jeans. The blond

ADVENTURES TO GO |

man wore a light sport coat. Like the car, nothing to make them stand out much in a crowd.

"Excuse me," I repeated, and tried again to go around.

The dark-haired man put his hand on the brake lever of my bike and squeezed, locking the front wheel. "I'm Larry," he said. "You're in trouble. We're here to help."

The others' names I never learned, so I thought of them as Curly and Moe. Curly, who had short, tight ringlets of hair, drove the car. Or, distracting myself from fear with absurd thoughts, I guessed they were Larry's brother Darryl and his other brother Darryl, from *Newhart*. I know, it's the twenty-first century, but classic TV is still classic.

"C'mon, Linc," Larry said. "Let's do this the easy way. What do you say?" Meanwhile, the blond man put his arm down. His jacket opened just far enough for me to glimpse the dark shape of a handgun.

"I said, no thanks!" I spoke loudly enough that people would notice, I hoped.

Of course nobody on the sidewalk or street paid attention, though. Louisville is not New York or Los Angeles, but it's big enough. People master from a young age the survival skill of keeping their heads down and walking quickly past trouble. Not that there was much to look at just then. A couple of pairs of eyes flashed my way for half a second and were quickly gone.

Larry put his other arm on my wrist and squeezed hard. "Listen, Linc," he said quietly, leaning confidentially toward me. "I've got a kid about your age. I'd really hate for this to get ugly." He squeezed my arm harder, until I nearly cried out in pain. "Nobody wants to hurt you. We just need to have a little conversation."

I've never been a fast runner, but I figured I didn't have to be. I knew the street, probably better than these guys did. I darted my eyes, planning an escape route, but then let out a yelp of pain as the grip on my arm turned vise-like.

"Your mom's got enough to worry about, hasn't she?" Larry said. "You don't really want her visiting you in the hospital. I don't want that, either. Like I said, though, we really do have to talk."

106

| THE ARTIFACT

"Let me help you with that," the blond man said, and hooked the lock on my bike around the one-hour-parking sign post. "Your wheels will be right here when you come back for them."

I understood the situation. They knew my name and apparently had been expecting me to come down this street. I figured they also knew where I lived and where Mom worked. Threats were implied that I didn't want to analyze and catalog just then.

I tried to break away and run but fell when my arm stayed in Larry's grip, and a few seconds later I found myself spinning down the street in the back seat of the car. All the tinted windows were now up. The blond man sat in front, Larry beside me. Curly drove, blending with traffic, stopping completely at stop signs and signaling dutifully when turning. Nothing to attract attention. I tried the door handle. It didn't open.

I didn't know exactly where we were headed, but it was in the general direction of Fort Knox.

NOBODY SAID ANYTHING FOR A WHILE. "ISN'T THIS WHERE YOU BLINDFOLD ME, so I can't tell anyone where I was taken?" I asked.

Nobody answered. Instead the blond man said, "Give me your phone."

"What?" I said, stalling. My phone was the last thing keeping me from feeling totally at these guys' mercy.

"Your phone. Give it to me."

"What?" I said again, and instantly reminded myself of Brett in "Pulp Fiction" before he is dared to say "what" again – as, of course, he ever so unwisely does.

No inspiration had come in the extra seconds. If I did not give him the phone, they would take it anyway. I handed it to the blond man. He popped off the back, removed the battery, and put the disassembled pieces in his pocket.

I asked where we were going. Nobody answered. No surprise. But they didn't blindfold me, either. I started memorizing the way, noting road numbers, turns, and landmarks. It wasn't as if I had any confidence that reporting this incident to the police and telling them where I'd been taken would help. Even if I got away to tell anyone anything, I'd probably just end up talking to Officer Benton or his best buddy.

ADVENTURES TO GO |

But memorizing the route was something to do, and it made me feel a little less helpless. Also, if I had to walk home, I might as well know the way. Later, I realized I should have been very frightened at not being blindfolded – it meant I wasn't expected to be able to say where I was taken.

Based on the position of the sun sinking in the west, I knew the car was still headed in a southerly direction, more or less toward Fort Knox, but the city lay miles behind. The driver had exited Interstate 65 and soon turned off the two-lane state highway. We zigged and zagged along county roads in the Kentucky countryside. I had no idea where we were.

I still memorized landmarks and kept track of right and left turns, however, repeating them over in my head. I'm generally very good at feats of memory. When I was still young enough not to be bored by going with Mom to the grocery store, but old enough to have started school and learned to read, she used to call me her "mobile shopping reminder." All I had to do was see the list once, while it was stuck under the magnet on the fridge, to know if she forgot anything at the store.

I would have given a lot, just then, to be shopping with Mom; I was genuinely terrified by now. The only thing that kept me from panicking and trying to kick out one of the car's windows, large men notwithstanding, was repeating in my head the series of *lefts* and *rights* and *big tree, falling-down barn* and other landmarks.

After what must have been an hour or more, the car finally turned off the paved road onto gravel. That road became less gravelly and finally just plain dirt, right before the car stopped at a gate in a chain-link fence. Inside the fence was a concrete block structure best described as a bunker. It was maybe twenty feet on each side, with a low metal roof and steel door. The area inside the fence, I guessed, was around a hundred feet per side. The fence looked ten feet high and was topped with razor wire.

This place was, literally, the end of the road. The driver rolled down his window and keyed in some numbers on a pad attached to a metal pole. I tried to see the numbers, but his hand blocked my view. The gate opened and shut, apparently automatically, after the car rolled through. Or perhaps someone in the bunker pushed a button.

All around, outside the fence, lay nothing but dense Kentucky woods, which can be as impenetrable as any jungle, fence or no fence. Big tree trunks were surrounded by smaller shrubs, vines, and thorny bushes. The

| THE ARTIFACT

driver pushed a button up front and the lock on the door beside me clicked. He and the others got out.

I didn't move. The blond man bent and looked inside the car. "You planning to sleep here, or are you going to come in and have some supper?"

I got out.

The men – call them kidnappers, because that's what they were – didn't bother with ropes or handcuffs. There was nowhere to run. I'd seen no other cars on the road for several miles, even if the gate were not closed.

A small plate a few inches square on the door of the bunker slid aside, a face peered out for a moment, and the door opened. We went in.

Inside, the bunker looked like an ordinary office: a desk, some chairs, a counter with a coffee maker, and some cabinets over a sink. And an elevator. I recognized the black circle and yellow triangles that indicated a bomb shelter or fallout shelter, on the wall beside the elevator. I guessed that explained why the bunker was here in the middle of nowhere, apparently now used for other purposes. It must have been built decades ago when people were more worried about all-out nuclear war, and some imagined themselves among survivors who wouldn't wish they had died in the blasts. I thought briefly of *Dr. Strangelove*. The day we saw it seemed a long time ago.

No one was there but me and the Three Stooges. Whoever had looked out was gone. Larry banged the door closed behind us.

"This way," he said, going to the elevator and punching four digits on a keypad beside it. I memorized those numbers. He pushed the call button. Inside, the control panel had only three buttons: *Up*, *Down*, and *Emergency Stop*. Larry pushed *Down*. The air smelled stale, recycled.

I couldn't know how far we went, but the floor dropped quickly. I nearly stumbled before steadying myself with a hand against the cold stainless-steel wall. The elevator kept going for perhaps twenty-five or thirty seconds, a long way down. On the way, I wondered if there were stairs leading back to the surface, in case of fire or power failure, and how long it would take to climb them.

The elevator stopped as abruptly as it started. My knees almost buckled. When the door opened, Larry and the other guys stepped out to the left. I followed, if only because I did not want to be trapped inside if the elevator door closed. But it stayed open after I stepped out and looked

ADVENTURES TO GO |

around. The hallway ran dozens of feet in either direction, doors here and there on both sides. The ends were lost in shadow. It occurred to me that I should get back in the elevator and take it back to the surface. But I'd noted Curly, the driver, taking the keys from the ignition of the car. Even if I made it around, under, or over the gate without being irreparably sliced up by razor wire, it would be a long walk back to the last outpost of civilization in my catalog of landmarks.

At that point, I had no idea just how much I would eventually long to find myself walking down a lonely country road.

CHAPTER XXIII

The three men walked purposefully away. I supposed their work with me was done. To my right a door opened. Miss B stepped out. She had been dressed in a sort of business-casual outfit when I'd last seen her, but now she wore a white lab coat.

"Lincoln!" she exclaimed. "Nice to see you again. Welcome to our little outpost in the wilderness."

Strangely, my first emotion was a slight feeling of comfort at seeing a familiar face. Which made no sense, as she was, for me, the beginning of all my current troubles. Maybe I was already suffering from the onset of Stockholm syndrome. Or maybe fear was just causing me to grasp at straws because I felt like I sort of knew her, though even her real name remained a mystery.

"I thought you said we wouldn't meet again," I said.

"Didn't expect things to work out this way," she shrugged. "The others were getting too aggressive. Not to mention your little stunt with the hammer. We need you to finish your contribution to the project while there's still time."

111

ADVENTURES TO GO |

"Time for what? Which others? Project? My contribution? I don't suppose you want to give me any details about the big picture. Like who these others really are, or why you sent people to kidnap me?"

"Don't think of it as kidnapping," Miss B said. "Consider us your colleagues. As for why, well, we need you to do something. The rest is all on a need-to-know basis. And you know all you need to, for now. More than you should, in fact." She walked toward me and pointed the way the others had gone. "Come along. There's someone I want you to meet."

"Larry, Curly, and Moe? I've already made their acquaintance."

"No." She smiled a little. "You have a nickname for me, too?"

"Maybe you'd like to tell me your real name?"

"No."

"Well, I think of you as Miss B. For Blue Eyes."

"I'm flattered. I've been called worse by test subjects." Right then, the blue eyes looked very cold. A chill ran down my spine.

"So you're the one I should have been afraid of, not someone called Bob, as you said that day at the picnic bench? The story about how you were there to keep the really bad guys from getting to me was totally bogus?"

"Maybe I am Bob. Or maybe Bob is one of my personae. But enough about Bob. You don't need to know."

She opened a door, looked briefly inside, and said, "Looks like the Doc stepped out for a minute. But where are my manners?" she said. "Come in and have a seat. Let's talk. He'll be back in a while. You can meet him later." She opened another door farther down the hall and gestured for me to enter. The room was an ordinary office, with desk and chairs, a potted plant under a light. If not for the absence of a window to remind occupants they were deep underground, it could have been the workspace of a lawyer or banker.

"Did you ever wonder why you were chosen to carry the artifact?" she asked, smiling enigmatically, when we were seated.

"I assume I was in the wrong place at the wrong time. I must have been convenient. Somebody who wanted the box was onto you, and you had to get rid of it."

"There's more to the story than that," Miss B said. "You were chosen. It was no accident I found you at the airport. Success in any endeavor,

112

| THE ARTIFACT

including one as high-risk/high-reward as ours, requires one to adapt to circumstances. We have had occasional disagreements with some of our competitors, but we do not generally operate on a random or chaotic level. The main reason you were given the artifact is that you were identified, several years ago, as someone who could use it effectively."

"Years ago?" I repeated. "Identified how?"

"Have you ever pondered how much information about each individual is available for ones who know how and where to look for it? Especially in the modern technological society? Some kinds of personal information have been around for decades, when computers still ran on punch cards and vacuum tubes, or even longer. Birth certificates, phone numbers and postal addresses, bank accounts, social security registration, tax filings, internet search histories, etc. Now that information is easily accessed by anybody who's interested and has the right technical skills. Accessed, and manipulated, if need be. School records, especially standardized test scores – did you ever notice one or two questions in each section seemed irrelevant or out of place? Those are our screener questions, used to identify potential recruits. You are highly qualified. Not everyone can use the artifact effortlessly, the way you did. You have the mental ability to do so much more." Miss B's voice trailed off as if contemplating heights of achievement I could soar to.

"Or consider the innocent altruism that leads you to donate blood. People who are not eager to be easy targets use complex passwords for things like email and bank accounts, change them on a regular basis, and guard them like state secrets. Then they go and donate blood, for no more reward than the chance to feel good about themselves. If there were full disclosure as to how much personal information they're handing out, free of charge, for anyone who cares to look, with every cubic milliliter of blood – DNA, antibodies, blood type, diseases you've had, trace elements that reveal foods you eat, water you drink, air you breathe – people would run and never look back when asked to donate blood."

I had donated blood several times. Still do. Once the info is out there, I guess it's out there. Besides, I'm no freeloader. Some day, I may need someone else's blood, and I want to feel like I give as much as I take.

"I think I'm starting to get the picture," I said. "No matter how paranoid I am, I'm not paranoid enough."

ADVENTURES TO GO |

"Paranoid, or realistic. They can be hard to tell apart sometimes. We also checked your medical records, of course, just to confirm what DNA and blood samples told us – you are a very healthy young man. Current on your vaccinations, never had any venereal diseases, so you are careful – good for you – appropriate weight for age and height, and fine overall cardiovascular health. Probably enhanced by the bicycling you do, which explains the broken clavicle you had a couple of years ago. Common injury for cyclists, and you healed nicely. But you do wear a helmet. That's good. It would be a shame to damage that marvelous brain of yours."

She glanced up from the folder, still flashing that enigmatic smile. I guess she hoped I would look alarmed, or at least impressed, by how thoroughly someone had snooped into my life. I tried to look stoic. Or at least, less afraid than I was.

"I assume there's a point to all this?" I asked. "Besides proving privacy is an illusion? Because that's not really surprising for anyone who pays attention to the news."

"Of course. Our research here at this facility shows strong academic and intellectual abilities are a good starting point in determining who can use the artifact most effectively. In addition, there's a genetic marker to indicate whether the memory loss is temporary or permanent. You scored high on all assessments. And you're young. That always seems to help. Older subjects tend not to fare so well."

"What you're saying is, you think I'm a good lab rat."

"Oh, so cynical. I'm offering you a chance to serve your country," she said.

"Yeah, about that. I'm no bum, I do my part. Make my contribution to society and all. But my dad served his country, too, and got killed for his trouble. So pardon me if I'm a little skeptical. I never asked or volunteered to be a martyr. I like my memories. Most of them, anyway. Even the bad ones, I'd like to keep. Maybe learn something from them."

"For instance, you hope to learn why it's a bad idea to destroy other people's property that was entrusted to you for safekeeping?"

"I have no idea what you mean," I said, hoping I did know. She had earlier mentioned my "little stunt with the hammer," which I took to be an allusion to destroying the decoy, but it would be nice to know for sure.

114

| THE ARTIFACT

"I hear you broke our toy. The artifact. That's unfortunate, but we still have work for you to do."

So it seemed they thought the box no longer existed. Or existed only as useless crumbs. Thank goodness for small favors. "Okay, I'm confused," I said. "First you just want me to transport your magic box, because, it was implied, you were being watched or followed or something, but now it turns out I was chosen specifically, and I was being spied on – even before the hidden cameras turned up in my house? Was anyone ever really trying to snatch the box from you?" I also wondered how long the house had been bugged. Months? Years? But if I asked, and even if she answered, I would have no reason to believe her.

"It is possible for spies to spy on other spies, you know. We're a suspicious lot. Anyway, that's water under the bridge. What matters is here and now and what comes next. You were not entrusted with the artifact only to move it from point A to point B. You were being auditioned. What would you do with it? What *could* you do with it? Fortunately, for us, at any rate, you passed the audition. With flying colors, I might add. Many do not."

"And I should be ever so grateful to get the part?"

"We have a lot of questions you can help us answer," Miss B said, ignoring the sarcasm. "Questions about the future. Questions about how your brain and central nervous system interact with the artifact."

"You'll have to find your answers some other way. I have no reason to cooperate. Besides, that day outside the museum, you told me you just wanted to keep the box where it could do no more harm."

"Oh, come now, be sensible. You have every reason to help. You want to see your mother again, don't you? And those lovely girlfriends? You volunteered yourself for this," Miss B said.

"I didn't volunteer for anything," I said. I didn't know what time it was, but it was late. *Mom must be frantic with worry*, I thought. *She'll call Lonnie, maybe Julie. Possibly even the police and hospitals.*

"By keeping the box, by using it, you volunteered," Miss B said. "If you'd given up the artifact, you'd probably be just a note in our never-to-be-published records. A promising subject if we needed you, but far from unique. You proved what we needed you to prove, that people who fit the profile can experience at least a limited number of visions with no

ADVENTURES TO GO |

lasting harm. But by not playing fair, you stayed on the radar. Now we are as interested in you as in the artifact itself. After all, we made the one you broke, and we can make another one. Probably. There are aspects of its function we do not fully understand, but you'll give us a chance to gather data to further our knowledge. At any rate, we still have the original artifact to work with."

"You mean – ?" Despite the weight of fear and anxiety, I felt a twinge of curiosity and excitement.

She nodded. "The one Howard Carter removed from the tomb so long ago and wisely kept secret."

"You, or people you work with, have had an artifact with mysterious, if not downright magical properties, since 1922, and you're just now getting around to investigating it?"

"Others have tried to crack its secrets, of course. With varying degrees of success. You know the story of the Enigma machine, an encoding device used by the Germans in World War II? And how the Allies supposedly cracked the Enigma code, which the Germans believed to be unbreakable?"

I nodded. "I watch movies and read books."

"Well, what the books and movies don't tell you is how the Allies got enough information to understand Enigma and build their own machine. We believe the British had knowledge of the future, which they probably got by using the same artifact we are now attempting to understand. We still have a lot to learn, but of course we did not give you our only reproduction model. We have learned to make functional models, consistently, even though we still have a lot of questions about how and why they work. Questions you may help us answer.

"So, you may as well play the game, by the rules, and soon we'll send you back to the city and let you get on with your delightful little life."

I was not naive enough to take that story at face value, of course. Not for one second, as badly as I wanted to. I knew far too much for them to just let me walk away. "I never asked to play the game at all." I felt like I was repeating myself. "I didn't know there was a game until you stowed the box in my backpack. Or had you forgotten? You know my mom and my friends will be looking for me by now. They've almost certainly called the police. Kidnapping is a federal crime, so the FBI will get involved."

"Now, Lincoln. I thought we'd gotten past all that. Your friends and mother will have no idea where to look for you. The police, as I believe you are well aware, have been infiltrated. And the FBI, well, they work for the same people we do. Or, at least, they are answerable to the same people. The FBI knows well enough to stick with chasing drug dealers and bank robbers. Oh, and just in case you decide it might be a good idea to get lost in the woods, we change the code on the elevator and the outside gate twice a day. Also, in addition to being tall and topped with razor wire, the fence is electrified with enough current to light up a small town."

"You're telling me there's not one honest cop in all of Louisville who will do their job? Or one Kentucky State Trooper or FBI agent? You're that confident in being above the law?"

She smiled complacently and didn't answer.

"What exactly do you want me to do?" I asked, to break the oppressive silence. This far underground, miles from the city, the bunker seemed deafeningly quiet now, except for the low hiss of the ventilation system.

Other sections were not so comfortingly quiet, I was soon to learn.

"What do we want you to do? Not much. Just save the world," she said. "But it's late. You must be tired. And hungry. Let's get you something to eat, and then I'll introduce you to the Doc and show you to your room. You two can get started in the morning."

She stood and opened the door. "After you," she said politely.

I got up and went back out in the hall. She was right. I was starving and exhausted. Fear will do that to you.

I FOLLOWED MISS B DOWN THE HALL OF MANY DOORS TO A SMALL BUT WELL-stocked cafeteria. It held a dozen tables and a serving line, complete with trays, plates, and silverware at one end. "Help yourself," she said. Steam rose from some of the dishes on the serving line, but the room was empty save for us two.

Despite feeling very hungry, I was nauseated by the sight and smell of food. I choked down some onion rings, washed down by bottled water, which seemed a safe choice. Miss B sat across from me and quietly sipped a cup of coffee.

ADVENTURES TO GO |

"You don't seem worried I'm going to escape," I said, dipping a ring in some ketchup. "I did notice we're in the middle of nowhere, the doors require a code, and the keys were not left in the car. So you don't have to watch me eat."

"Oh, but I do," she said. "Have to be sure you keep your energy levels up."

When I finished, she led me down the hall. "Let me introduce you to the Doc. I know he's been anxious to meet you. Then we'll let you get some rest. Busy day tomorrow."

She opened a door on the left side of the hall. Inside was a large room outfitted with computer monitors, microscopes, and tables with built-in sinks and lots of drawers. The room reminded me of the biology lab at school – except for the thing in the middle, a medical-industrial-looking chair. It was like ones I recalled seeing in dentists' exam rooms, yet somehow darker. Shiny, sinister instruments glittered over black vinyl. Nor did the dentists' chairs I'd seen have restraining straps and buckles for occupants. Or victims. Or "test subjects," as Miss B had said.

"Dr. Eisenberg, meet Lincoln. I believe he prefers to be called Linc."

A man sat at a desk facing the far right wall. He stood and turned. Round, steel-framed glasses perched on a sharp, pointed nose. A fringe of white hair circled a mostly bald head. I guessed he was in his sixties.

He smiled when he saw me, but the smile rose no further than thin lips over his narrow chin.

"Oh, so you are the wunderkind. So glad to finally make your acquaintance," he said.

I looked from him to Miss B and back. "I don't know about *wunderkind*. As far as I know, I'm just a regular guy. So, now that I've met everyone and had the tour, why don't you call Larry and the boys to take me home? I promise not to tell anyone where I've been."

"Of course you won't, dear," Miss B said, and patted my shoulder. "Keep me posted on the results," she said to Dr. Eisenberg, on her way out.

He examined me briefly – took my blood pressure and heartbeat, shined a small flashlight in my eyes, and looked in my ears, for some reason.

"I'd like to get a blood sample, too, but I suppose that can wait." He filled a syringe with clear liquid from a small vial and asked, "Right or left?"

118

| THE ARTIFACT

"If you mean which of your own butt cheeks you should inject that into, it's totally up to you," I said.

"Oh, you do have a sense of humor. That always helps. Now then, right or left?"

"I'm not volunteering. Forget it. I've had it with you people, whoever the hell you are. I want to go home."

"Come now. This injection is not at all harmful or unpleasant. You don't want me to call the boys to strap you in the chair, just for a simple shot, do you? I believe you are far smarter than that."

"At least tell me what's in the syringe."

"Certainly. Informed consent. This is a combination of a a sleep aid, which will act in the short term to make sure you are well-rested in the morning, and a compound that stimulates production of neurotransmitters. The neural stimulator should have a more lasting effect than the sleep aid, and it will enhance your natural ability to interact with the artifact. It seems to help avoid the worst short-term memory losses, too. As I said, nothing to be the least bit afraid of."

He gave me the shot and pushed a button on the wall that apparently activated an intercom. "He'll be sound asleep in no time," Eisenberg said. "You have a room assigned for him?"

"I'll be right there." I recognized the voice as Miss B's.

Down the hall again through a door on the right. I collapsed on a twin bed and passed out before I could repeat my demand to be taken home.

119

CHAPTER XXIV

This is where my tale began.

The next morning, as I thought of it – somehow there was a morning feel, despite the absence of daylight or a clock in the room – I awoke to the buzz of an overhead fluorescent light and a knock at the door. Confused, I sat up and looked around. The horrifying memories of the evening before came flooding back.

I was in a small room that reminded me of a college dorm. Not that I had ever lived in a college dorm, though I hoped I soon would.

A second knock at the door. I said nothing, but the door opened. A young woman looked in. She was maybe twenty-five and wore a lab coat. "I'm Jeanette. Dr. Eisenberg's assistant," she said, speaking with quick efficiency. "He wants you in the lab in half an hour." I noticed she had one large freckle on her left upper lip. When it's hard to understand or process what's happening, sometimes it helps to zoom in on one detail, like that freckle, and hope the rest will come into focus. It did not.

So now you're up to speed on how I came to be in the bunker, at the mercy of Dr. Eisenberg and Miss B, about to experience the weirdest parts of my already too-weird story.

120

In the hall outside the room that morning were others who must have been victims of the experiments, people brought there to *help with the research*, as Miss B and Dr. Eisenberg called it. I don't think I was supposed to see them, then or any other time. They were quickly ushered away by Jeannette and another assistant whose name I never learned. I also don't think I will ever stop seeing them. Or hearing and smelling them. These test subjects – or victims – had apparently forgotten how to take themselves to the bathroom. I wondered if they had forgotten how to feed themselves, too. They were kept around, I suppose, to see if any of their memories would ever come back.

One of them made whimpering sounds, like a lost puppy or kitten that knows something bad is happening but is unable to do anything about it. No words, just inhuman mewling.

The other was clearly angry. "Someone stole my shoes," he shouted several times. When Jeannette came soon, to take him away, he asked, "Did you steal my shoes?"

"No, they're in your room," she said. "Come this way, and you can have them back." I looked at his feet. He wore an ordinary pair of white athletic shoes. I understood, after a moment – like the first victim I saw that morning, he knew something bad had been done, but he was unable even to define the offense. Footgear or its absence was not what bothered him, but he no longer had the capacity to verbalize his grievance.

A third victim, farther down the hall, sat in a wheelchair. I wondered if she had forgotten how to walk or simply had no will to do so. She stared, vacant, unblinking eyes tracking any motion, however slight, making no other response to anything around her.

Of all the pitiful visions, the eyes were the worst. All the victims' eyes, searching for something they would never find, stay with me. The cries of anguish and rage mostly echo away, along with the smell of human waste. Years later, the eyes turn up in nightmares.

At the time, my main thought was, I have to get out of here before I turn into one of those zombies.

Dr. Eisenberg asked me to sit at the desk by the wall, in the chair facing out into the room. While I looked around at microscopes and what I thought were centrifuges, he said, "I apologize for how this is being done. But in decades to come, you may be remembered as the hero who helped change the world for the better. Think of what we can do if everyone can see the future. Crime will disappear because everyone will know before it happens. No one need ever die in a flood or fire or hurricane or terrorist bombing again. A renaissance lies in store for all humanity. We're making it possible right here and now. *You* are making it possible."

"I don't want to make it possible. I want to go home," I said.

"And you will. But we have some work to do first."

I thought of asking him if he figured people who worked on the Manhattan Project or the Chernobyl nuclear plant had similar overblown assumptions about how their work would change the world, turn it into a paradise. Or I could have pointed out that knowing about a problem and solving the problem are very different operations. People still die in hurricanes, despite weather satellites and advance warnings, not because they don't know the storms are coming, but because they're too silly or stubborn to leave, or because they have nowhere to go and no way to get there. Or consider alcoholics and drug addicts, who know very well there are dark days ahead on the path they follow, but they keep going. Until, you know, they don't. Then there's climate change. We all know what we're doing, if we are paying attention at all, but we keep doing it. Humans are like that about a thousand other things. Getting us to do the right thing takes a lot more than knowledge of how doing the wrong thing will turn out.

In retrospect, I think Dr. Eisenberg was no different than a great many people. He had his place in the order of things. As far as he was concerned, he was like a soldier going into battle. He would do what needed to be done (from his point of view, anyway). If he didn't, someone else would, or the world would suffer from his inaction. He was going to do his experiments, and damn the minor consequences. I was just his lab rat.

"What exactly do you want me to do?" I asked. "I don't even have the box anymore. Why can't you people just leave me alone?"

| THE ARTIFACT

Dr. Eisenberg got up and opened a cabinet under one of the lab tables. He took out an ordinary-looking brown cardboard carton, about the size of a large shoebox, and put it on the desk beside me and sat back down.

"Open it," he said.

I pushed the flaps aside and saw packing peanuts and something wrapped in brown paper. I started to lift the wrapped object. It was heavy. I had to use both hands to pull it out. Eisenberg set the cardboard box on the floor to make room on the desk beside me.

"Go ahead, unwrap it."

Under the paper was a ceramic jar. It looked like polished stone. Or perhaps it was made of clay. A foot high and about six inches in diameter, the jar was decorated with an image of a bird. Thanks to *The Book of the Dead* and my other reading about ancient Egypt, I knew the bird figure represented an ibis. It symbolized the god Thoth, the deity who supposedly gave humans divine inspiration. I assumed this was the jar Miss B had told me about. I wondered what happened to the cedar box it had occupied, and who managed to open it. I kept the paper between my fingers and the artifact, instinctively reluctant to touch it, only partly because it looked like something that should be in a museum, behind glass. Or better yet, undisturbed in the ancient tomb from which it had been plundered. I was also reluctant to touch it because I could guess what it was, and I knew what the reverse-engineered model could do to a person. Just being near it seemed risky.

"You recognize the iconography, don't you?" Eisenberg asked, watching me closely with owlish eyes behind round glasses.

"Don't know." I shrugged. "Kinda looks Egyptian, to me. Is it?" I kept quiet about my suspicions and waited to see what Eisenberg would say. *Listen and learn* seemed to be the only viable strategy at the moment.

"Ah, passive aggression." The good doctor smiled. "The privilege of the well-informed when they feel powerless and threatened.

"This is a canopic jar," he continued. "As you probably know. I understand you have more than a passing interest in secrets of the ancients. Nor is this just any canopic jar. It's the original artifact from which the object you destroyed was reverse-engineered. But there is still much we do not understand about its design, construction, and operation. To learn more, we need to see it at work. We need an adept operator. As I think Miss

ADVENTURES TO GO |

Barron explained, you are among the few subjects well-suited to operate the device."

"Barron? That's her name?" I asked. Eisenberg ignored the question. "Anyway, she told me the box I had was reverse-engineered from a cedar box. A box no one had opened."

"We've made some progress since she spoke to you before," Eisenberg said. "Or did you expect constant updates? That's not important right now, anyway. Go ahead, touch the artifact." He ignored my attempt to sidetrack the discussion. "You won't hurt it."

"That's not what I'm worried about. I have some idea it might hurt me."

"No, go ahead, touch it."

"What's in it?" I asked. He could see I was still stalling, so he said, "I'll go first. See? Nothing to be afraid of." He touched the jar briefly beside the image of Thoth, and then took my hand and placed it on the jar. I felt an electric shock, which seemed not to affect the doctor, even though he was touching my hand as I jerked it away.

"It recognizes you," he said, smiling broadly. "That's wonderful. We are going to do great things. You'll answer a lot of questions about the future. And maybe about the artifact itself."

"What's in the jar?" I asked again, massaging my tingling fingers. I knew what such jars were originally made to hold – the viscera removed in the process of mummification – but I wasn't going to assume that's what this one held.

"We're not entirely sure," he said.

"You mean you haven't looked?" Despite my fear and resentment, I was curious.

"Of course we looked. Or tried to. But the contents seem to be indeterminate."

"If you want me to cooperate, I at least deserve a simple answer to a simple question," I said.

"It's not a simple question, though. Or maybe it is. Nevertheless, there's no good simple answer. Except the one I gave you: The contents of the jar are indeterminate."

"You're going to have to do better than that," I insisted. "Did you try, oh, I don't know, taking off the lid and having a look inside? Or, if you're

124

| THE ARTIFACT

afraid to break the seal on the jar and let twenty-first century air in, X-ray it. Or scan it somehow."

"If only we'd had the boy genius to instruct us before now!" Eisenberg said, slapping his forehead in mock frustration. "You think we haven't tried that? But the jar is like the box in Schrodinger's experiment with the cat. You know about that?"

I nodded. "I may be only 17, but I'm not stupid. Also, I paid attention in physics and chemistry classes. It was just a thought experiment to illustrate the weirdness of quantum mechanics and the absurd notion that a cat could be alive and dead at the same time. As far as Schrodinger was concerned, the idea was ridiculous. But you're telling me, even though you don't understand what's in the jar or how it works, you managed to reproduce it?"

"Well, not me, personally. We have other people, engineers, physicists, gear jockeys and electron chasers of all sorts" – he gestured dismissively – "who are responsible for reproduction and assembly. But the jar does seem to be analogous to Schrodinger's metaphorical box. In Schrodinger's idea, the cat is, of course, a stand-in for subatomic quanta of energy and particles, especially their wave-particle duality. The cat's being neither alive nor dead, or both alive and dead at once, depending on whom you ask, corresponds to particles existing as a wave of energy, or not."

"I knew that," I said, "Like I told you, I stayed awake in class that day."

"So you did. Except, to stretch the metaphor, our scans of the jar show if the cat is dead or alive without opening the box. However, this particular cat sometimes dies and comes back to life. Or, it is not a cat at all, but something entirely different. I think the jar acts that way because the future is always changing. Always in flux, since it hasn't happened yet. The future doesn't really even exist until it is created by the present. So, like the hypothetical cat, tomorrow, next year, next century – they exist in a quantum possibility state, such that the waveforms do not collapse into a definite state until they are observed. Normally, they cannot be observed until the future becomes the present. But the jar lets some people, like you, collapse waveforms no one else has yet observed. Actually, it seems to allow most people some limited vision of future events, but at a much greater cost than for you. We believe you can see the future without significant permanent memory loss."

125

ADVENTURES TO GO |

I opened my mouth to comment but quickly closed it.

"You don't believe me?" Eisenberg asked.

"It's a lot to take in," I said, stopping myself from saying what I really thought, which was *Thanks, Doc, you just told me how to escape from your little shop of horrors.* "I don't recall giving you permission to define 'significant' for me," I said aloud. "All my memories are mine, insignificant or otherwise."

"The injection we gave you should help counter memory loss," he said. "That's the theory, anyway. Compare the sacrifice you are being asked to make with the sacrifice soldiers make when they are sent off to battle. No risk, no reward."

"Yeah, I know about soldiers and what happens to them," I said. "But at least they volunteer."

"Not always. Sometimes they are drafted."

"I'm sorry for them, then. That doesn't change what you're doing or how wrong it is."

"Lincoln, we could argue the question forever, but I'm afraid you've been chosen. Drafted. End of story. The sooner you do your part, the sooner you can go home."

Or join the living dead, I said to myself. Not that I planned on sticking around that long. Nor was I naive enough to believe they would ever voluntarily let me go. But I've noticed when people use your first name the superfluous way Eisenberg had just used mine, you're firmly planted in BS territory. No going back, no point arguing.

I said, "Let's get on with it, then."

"Great. The first step is to prepare. Establish a baseline to evaluate your results, so we know how the work may or may not be affecting your memory. I'm going to ask you some questions. You must answer honestly, so what you remember now can be compared to what you remember later. We have a series of one hundred items that have proven very predictive of any new memory problems."

I let that statement sink in. While Eisenberg called up the list of questions on his tablet, I wondered how many minds had been destroyed in the process of creating the list, besides those of the victims I had seen out in the hall.

The questions ranged from whether I had any pets to the name of my first-grade teacher. They also covered places I had visited, movies I'd seen

126

| THE ARTIFACT

and books I had read, general knowledge of the world, like state capitals and presidents, feelings about other people, including family, and sexual preferences and experiences. Some of those questions I refused to answer. I told Eisenberg they were none of his business.

"Don't worry, Lincoln. You have nothing to be embarrassed about. I've heard it all. People who hate their parents. People who love – and are loved by – their parents in very much ... unusual ways. Answers that involve everything from Barbie dolls and odd habits of self-gratification to fruit fetishes. One subject had a fixation with cantaloupes. Very ripe ones. They reminded her of – well, that's not important. The point is, I won't find anything you say very shocking."

"I'm not embarrassed," I said. "I don't care if you are shocked. Some things are still not your business."

He sighed. "You're a smart boy, Linc. Look around you. You're here to do a job. Nothing's going to change that. You can cooperate, let us do it the easy way, or you can make things harder for everyone. Either way, you don't leave until the job is done."

I answered the questions, and did not bother trying to explain further that embarrassment played no part in my reluctance.

127

CHAPTER XXV

So it went, day after day, or what felt like days, since I saw no clocks. I woke up, had a shower, ate breakfast, and answered questions. I used the artifact. I had visions of the future, or possible futures. I answered more questions. I ate. I slept. I awoke and was taken back to the lab to do it again. Jeanette gave me clean sheets and left clean clothes every other day. In that context, a day was a cycle of breakfast, work with Eisenberg, lunch, more work with Eisenberg, dinner, and sleep.

I was given a shot of something every morning, too. I asked what it was, and Eisenberg said, "The same thing you had the first time we met. It's called MJ12."

I thought for a minute. Those letters and numbers seemed familiar. "MJ12, like the UFO and alien conspiracy stories?"

Eisenberg smiled a disturbing, crooked grin. "I think of it as Magic Juice 12. Keeps your brains from being fried when you use the box."

He always asked me the test questions before each day's work to see if my memories were disappearing. I always passed the test. At least, it seemed to me I did, and Eisenberg said I did. There was no way to be certain, though, as both sources of information – my memory and the good doctor – were of dubious reliability. My memory had always been

128

fabulous, but I'd learned the paradox: You don't necessarily remember forgetting until you are confronted with questions you should remember how to answer but can't. I was also scanned in the MRI or CT machine or X-rayed at least a dozen times. I expect that kind of superfluous scanning is risky and not recommended, except for ones who seem likely to have some disease. Nevertheless, Eisenberg wanted to see how my brain might differ from other people's brains, or what effect using the jar might have. No one ever shared the results of the scans with me.

After the memory check, a typical session would begin with a background summary on whatever topic Eisenberg wanted to investigate – politics, economics, military conflict, foreign affairs, etc. Questions varied. Which world leader was about to have a career-ending scandal exposed? Which leader was about to be deposed in a coup? Who was planning an invasion of what country? Who was developing nuclear weapons? What would inflation or interest rates be in six months or a year? In each case, I needed to know enough to pose a clear question in my mind and understand the resulting vision that came to me.

When I had enough context, both to understand the question Eisenberg asked and to recognize an answer when I saw it, the jar would be put in front of me, and I would wrap my hands around it and see the future. Or possible futures. Sometimes one was as clear as another. The feeling of being shocked gradually lessened. I was building up a tolerance, I guessed, like an addict needing more and more of the substance to achieve an effect. I wasn't sure what that tolerance meant, but I did not think it was a good sign.

You may ask why I cooperated, why I kept putting my hands on the jar and looking for visions of things to come. I felt like I had no choice – until I was confident my plan for escape would work. There was no alternative. No appealing alternative, anyway. Spock, on the original *Star Trek*, said there are always alternatives. Which may be technically true, but it doesn't mean the alternatives are always good. Of course, Eisenberg and Miss B continued to dangle the promise of release when I finished helping them. Not that I believed them. Nor was there any definition of what would count as finishing.

Besides, I liked it. That little tingle in my hands, up my arms, and the lab fading away and being replaced by the sensation of another time,

ADVENTURES TO GO |

another place, it was the closest I could come to escape without escaping. Better, in a way, because it became so effortless. I understand a little better now why addicts keep drinking or using the drug even when they know it's killing them. It's a way of living in the moment, ignoring future consequences. Yes, I get the irony – live in this present moment to see a moment that hasn't happened yet.

Aside from the momentary thrill, using the jar was addictive because it satisfied a basic human longing: the need to find answers, to solve mysteries. To stop using it would be like not reading the last chapter of a murder mystery, or never finding the right word for seven-down in the crossword puzzle. You could refuse to do it, but it would nag at you.

I was working on the plan to escape, though. I would have gone home in a heartbeat if I'd had the chance. Using an ancient Egyptian artifact to see the future was a thrill, but not one I would trade my life for. I think I had appreciated how good my life was – great mom, great friends, plans for college – even before I was kidnapped. But missing them reinforced the point.

Eisenberg always took care to move at least six feet away while I was using the jar. "There's a potential bleed-over," he explained. "Even for people like me. I have no talent for seeing the future, even with the aid of the artifact. But I might suffer memory loss if I stayed close for long. The artifact generates some sort of field, like electromagnetism, except it's not any kind of electricity or magnetism we understand or can measure accurately or consistently. But it follows the inverse square law. Effects decrease or increase exponentially as you move away or come closer to the surface of the jar."

Each day's visions also included a look ahead at stock markets. "How do you think all this is funded?" Eisenberg asked, gesturing around the lab.

"I thought the government was allowed to print money," I said.

"Well, of course. But even though the *New York Times* or *Wall Street Journal* will never know what we do here, or be allowed to report it if they did, someone still has to convince the politicians, or some bureaucrat who has the politicians' ear, to approve money we get in the federal budget. So we don't limit ourselves to those unreliable sources of funding. Why would we, when, for us, investing in the Dow or NASDAQ is like picking up money lying in the street?"

130

| THE ARTIFACT

I also saw things I can't unsee, to this day, no matter how much I would like to. Plane crashes, earthquakes, floods, people washed away or mutilated by falling bombs or falling buildings.

I saw the assassination of a president of the United States.

That vision stopped me cold. "I don't want to see this," I said. It was like the film of JFK being shot, but worse. Much worse. Partly because seeing it in a vision was just like being there, and partly because it was … bloodier. I won't describe it further, but after that vision, an ominous cloud formed in my memory. I felt like someone on a beach who falls asleep in the sun and is awakened from a pleasant nap to see the beach abandoned, a tsunami bearing down. It is too late to run. Nevertheless, the ant-sized human tries to flee as the giant wave sweeps in.

I also saw the aftermath of the assassination, the struggles for power, the naked aggression and chaos and more assassinations. It was a bloody tide of chaos, violence, and senseless death. Seeing it felt like trying to run in wet sand in a nightmare, the sort where your muscles are paralyzed, no chance of escape. To this day, the memory is painful to think about. I don't even like to write about it.

"I can't do this anymore," I said, after describing what I'd seen.

"Okay. Take a break," Eisenberg said.

"That's not what I mean," I said. "All this. I'm done. It's too much. No more."

Eisenberg took off his glasses and put them on the desk. The red indentations where the frame sat on his nose were all I could think of.

"Because you see it, that doesn't mean it happens, Lincoln. In fact, the opposite is often the case. Have you forgotten what I told you? The future is an uncollapsed waveform. It's indeterminate."

"That doesn't make it easier to see. Anyway, I thought the theory was that seeing the future collapses the waveform. Determines the indeterminate."

"It does. If nothing is done to change circumstances surrounding that future. But circumstances can usually be changed. That plane crash you saw yesterday, looking three weeks ahead, that crash will probably never happen. Thanks to you, all those people will live, I expect. Including one very important United States Senator whose vote will help change the world for decades to come. That means your work will also change the

ADVENTURES TO GO |

world for the better. The Senator who was scheduled to be on that flight will not be there when it crashes. Or the flight will never happen at all. Because of your vision, steps will be taken."

"'Steps' will be taken?" I echoed. "What kind of steps?"

"Oh, I don't know. Any number of possibilities. Maybe airline computer problems cause hundreds of flights to be canceled that day and rescheduled for a later day. Perhaps the Senator will be on another flight that lands safely at its destination, without incident. Or a bomb scare, caused by what turns out to be just a box of lawn mower parts. A flight crew union goes on strike. Something simple might happen – a technician damages a circuit, causing the plane to fail its preflight inspection. Or the pilot of that particular plane is late to work because his car won't start, and no other pilots are available. Fortunately for you and me, we don't have to figure it out or make those decisions. That's someone else's job.

"Of course, it's possible the plane will in fact be allowed to crash, with the Senator on board. Depends on conclusions drawn by others. It's out of our hands. Which is fine by me.

"That assassination you saw – I expect it will never happen, though. The president will be somewhere else that day. If we'd been operational in 1963, I doubt JFK would have died the way he did."

I thought for a moment and said, "You don't know what would have happened if he had lived. It might have led to a worse future."

Eisenberg arched his eyebrows and said nothing. He was a good listener, one reason I was developing a case of Stockholm syndrome. Knowing you should resent your captors doesn't prevent a kind of attachment to the only human contacts you have.

"Anyway, whether another assassination happens or not, I still saw it," I went on. "It was horrible to watch."

"Not as horrible as if it really happens. Have you ever seen the video from November 22, 1963?"

"I have," I said, nodding. "I also read that book – *11/22/63*. As awful as the death of JFK was, maybe the world that follows is even worse if he doesn't die. It's like the question about whether you would go back in time and kill Hitler if you could. I wouldn't, because I'm not a murderer. But even if I were willing to do it, Hitler's replacement might kill ten million people in concentration camps, instead of six million. Or Hitler-two-

132

| THE ARTIFACT

point-o might be smart enough to know the Enigma machine's code was not invulnerable, or might have developed atom bombs first. So you can't tell me that playing God is a good idea. The possible outcomes are too variable and complex."

"Maybe so." Eisenberg smiled the most chilling smile I've ever seen and said again, "Maybe so. Playing God is a big responsibility, but someone has to do it. You don't get great results by praying, asking the real God, if there is one, to intervene in human affairs. If history proves anything, it proves we are allowed to screw up as badly as we like, without divine intervention. Now, then, back to work. The world needs saving every day. We supply the knowledge to save it."

CHAPTER XXVI

Of course, I had my own set of test memories – I repeated the list of landmarks leading back to Louisville, the ones I memorized when I was brought to the bunker. I repeated them morning and night and during lunch in order to keep them safe and fresh. As far as I could tell, those memories were unimpaired.

The danger was that I might forget that they should exist at all. What if I forgot there was even anything about that trip to remember? I'm no neurologist, but my brain must have its limits. If I reached a threshold for whatever punishment using the artifact served up, would I start to forget, and stop even remembering what questions I could no longer answer?

On what felt like the fourth or fifth day, I decided it was time for a change. I had a plan to escape, but I wanted to be confident I could carry it out before I tried. A second chance seemed unlikely. Conversely, I couldn't wait forever to try to escape. I would never be absolutely certain of success. The longer I waited, the chances of failure would only increase.

Obviously, the other way out, besides enacting my plan, was to stop being a promising lab rat. Which was dangerous, because what usually happens to lab rats who cease to be useful? I wasn't sure, but in this case, *nothing good* seemed the likely answer.

| THE ARTIFACT

I experimented with not providing good results, telling Eisenberg I couldn't see anything even when I did. He just kept asking, if not the same question, then different ones, until I gave him an answer. The chances that failing to cooperate, either covertly or overtly, would result in them letting me go seemed slim to nonexistent. Once a lab rat, always a lab rat, cooperative or not, from Eisenberg's point of view.

From time to time, coming and going, I saw the other test subjects. Or, more correctly, test victims. I think Miss B and Eisenberg and their minions tried to keep them mostly out of sight. Nevertheless, we sometimes passed in the hall. I knew I had to get out before I turned into one of those zombies. Then there would be no escape. The thought of Mom and my friends also kept me going. I had to escape while I still knew who they were.

I wondered if any other test subjects had escaped. Maybe they had, or maybe they all had been too full of visions of the future to think clearly about the present.

What I had realized but not said when Eisenberg gave me his speech on how the jar was like the box in Schrodinger's experiment was, *You mean I don't just see the future – I also create it*. I had kept thinking when I had a chance, while eating in the cafeteria, while falling asleep, whenever I was not reciting my personal memory check, about the mystery of what exactly the jar did. If seeing was creating, I needed to create a future where circumstances were right for me to escape. If the jar, and consequently the box modeled after it, let the user influence or create the future, it helped explain how Miss B had gotten the box in my backpack and on its way to Louisville with me. She must have used it not only to distract me with a vision but to create the future she wanted. I wondered what memories that vision had cost her, and if she had gotten them back.

I had found that I could, in fact, seem to influence the vision, to see what I wanted, and the thing I wanted was likely to happen. Or as Eisenberg would have said, I not only collapsed the waveforms, but I could influence *how* they collapsed. As a test, I decided the stock markets would go down. Far down, two days in a row.

"The finance section is not going to like this," Eisenberg said, when I told him what I saw. Then he shrugged and said, "Well, they have their problems and we have ours, don't we?" He began explaining the background of conflicts in the Middle East. The main questions of the

ADVENTURES TO GO |

day concerned the influence of Arab-Israeli affairs on U.S. politics and oil prices.

On the third day after I began my experiment in controlling stock prices, I knew it was working. Eisenberg provided background information so I had the necessary context to understand my visions of the future. He was always interested in finance and Wall Street, so that news kept coming my way. I don't know if he ever suspected I was practicing my skills at influencing the visions. If so, what could he have done about it? I was the center of his research. Me, and the jar, of course. Whatever else he was, he was a scientist. He was a fellow addict. A curiosity junkie. I recognized the signs. I think he cared more about how I could do what I did than about outcomes of a lot of incidents in politics and business.

The next day – day six, by my count, though I still had no access to windows, calendars, or clocks – as a sort of warm-up exercise, Eisenberg gave me the jar and asked me to look ahead at stock market indices. Instead, I looked elsewhere, to the afternoon of that day, right after lunch, there in the bunker somewhere under the Kentucky wilderness, and I chose to see myself being allowed to escape.

Holding the jar, I saw Larry the kidnapper drive through the gate and enter the bunker. I watched the codes he entered at the gate and elevator. Or would enter. In my vision, the trees around the small parking lot outside cast short shadows in the woods under summer sun, so the time was near noon. I also focused intently on the keys, which he left in the car. Or would leave, assuming I could influence his actions the way I seemed to influence the NASDAQ and S&P.

The hall was rarely deserted for long. People like Larry and Jeanette came and went to bring supplies, attend to the zombies, or do who knew what else. Miss B periodically left her office and made rounds to supervise. As far as I could tell, everyone there deferred to her authority.

But that morning I chose to see the hall empty for ten minutes, and the area outside the bunker abandoned as well – all except the car with keys in the ignition. I chose to see Dr. Eisenberg appear to have stomach cramps and excuse himself to use the bathroom. I chose to see myself leave the room while he was gone, walk down the hall, punch in the numbers on the elevator, and exit the building.

Which is what I did.

136

| THE ARTIFACT

It all happened without a hitch, except I forgot how quickly the elevator moved, so I stumbled to my knees when it started up.

CHAPTER XXVII

Outside, the sunlight was blinding. Blinking, stumbling on bruised knees, I made my way to the car. The keys were there, just as I had seen them. The gate rolled smoothly open when I entered the numbers on the keypad.

I drove away from the bunker, looking nervously behind me all the time, though there had been no other vehicles in the parking lot, and proceeded to become completely lost.

The list of landmarks I believed I had kept safe in my memory, reciting them daily forward and backward, was completely useless. It turned out more than my memories of the landmarks and turns were scrambled. Eventually, I found myself in Elizabethtown, unable to remember which road would take me back to Louisville. I knew I was in Elizabethtown only because I saw the sign. Feeling panicky, the fuel gauge on the car barely above empty, I made a U-turn through an emergency-vehicles-only lane and was quickly pulled over by a Kentucky State Trooper who witnessed my erratic driving.

Of course, his first thought must have been that I was drunk or stoned. I had no driver's license to show him, it having been confiscated when I was kidnapped by the Stooges, along with my phone.

I told him my name, my age, and my mother's name. I could not remember my address or anyone's phone number.

Trooper Green put me in the back of his car, though it was all done in very undramatic fashion. I was spared the handcuff treatment. He could probably see I needed help of some sort and was not inclined to run away. He talked on his radio for a minute, and then turned to look back at me. "Lot of people are looking for you, young man. Including your mother, I understand."

I just nodded. I was glad to look out the window and see sunshine and blue sky and trees and grass while someone else did the driving. I wondered what happened in the bunker after I escaped. Despite looking repeatedly over my shoulder and in the rearview mirror, I had spotted no pursuers. Did Miss B and Doc understand what I had done? Surely they must. However, I can only speculate. Maybe they chalked my escape up to luck – bad for them, good for me.

I later realized what you've probably noticed already. Trusting Trooper Green so easily, instead of running away, was further proof of how scrambled my brains were. How did I know he wasn't working for Miss B, or whomever she reported to? As Hercule Poirot would have said, my little gray cells had grown dull.

IT TURNED OUT I HAD BEEN MISSING FOR ALMOST THREE MONTHS. MY SENSE of time as well as geography was badly disrupted. If I had been thinking clearly, I would have noticed as soon as I escaped from the bunker that the sun in the sky was lower, even at noon, and a few trees were beginning to drop leaves and show autumn colors. Not many and not much, but enough to notice if you didn't have other things to think about.

WHEN WE GOT TO THE STATE POLICE POST, TROOPER GREEN TOLD ME TO SIT beside the desk. He sat down across from me and asked more questions, mostly about where I'd been. I started to tell him a story about being on a camping trip and getting lost in the woods. By then he knew how long I 'd been missing. "For three months? I'm not buying it," he said. I must not have looked as half-starved and ragged as someone lost in the woods that long should look. I guess I invented the story of getting lost because I was too used to keeping secrets about anything related to the artifacts.

Nor was I thinking straight, even before I escaped, I later realized. If I had been, I would have created the future in which I made it home on my own. I would have used the jar to envision myself pulling up in front of our house in Louisville. I would have known I'd been gone for months, not days.

So I told Trooper Green the whole story, or parts of the whole story he was likely to believe. I said I and others were having our memories tested by memorizing what seemed like random lists. I described the people involved – Miss B, Jeanette, Dr. Eisenberg, and the zombies, who might have friends or families looking for them, too. It wouldn't help to discuss canopic jars or try to explain what was so special about a certain specimen of that particular class of artifact. He would just assume I was starting another tall tale. He listened carefully and made notes.

"Where exactly did all this happen?" he asked.

I told him what I knew, which wasn't much. I had already described the bunker and its insides. As for how to find it, my memory was obviously untrustworthy.

"Sounds like one of the old bomb shelters," he said. "They've been abandoned for decades. Built during the Cold War for the high-muckety-mucks to hide out in until the surface would supposedly be fit to live on again."

He asked for directions.

"If I had known where I was, I'd be home by now," I said. "I wouldn't have gotten lost."

Mom arrived shortly thereafter. A joyously tearful reunion ensued. Mom called Lonnie, who called Julie, and they were waiting at our house when we got home. Cue another tearful, joyous reunion.

A WEEK LATER, MOM GOT A PHONE CALL FROM THE STATE POLICE: A BUNKER matching the description I'd given had been located and searched, but it was abandoned. Empty. Not even a fingerprint. Inquiries were being made

| THE ARTIFACT

regarding the car I had been driving, but that investigation was also going nowhere fast. The license was registered to a state agency, but inquiries revealed little else. Calls were not returned, records turned up mysteriously missing, and everyone thought that particular vehicle must have been somebody else's responsibility.

The lack of results didn't surprise me, of course, but if anyone had tried to tell the State Troopers not to bother, they would no doubt have tilted at that windmill with even greater enthusiasm and determination. Trooper Green, at least, seemed to be doing his best to get actual results.

I knew he would get exactly nowhere. No matter. I was just glad to be home.

CHAPTER XXVIII

A lot can happen in three months. Lonnie and Julie were a definite, open, matching-outfits couple now. When I went missing, they leaned on each other for emotional support. Lonnie told Julie the whole story, and admitted we should have told her about the artifact from the start. Julie believed her, and, after some initial skepticism, decided she might have overreacted. That first time I saw her after my escape, I also told her we were just protecting her. To that she replied, "I'm a big girl, Linc. Don't need to be protected from the truth, by you or anyone else."

"Duly noted," I said. All was forgiven, and friendship resumed, even closer than before. When I found my way back, mentally and emotionally, Lonnie and Julie did not let me feel left out. Not in any way.

When he found out she was in a sexual relationship with Lonnie, Julie's dad kicked her out. She told us what he said: "If you want to go to hell, you'll have to do it somewhere else."

"I told him he didn't have to tell me twice," Julie said. "I added, 'I don't need to go to hell – I'm already there, as long as you're around.'"

"I know you don't need to be protected, but you might need a place to sleep," I said. "Mom would be happy for you to stay with us."

So Julie stayed at our house awhile.

MEANWHILE, I HAD MY OWN CHALLENGES TO DEAL WITH. THE BURDEN OF knowing the future, or possible futures, is almost as bad as losing memories. Once you see, you can't unsee just because you want to. The future is not set in stone, and tragedies foreseen may be prevented or avoided, but they still become bad memories. Even if they never happened, the memory of seeing and feeling them is the same. Knowing too much about the future is like seeing a horror movie you did not choose to watch. Except the movie is real, for the seers. They saw it happen.

I think memory loss from using the box or the original jar may be partly the brain's attempt to deal with trauma. I learned a term used by psychologists and psychiatrists: dissociative amnesia. It describes what the brain does when it witnesses or experiences something so traumatic or stressful that it just can't process the knowledge. The memories get put in isolation, a kind of quarantine, like white blood cells surrounding a cell infected by a virus. The bad memories are thus unavailable to the conscious mind. At least for a while. It's a useful coping strategy, because what you cannot remember, you do not have to think about. The amnesia caused by using the box or jar was unpredictable. Knowing how to navigate streets and roads was not a traumatic memory. I guess losing those kinds of memories was collateral damage, fortunately temporary.

How much time had passed and how to get from Elizabethtown to Louisville were not the only things I had forgotten. The lacunae in my memory seemed pretty random. Thankfully, I still remembered Mom, Julie, and Lonnie. But I had forgotten that we won the lottery. I had forgotten that humans landed on the Moon or what I liked in my oatmeal (brown sugar, apples, and cinnamon). Knowing hot was on the left and cold on the right in faucets and the shower seemed new to me. But these memories came back, slowly, as memories had come back the first time. Apparently they were not really, totally lost, just misfiled. It took some time to put them in alphabetical order again.

Lonnie and Julie (who both opted to stay in Louisville and go to U of L) and I spent a lot of that fall seeing old movies. These included many I had seen before but could not remember. They told me *Casablanca* was one of my favorites, that I'd watched it a dozen times or more at the Uptown

ADVENTURES TO GO |

or on TV or streaming. It seemed all new to me, which was both sad and, in a peculiar way, kind of fun. Who hasn't envied someone the opportunity to see a great movie for the first time? I don't recommend the ordeal I went through, but, hey, silver linings.

Not everything came back. I have about a week's worth of memories of what happened in the bunker. As for the other eleven weeks or so that I was missing – was I even in the bunker the whole time? If not, where? Doing what? I don't have those answers. You can let your imagination run wild, but right now, I'd just as soon not know. I'm not yet ready to remember what might be another horror movie.

There was also some good news. The case my mom was working to save land and trees from the developer's chainsaws and bulldozers had taken a sharp turn for the better. The U.S. Supreme Court had agreed to hear the case. No outcome was guaranteed, but whatever happened, Mom would at least join the small, elite group of attorneys who had the opportunity to argue a case there.

Naturally, going to college was off the schedule for me for a while. School had already started, and I was still busy looking over my shoulder and trying to remember my life when October rolled around. Mom, Julie, and Lonnie had a family meeting (because Julie and Lonnie felt like family) and decided I should take a "gap year," as the Brits call it. Thanks to the lottery winnings, money was not an issue in that regard.

We cashed in the lottery ticket, and I used part of the money, with help from Mom and some of her contacts, to establish a new identity, complete with new name, new photo ID, and new address, should they ever be needed. I wasn't sure how much of it was legal. In fact, I was pretty sure a lot of laws were broken to get my new identity. In the Witness Protection Program, that trope much-beloved by writers of crime dramas, people are often given new, officially approved identities. But I'm sure you don't just waltz into the New Identities Department, pay the forty-nine dollar fee, and walk out a different person. We were doing it on our own, because which authorities could be trusted? There was no way to be sure. You could hope the U.S. Marshals, who, I learned, run the program, had not been compromised by the likes of Miss B and Dr. Eisenberg and colleagues, but how could we know?

144

| THE ARTIFACT

For a long time, I wondered why they left me alone after I escaped. I still wonder sometimes. The most optimistic conclusion I can draw is that they consigned me to the zombie scrap heap, assuming my brains had been fried by forbidden technology. Or did the explanation lie in something I did not remember, as my memories of the time in the bunker remained dreadfully incomplete? I remember faking, pretending to not have answers to the Doc's questions, but what if, later, I really didn't have any answers? It's possible I had almost outlived my usefulness as a lab rat. But they found me in the first place, and they could still be watching, so they might know I did not remain a zombie, whatever I had been.

At any rate, I have never had to use the new identity. I get to go on being me, thus far, at least.

They. Them. A few months before, I would have thought such vague, anonymous terms for obscure villains were silly at best, or premises for a good story, like Stephen King's *Firestarter* or *The Stand*. I was no longer so quick to dismiss. Part of me still thought I was being paranoid, and another part knew the old saying is true: being paranoid doesn't mean no one's out to get you. I hoped they assumed I was neither a threat nor of any further use to them and remembered nothing that could form a coherent, believable story, should I decide to tell it to anyone. I still wonder, to this day, if I'm being watched, and look over my shoulder more than most people and avoid assuming the best about people I don't know.

I am probably worrying about nothing. Wild conspiracy theories masquerade as news now. Who would believe my crazy story is anything but harmless fiction?

I also worried about the world I lived in every day – the world we all live in – and how it differs from the way it might look if I had never heard of the artifacts, either the modern reproduction or the ancient one. What changes, big or small, had I helped Miss B and the others make? What world leaders had I helped rise to power? Which had I caused to be overthrown? What wars had I played a part in ending – or starting? I told myself people make important decisions to create the future every day. Deciding is what human existence is all about. Choice always leads to consequences, big or small. Knowing that helped. But only a little.

So I keep that new identity handy, and a bag packed, just in case I have to go. Sooner or later, the world takes everyone's innocence. Miss B and

ADVENTURES TO GO |

the Doc, or others like them, and their consorts and competitors, are still out there. Maybe they decided I have done my part. For the time being. Maybe they'll be back.

But they don't know what I still have hidden under the basement steps. If they ever figure it out, they'll surely be back. Yet another good reason to leave the artifact right there, unused, unless absolute necessity requires it.

Humans are meant to absorb only so much sorrow and grief without breaking. That's why I don't look for more sorrow or grief in the future. What comes in the present and past are more than enough.

For now, I'm happy to find out about the future when everyone else does – the moment it happens, or some time thereafter.

146

CHAPTER XXIX

"What are you going to do, now?" Lonnie asked one afternoon in early December. The air was cool but not cold. I guessed there were warm days in December before climate change. But snow before January was pretty much a thing of the past.

We sat in our same old spot, the picnic table in Willow Park. Julie was working that afternoon, at a very boring job in the convenience store where we'd bought lottery tickets a few months before. That day seemed like ancient history. I had a whole new appreciation of how comfortable it feels for things to be routine and uneventful, so I kind of envied Julie her boring job. But not enough to apply for one myself, just yet.

"Maybe I'll go to Egypt and see the pyramids. Wanna come with?"

Lonnie looked tempted for a moment, then said, "Better not. I've got school. The museum. Ideas for new paintings. And I'd miss Julie too much."

"She can come, too."

"Her whole life is here, like mine. But I'll miss you, too, every minute you're gone."

147

We watched red and yellow leaves drift from trees for a while before going back to my house. Mom was at the office, so we had the whole place to ourselves. Lonnie showed me some of the ways she would miss me.

A COUPLE OF DAYS LATER, I SAW JEANETTE, DR. EISENBERG'S ASSISTANT, WHO had given me clean sheets every other day, at Kroger. Her cart was full of goodies that looked like preparations for a holiday dinner. I looked twice to make sure I wasn't hallucinating, and said hello. I knew she was Jeanette because of that one large freckle on her left upper lip.

Of course, she pretended not to know me. "I think you have me confused with someone else."

There was so much I would have liked to ask her, but she obviously wasn't going to answer questions. Can't blame her.

I paid for my cornflakes and orange juice and went on my way.

LIFE IS GOOD.

Egypt was great, and I highly recommend it. That's a whole other story, though. If you go, just be extremely careful what you touch.

After the gap year, I started college at a small liberal arts school in another city in Kentucky, within easy driving distance of Louisville. I guess someday I'll be an archeologist as well as an architect. There are still a lot of things to build and a lot of mysteries waiting to be solved. Including what happens tomorrow, or a minute or a second from now.

| THE ARTIFACT

NOTES AND CONFESSIONS
FROM THE AUTHOR

MY UPTOWN THEATRE IS FICTIONALIZED. IT ONCE EXISTED, BUT IN THE MUNdane so-called real world, the Schuster Building no longer houses a theater.

There are, as far as I know, no abandoned Cold War era bomb shelters in Kentucky. At any rate, if there are, the one in this story is purely fictional.

The Louisville Metro Police Department is quite real, of course, as are the Kentucky State Police and the many brave people who serve the city and state, but Officer E. Benton and his colleagues and Trooper Green are purely fictional.

Howard Carter did indeed open the tomb of the Pharaoh Tutankhamen, and did keep a journal or diary, sometimes writing several paragraphs on a given day's activity, at other times making only brief notes about travel or visitors, but of course the mysterious uncatalogued artifact is my invention. If a lost diary of Howard Carter is some day discovered in an attic in London, won't that be exciting?

The MK-Ultra-Delta project was real.

The Speed Museum is also real, though Linc's opinions of its architecture, like Linc himself, are fictional.

THE AUTHOR

DAVID ROGERS' POEMS, STORIES, AND ARTICLES HAVE APPEARED IN VARIOUS print and electronic outlets, including StarLine, Third Flatiron, and Daily Science Fiction. His collection of short fiction, Emergency Exits, is available from Amazon. He lives near Mammoth Cave, Kentucky and has been an avid reader in many genres for decades. More at Davidbooks.com and Twitter @Davidbook

HISTORICAL EMPORIUM
Est. 2003

Buy at... HISTORICAL EMPORIUM

Whose **REPUTATION** is *celebrated* world-wide as the pre-eminent clothing source for the **ADVENTUROUS** and *Fashionable*.

We are...

REVERED
by our customers

REVILED
by our competitors

RESPECTED
by all who know us

NO LOCAL DEALER CAN COMPETE WITH OUR QUALITY, VARIETY AND INCOMPARABLE CUSTOMER SERVICE!

ACCEPT NO SUBSTITUTE!
If you require **clothing and supplies** as stylish and **stout-hearted** as you, contact us immediately to be outfitted.

800-997-4311

"The **ONLY** shop for me!" -P.W.

HistoricalEmporium.com

Dark Corners
Elmedina Hota

ELMEDINA HOTA IS AN ARTIST BASED IN SARAJEVO, BOSNIA AND HERZEGOVINA. FOR MORE ABOUT HER BREATHS OF LIFE VISIT INSTAGRAM & TWITTER: @HELLMEDINCIC

Purgatory

Many years have passed,
fractions of his soul were fading away,
as if they were the petals of a rose
took by the wind for a play

Seeking for the brightness
in that playful dream,
an emptiness was accompanied
by a silent scream,
echoing through his mind,
reverting him to the dark,
so it disappeared:
the bright silver song of a lark

Full of beauty, of a heart and soul,
his was strange to him,
full of self-loathing,
empty, hopeless, his mind used to stroll,
reflections of the mirrors to him were revolting

Such beauty of a human being deserves no Hell,
nor was it selfless enough for Heaven,
taking his own life to his loved ones was a dispel,
none of the deadly sins yet as strong as the seven

In loving memory of Ivan Ćosić,
who lost his lifelong battle with mental illness.
1991-2013
R.I.P.

SUSAN GLASPELL

SUSAN GLASPELL (1876-1948) MADE waves in her multi-faceted career. More than an author and journalist, she was a Pulitzer Prize-winning playwright and actress.

During her stint as a reporter, in 1900, Glaspell covered a murder case for the Des Moines Daily News.

Trifles, the one act play she wrote, is based on that very case. The story that follows is a short story version of that play Glaspell also wrote titled, ***A Jury of Her Peers***.

ADVENTURES TO GO |

When Martha Hale opened the storm-door and got a cut of the north wind, she ran back for her big woolen scarf. As she hurriedly wound that round her head her eye made a scandalized sweep of her kitchen. It was no ordinary thing that called her away--it was probably further from ordinary than anything that had ever happened in Dickson County. But what her eye took in was that her kitchen was in no shape for leaving: her bread all ready for mixing, half the flour sifted and half unsifted.

Arthur Streeton, At Templestowe, 1889She hated to see things half done; but she had been at that when the team from town stopped to get Mr. Hale, and then the sheriff came running in to say his wife wished Mrs. Hale would come too--adding, with a grin, that he guessed she was getting scary and wanted another woman along. So she had dropped everything right where it was.

"Martha!" now came her husband's impatient voice. "Don't keep folks waiting out here in the cold."

She again opened the storm-door, and this time joined the three men and the one woman waiting for her in the big two-seated buggy.

After she had the robes tucked around her she took another look at the woman who sat beside her on the back seat. She had met Mrs. Peters the year before at the county fair, and the thing she remembered about her was that she didn't seem like a sheriff's wife. She was small and thin and didn't have a strong voice. Mrs. Gorman, sheriff's wife before Gorman went out and Peters came in, had a voice that somehow seemed to be backing up the law with every word. But if Mrs. Peters didn't look like a sheriff's wife, Peters made it up in looking like a sheriff. He was to a dot the kind of man who could get himself elected sheriff--a heavy man with a big voice, who was particularly genial with the law-abiding, as if to make it plain that he knew the difference between criminals and non-criminals. And right there it came into Mrs. Hale's mind, with a stab, that this man who was so pleasant and lively with all of them was going to the Wrights' now as a sheriff.

"The country's not very pleasant this time of year," Mrs. Peters at last ventured, as if she felt they ought to be talking as well as the men.

Mrs. Hale scarcely finished her reply, for they had gone up a little hill and could see the Wright place now, and seeing it did not make her feel like talking. It looked very lonesome this cold March morning. It had always been a lonesome-looking place. It was down in a hollow, and the poplar trees around it were lonesome-looking trees. The men were looking at it and talking about what had happened. The county attorney was bending to one side of the buggy, and kept looking steadily at the place as they drew up to it.

"I'm glad you came with me," Mrs. Peters said nervously, as the two women were about to follow the men in through the kitchen door.

Even after she had her foot on the door-step, her hand on the knob, Martha Hale had a moment of feeling she could not cross that threshold. And the reason it seemed she couldn't cross it now was simply because she hadn't crossed it before. Time and time again it had been in her mind, "I ought to go over and see Minnie Foster"--she still thought of her as Minnie Foster, though for twenty years she had been Mrs. Wright. And then there was always something to do and Minnie Foster would go from her mind. But now she could come.

The men went over to the stove. The women stood close together by the door. Young Henderson, the county attorney, turned around and said, "Come up to the fire, ladies."

Mrs. Peters took a step forward, then stopped. "I'm not--cold," she said.

And so the two women stood by the door, at first not even so much as looking around the kitchen.

The men talked for a minute about what a good thing it was the sheriff had sent his deputy out that morning to make a fire for them, and then Sheriff Peters stepped back from the stove, unbuttoned his outer coat, and leaned his hands on the kitchen table in a way that seemed to mark the beginning of official business. "Now, Mr. Hale," he said in a sort of semi-official voice, "before we move things about, you tell Mr. Henderson just what it was you saw when you came here yesterday morning."

The county attorney was looking around the kitchen.

"By the way," he said, "has anything been moved?" He turned to the sheriff. "Are things just as you left them yesterday?"

Peters looked from cupboard to sink; from that to a small worn rocker a little to one side of the kitchen table.

"It's just the same."

ADVENTURES TO GO |

"Somebody should have been left here yesterday," said the county attorney.

"Oh--yesterday," returned the sheriff, with a little gesture as of yesterday having been more than he could bear to think of. "When I had to send Frank to Morris Center for that man who went crazy--let me tell you. I had my hands full yesterday. I knew you could get back from Omaha by today, George, and as long as I went over everything here myself--"

"Well, Mr. Hale," said the county attorney, in a way of letting what was past and gone go, "tell just what happened when you came here yesterday morning."

Mrs. Hale, still leaning against the door, had that sinking feeling of the mother whose child is about to speak a piece. Lewis often wandered along and got things mixed up in a story. She hoped he would tell this straight and plain, and not say unnecessary things that would just make things harder for Minnie Foster. He didn't begin at once, and she noticed that he looked queer--as if standing in that kitchen and having to tell what he had seen there yesterday morning made him almost sick.

"Yes, Mr. Hale?" the county attorney reminded.

"Harry and I had started to town with a load of potatoes," Mrs. Hale's husband began.

Harry was Mrs. Hale's oldest boy. He wasn't with them now, for the very good reason that those potatoes never got to town yesterday and he was taking them this morning, so he hadn't been home when the sheriff stopped to say he wanted Mr. Hale to come over to the Wright place and tell the county attorney his story there, where he could point it all out. With all Mrs. Hale's other emotions came the fear now that maybe Harry wasn't dressed warm enough--they hadn't any of them realized how that north wind did bite.

"We come along this road," Hale was going on, with a motion of his hand to the road over which they had just come, "and as we got in sight of the house I says to Harry, 'I'm goin' to see if I can't get John Wright to take a telephone.' You see," he explained to Henderson, "unless I can get somebody to go in with me they won't come out this branch road except for a price I can't pay. I'd spoke to Wright about it once before; but he put me off, saying folks talked too much anyway, and all he asked was peace and quiet--guess you know about how much he talked himself. But I thought

156

| A JURY OF HER PEERS

maybe if I went to the house and talked about it before his wife, and said all the women-folks liked the telephones, and that in this lonesome stretch of road it would be a good thing--well, I said to Harry that that was what I was going to say--though I said at the same time that I didn't know as what his wife wanted made much difference to John--"

Now there he was!--saying things he didn't need to say. Mrs. Hale tried to catch her husband's eye, but fortunately the county attorney interrupted with:

"Let's talk about that a little later, Mr. Hale. I do want to talk about that but, I'm anxious now to get along to just what happened when you got here."

When he began this time, it was very deliberately and carefully:

"I didn't see or hear anything. I knocked at the door. And still it was all quiet inside. I knew they must be up--it was past eight o'clock. So I knocked again, louder, and I thought I heard somebody say, 'Come in.' I wasn't sure--I'm not sure yet. But I opened the door--this door," jerking a hand toward the door by which the two women stood. "and there, in that rocker"--pointing to it--"sat Mrs. Wright."

Everyone in the kitchen looked at the rocker. It came into Mrs. Hale's mind that that rocker didn't look in the least like Minnie Foster--the Minnie Foster of twenty years before. It was a dingy red, with wooden rungs up the back, and the middle rung was gone, and the chair sagged to one side.

"How did she--look?" the county attorney was inquiring.

"Well," said Hale, "she looked--queer."

"How do you mean--queer?"

As he asked it he took out a note-book and pencil. Mrs. Hale did not like the sight of that pencil. She kept her eye fixed on her husband, as if to keep him from saying unnecessary things that would go into that note-book and make trouble.

Hale did speak guardedly, as if the pencil had affected him too.

"Well, as if she didn't know what she was going to do next. And kind of--done up."

"How did she seem to feel about your coming?"

"Why, I don't think she minded--one way or other. She didn't pay much attention. I said, 'Ho' do, Mrs. Wright? It's cold, ain't it?' And she said. 'Is it?'--and went on pleatin' at her apron.

ADVENTURES TO GO |

"Well, I was surprised. She didn't ask me to come up to the stove, or to sit down, but just set there, not even lookin' at me. And so I said: 'I want to see John.'

"And then she--laughed. I guess you would call it a laugh.

"I thought of Harry and the team outside, so I said, a little sharp, 'Can I see John?' 'No,' says she--kind of dull like. 'Ain't he home?' says I. Then she looked at me. 'Yes,' says she, 'he's home.' 'Then why can't I see him?' I asked her, out of patience with her now. 'Cause he's dead' says she, just as quiet and dull--and fell to pleatin' her apron. 'Dead?' says, I, like you do when you can't take in what you've heard.

"She just nodded her head, not getting a bit excited, but rockin' back and forth.

"'Why--where is he?' says I, not knowing what to say.

"She just pointed upstairs--like this"--pointing to the room above.

"I got up, with the idea of going up there myself. By this time I--didn't know what to do. I walked from there to here; then I says: 'Why, what did he die of?'

"'He died of a rope around his neck,' says she; and just went on pleatin' at her apron."

Hale stopped speaking, and stood staring at the rocker, as if he were still seeing the woman who had sat there the morning before. Nobody spoke; it was as if every one were seeing the woman who had sat there the morning before.

"And what did you do then?" the county attorney at last broke the silence.

"I went out and called Harry. I thought I might--need help. I got Harry in, and we went upstairs." His voice fell almost to a whisper. "There he was--lying over the--"

"I think I'd rather have you go into that upstairs," the county attorney interrupted, "where you can point it all out. Just go on now with the rest of the story."

"Well, my first thought was to get that rope off. It looked--"

He stopped, his face twitching.

"But Harry, he went up to him, and he said. 'No, he's dead all right, and we'd better not touch anything.' So we went downstairs.

158

| A JURY OF HER PEERS

"She was still sitting that same way. 'Has anybody been notified?' I asked. 'No, says she, unconcerned.

"'Who did this, Mrs. Wright?' said Harry. He said it businesslike, and she stopped pleatin' at her apron. 'I don't know,' she says. 'You don't know?' says Harry. 'Weren't you sleepin' in the bed with him?' 'Yes,' says she, 'but I was on the inside. 'Somebody slipped a rope round his neck and strangled him, and you didn't wake up?' says Harry. 'I didn't wake up,' she said after him.

"We may have looked as if we didn't see how that could be, for after a minute she said, 'I sleep sound.'

"Harry was going to ask her more questions, but I said maybe that weren't our business; maybe we ought to let her tell her story first to the coroner or the sheriff. So Harry went fast as he could over to High Road-- the Rivers' place, where there's a telephone."

"And what did she do when she knew you had gone for the coroner?" The attorney got his pencil in his hand all ready for writing.

"She moved from that chair to this one over here"--Hale pointed to a small chair in the corner--"and just sat there with her hands held together and lookin down. I got a feeling that I ought to make some conversation, so I said I had come in to see if John wanted to put in a telephone; and at that she started to laugh, and then she stopped and looked at me--scared."

At the sound of a moving pencil the man who was telling the story looked up.

"I dunno--maybe it wasn't scared," he hastened: "I wouldn't like to say it was. Soon Harry got back, and then Dr. Lloyd came, and you, Mr. Peters, and so I guess that's all I know that you don't."

He said that last with relief, and moved a little, as if relaxing. Everyone moved a little. The county attorney walked toward the stair door.

"I guess we'll go upstairs first--then out to the barn and around there."

He paused and looked around the kitchen.

"You're convinced there was nothing important here?" he asked the sheriff. "Nothing that would--point to any motive?"

The sheriff too looked all around, as if to re-convince himself.

"Nothing here but kitchen things," he said, with a little laugh for the insignificance of kitchen things.

ADVENTURES TO GO |

The county attorney was looking at the cupboard--a peculiar, ungainly structure, half closet and half cupboard, the upper part of it being built in the wall, and the lower part just the old-fashioned kitchen cupboard. As if its queerness attracted him, he got a chair and opened the upper part and looked in. After a moment he drew his hand away sticky.

"Here's a nice mess," he said resentfully.

The two women had drawn nearer, and now the sheriff's wife spoke.

"Oh--her fruit," she said, looking to Mrs. Hale for sympathetic understanding.

She turned back to the county attorney and explained: "She worried about that when it turned so cold last night. She said the fire would go out and her jars might burst."

Mrs. Peters' husband broke into a laugh.

"Well, can you beat the women! Held for murder, and worrying about her preserves!"

The young attorney set his lips.

"I guess before we're through with her she may have something more serious than preserves to worry about."

"Oh, well," said Mrs. Hale's husband, with good-natured superiority, "women are used to worrying over trifles."

The two women moved a little closer together. Neither of them spoke. The county attorney seemed suddenly to remember his manners--and think of his future.

"And yet," said he, with the gallantry of a young politician. "for all their worries, what would we do without the ladies?"

The women did not speak, did not unbend. He went to the sink and began washing his hands. He turned to wipe them on the roller towel-- whirled it for a cleaner place.

"Dirty towels! Not much of a housekeeper, would you say, ladies?"

He kicked his foot against some dirty pans under the sink.

"There's a great deal of work to be done on a farm," said Mrs. Hale stiffly.

"To be sure. And yet"--with a little bow to her--'I know there are some Dickson County farm-houses that do not have such roller towels." He gave it a pull to expose its full length again.

160

| A JURY OF HER PEERS

"Those towels get dirty awful quick. Men's hands aren't always as clean as they might be."

"Ah, loyal to your sex, I see," he laughed. He stopped and gave her a keen look, "But you and Mrs. Wright were neighbors. I suppose you were friends, too."

Martha Hale shook her head.

"I've seen little enough of her of late years. I've not been in this house--it's more than a year."

"And why was that? You didn't like her?"

"I liked her well enough," she replied with spirit. "Farmers' wives have their hands full, Mr. Henderson. And then--" She looked around the kitchen.

"Yes?" he encouraged.

"It never seemed a very cheerful place," said she, more to herself than to him.

"No," he agreed; "I don't think anyone would call it cheerful. I shouldn't say she had the home-making instinct."

"Well, I don't know as Wright had, either," she muttered.

"You mean they didn't get on very well?" he was quick to ask.

"No; I don't mean anything," she answered, with decision. As she turned a little away from him, she added: "But I don't think a place would be any the cheerfuller for John Wright's bein' in it."

"I'd like to talk to you about that a little later, Mrs. Hale," he said. "I'm anxious to get the lay of things upstairs now."

He moved toward the stair door, followed by the two men.

"I suppose anything Mrs. Peters does'll be all right?" the sheriff inquired. "She was to take in some clothes for her, you know--and a few little things. We left in such a hurry yesterday."

The county attorney looked at the two women they were leaving alone there among the kitchen things.

"Yes--Mrs. Peters," he said, his glance resting on the woman who was not Mrs. Peters, the big farmer woman who stood behind the sheriff's wife. "Of course Mrs. Peters is one of us," he said, in a manner of entrusting responsibility. "And keep your eye out, Mrs. Peters, for anything that might be of use. No telling; you women might come upon a clue to the motive--and that's the thing we need."

ADVENTURES TO GO |

Mr. Hale rubbed his face after the fashion of a showman getting ready for a pleasantry.

"But would the women know a clue if they did come upon it?" he said; and, having delivered himself of this, he followed the others through the stair door.

The women stood motionless and silent, listening to the footsteps, first upon the stairs, then in the room above them.

Then, as if releasing herself from something strange. Mrs. Hale began to arrange the dirty pans under the sink, which the county attorney's disdainful push of the foot had deranged.

"I'd hate to have men comin' into my kitchen," she said testily--"snoopin' round and criticizin'."

"Of course it's no more than their duty," said the sheriff's wife, in her manner of timid acquiescence.

"Duty's all right," replied Mrs. Hale bluffly; "but I guess that deputy sheriff that come out to make the fire might have got a little of this on." She gave the roller towel a pull. 'Wish I'd thought of that sooner! Seems mean to talk about her for not having things slicked up, when she had to come away in such a hurry."

She looked around the kitchen. Certainly it was not "slicked up." Her eye was held by a bucket of sugar on a low shelf. The cover was off the wooden bucket, and beside it was a paper bag--half full.

Mrs. Hale moved toward it.

"She was putting this in there," she said to herself--slowly.

She thought of the flour in her kitchen at home--half sifted, half not sifted. She had been interrupted, and had left things half done. What had interrupted Minnie Foster? Why had that work been left half done? She made a move as if to finish it,--unfinished things always bothered her,--and then she glanced around and saw that Mrs. Peters was watching her--and she didn't want Mrs. Peters to get that feeling she had got of work begun and then--for some reason--not finished.

"It's a shame about her fruit," she said, and walked toward the cupboard that the county attorney had opened, and got on the chair, murmuring: "I wonder if it's all gone."

| A JURY OF HER PEERS

It was a sorry enough looking sight, but "Here's one that's all right," she said at last. She held it toward the light. "This is cherries, too." She looked again. "I declare I believe that's the only one."

With a sigh, she got down from the chair, went to the sink, and wiped off the bottle.

"She'll feel awful bad, after all her hard work in the hot weather. I remember the afternoon I put up my cherries last summer.

She set the bottle on the table, and, with another sigh, started to sit down in the rocker. But she did not sit down. Something kept her from sitting down in that chair. She straightened--stepped back, and, half turned away, stood looking at it, seeing the woman who had sat there "pleatin' at her apron."

The thin voice of the sheriff's wife broke in upon her: "I must be getting those things from the front-room closet." She opened the door into the other room, started in, stepped back. "You coming with me, Mrs. Hale?" she asked nervously. "You--you could help me get them."

They were soon back--the stark coldness of that shut-up room was not a thing to linger in.

"My!" said Mrs. Peters, dropping the things on the table and hurrying to the stove.

Mrs. Hale stood examining the clothes the woman who was being detained in town had said she wanted.

"Wright was close!" she exclaimed, holding up a shabby black skirt that bore the marks of much making over. "I think maybe that's why she kept so much to herself. I s'pose she felt she couldn't do her part; and then, you don't enjoy things when you feel shabby. She used to wear pretty clothes and be lively--when she was Minnie Foster, one of the town girls, singing in the choir. But that--oh, that was twenty years ago."

With a carefulness in which there was something tender, she folded the shabby clothes and piled them at one corner of the table. She looked up at Mrs. Peters, and there was something in the other woman's look that irritated her.

"She don't care," she said to herself. "Much difference it makes to her whether Minnie Foster had pretty clothes when she was a girl."

ADVENTURES TO GO |

Then she looked again, and she wasn't so sure; in fact, she hadn't at any time been perfectly sure about Mrs. Peters. She had that shrinking manner, and yet her eyes looked as if they could see a long way into things.

"This all you was to take in?" asked Mrs. Hale.

"No," said the sheriffs wife; "she said she wanted an apron. Funny thing to want, " she ventured in her nervous little way, "for there's not much to get you dirty in jail, goodness knows. But I suppose just to make her feel more natural. If you're used to wearing an apron--. She said they were in the bottom drawer of this cupboard. Yes--here they are. And then her little shawl that always hung on the stair door."

She took the small gray shawl from behind the door leading upstairs, and stood a minute looking at it.

Suddenly Mrs. Hale took a quick step toward the other woman, "Mrs. Peters!"

"Yes, Mrs. Hale?"

"Do you think she--did it?"

A frightened look blurred the other thing in Mrs. Peters' eyes.

"Oh, I don't know," she said, in a voice that seemed to shink away from the subject.

"Well, I don't think she did," affirmed Mrs. Hale stoutly. "Asking for an apron, and her little shawl. Worryin' about her fruit."

"Mr. Peters says--." Footsteps were heard in the room above; she stopped, looked up, then went on in a lowered voice: "Mr. Peters says--it looks bad for her. Mr. Henderson is awful sarcastic in a speech, and he's going to make fun of her saying she didn't--wake up."

For a moment Mrs. Hale had no answer. Then, "Well, I guess John Wright didn't wake up--when they was slippin' that rope under his neck," she muttered.

"No, it's strange," breathed Mrs. Peters. "They think it was such a-- funny way to kill a man."

She began to laugh; at sound of the laugh, abruptly stopped.

"That's just what Mr. Hale said," said Mrs. Hale, in a resolutely natural voice. "There was a gun in the house. He says that's what he can't understand."

"Mr. Henderson said, coming out, that what was needed for the case was a motive. Something to show anger--or sudden feeling."

164

| A JURY OF HER PEERS

'Well, I don't see any signs of anger around here," said Mrs. Hale, "I don't--" She stopped. It was as if her mind tripped on something. Her eye was caught by a dish-towel in the middle of the kitchen table. Slowly she moved toward the table. One half of it was wiped clean, the other half messy. Her eyes made a slow, almost unwilling turn to the bucket of sugar and the half empty bag beside it. Things begun--and not finished.

After a moment she stepped back, and said, in that manner of releasing herself:

"Wonder how they're finding things upstairs? I hope she had it a little more red up up there. You know,"--she paused, and feeling gathered,--"it seems kind of sneaking: locking her up in town and coming out here to get her own house to turn against her!"

"But, Mrs. Hale," said the sheriff's wife, "the law is the law."

"I s'pose 'tis," answered Mrs. Hale shortly.

She turned to the stove, saying something about that fire not being much to brag of. She worked with it a minute, and when she straightened up she said aggressively:

"The law is the law--and a bad stove is a bad stove. How'd you like to cook on this?"--pointing with the poker to the broken lining. She opened the oven door and started to express her opinion of the oven; but she was swept into her own thoughts, thinking of what it would mean, year after year, to have that stove to wrestle with. The thought of Minnie Foster trying to bake in that oven--and the thought of her never going over to see Minnie Foster--.

She was startled by hearing Mrs. Peters say: "A person gets discouraged--and loses heart."

The sheriff's wife had looked from the stove to the sink--to the pail of water which had been carried in from outside. The two women stood there silent, above them the footsteps of the men who were looking for evidence against the woman who had worked in that kitchen. That look of seeing into things, of seeing through a thing to something else, was in the eyes of the sheriff's wife now. When Mrs. Hale next spoke to her, it was gently:

"Better loosen up your things, Mrs. Peters. We'll not feel them when we go out."

165

ADVENTURES TO GO |

Mrs. Peters went to the back of the room to hang up the fur tippet she was wearing. A moment later she exclaimed, "Why, she was piecing a quilt," and held up a large sewing basket piled high with quilt pieces.

Mrs. Hale spread some of the blocks on the table.

"It's log-cabin pattern," she said, putting several of them together, "Pretty, isn't it?"

They were so engaged with the quilt that they did not hear the footsteps on the stairs. Just as the stair door opened Mrs. Hale was saying:

"Do you suppose she was going to quilt it or just knot it?"

The sheriff threw up his hands.

"They wonder whether she was going to quilt it or just knot it!"

There was a laugh for the ways of women, a warming of hands over the stove, and then the county attorney said briskly:

"Well, let's go right out to the barn and get that cleared up."

"I don't see as there's anything so strange," Mrs. Hale said resentfully, after the outside door had closed on the three men--"our taking up our time with little things while we're waiting for them to get the evidence. I don't see as it's anything to laugh about."

"Of course they've got awful important things on their minds," said the sheriff's wife apologetically.

They returned to an inspection of the block for the quilt. Mrs. Hale was looking at the fine, even sewing, and preoccupied with thoughts of the woman who had done that sewing, when she heard the sheriff's wife say, in a queer tone:

"Why, look at this one."

She turned to take the block held out to her.

"The sewing," said Mrs. Peters, in a troubled way, "All the rest of them have been so nice and even--but--this one. Why, it looks as if she didn't know what she was about!"

Their eyes met--something flashed to life, passed between them; then, as if with an effort, they seemed to pull away from each other. A moment Mrs. Hale sat there, her hands folded over that sewing which was so unlike all the rest of the sewing. Then she had pulled a knot and drawn the threads.

"Oh, what are you doing, Mrs. Hale?" asked the sheriff's wife, startled.

166

| A JURY OF HER PEERS

"Just pulling out a stitch or two that's not sewed very good," said Mrs. Hale mildly.

"I don't think we ought to touch things," Mrs. Peters said, a little helplessly.

"I'll just finish up this end," answered Mrs. Hale, still in that mild, matter-of-fact fashion.

She threaded a needle and started to replace bad sewing with good. For a little while she sewed in silence. Then, in that thin, timid voice, she heard:

"Mrs. Hale!"

"Yes, Mrs. Peters?"

'What do you suppose she was so--nervous about?"

"Oh, I don't know," said Mrs. Hale, as if dismissing a thing not important enough to spend much time on. "I don't know as she was--nervous. I sew awful queer sometimes when I'm just tired."

She cut a thread, and out of the corner of her eye looked up at Mrs. Peters. The small, lean face of the sheriff's wife seemed to have tightened up. Her eyes had that look of peering into something. But next moment she moved, and said in her thin, indecisive way:

'Well, I must get those clothes wrapped. They may be through sooner than we think. I wonder where I could find a piece of paper--and string."

"In that cupboard, maybe," suggested to Mrs. Hale, after a glance around.

One piece of the crazy sewing remained unripped. Mrs. Peter's back turned, Martha Hale now scrutinized that piece, compared it with the dainty, accurate sewing of the other blocks. The difference was startling. Holding this block made her feel queer, as if the distracted thoughts of the woman who had perhaps turned to it to try and quiet herself were communicating themselves to her.

Mrs. Peters' voice roused her.

"Here's a bird-cage," she said. "Did she have a bird, Mrs. Hale?"

'Why, I don't know whether she did or not." She turned to look at the cage Mrs. Peters was holding up. "I've not been here in so long." She sighed. "There was a man round last year selling canaries cheap--but I don't know as she took one. Maybe she did. She used to sing real pretty herself."

Mrs. Peters looked around the kitchen.

167

ADVENTURES TO GO |

"Seems kind of funny to think of a bird here." She half laughed--an attempt to put up a barrier. "But she must have had one--or why would she have a cage? I wonder what happened to it."

"I suppose maybe the cat got it," suggested Mrs. Hale, resuming her sewing.

"No; she didn't have a cat. She's got that feeling some people have about cats--being afraid of them. When they brought her to our house yesterday, my cat got in the room, and she was real upset and asked me to take it out."

"My sister Bessie was like that," laughed Mrs. Hale.

The sheriff's wife did not reply. The silence made Mrs. Hale turn round. Mrs. Peters was examining the bird-cage.

"Look at this door," she said slowly. "It's broke. One hinge has been pulled apart."

Mrs. Hale came nearer.

"Looks as if someone must have been--rough with it."

Again their eyes met--startled, questioning, apprehensive. For a moment neither spoke nor stirred. Then Mrs. Hale, turning away, said brusquely:

"If they're going to find any evidence, I wish they'd be about it. I don't like this place."

"But I'm awful glad you came with me, Mrs. Hale." Mrs. Peters put the bird-cage on the table and sat down. "It would be lonesome for me-- sitting here alone."

"Yes, it would, wouldn't it?" agreed Mrs. Hale, a certain determined naturalness in her voice. She had picked up the sewing, but now it dropped in her lap, and she murmured in a different voice: "But I tell you what I do wish, Mrs. Peters. I wish I had come over sometimes when she was here. I wish--I had."

"But of course you were awful busy, Mrs. Hale. Your house--and your children."

"I could've come," retorted Mrs. Hale shortly. "I stayed away because it weren't cheerful--and that's why I ought to have come. I"--she looked around--"I've never liked this place. Maybe because it's down in a hollow and you don't see the road. I don't know what it is, but it's a lonesome place,

168

| A JURY OF HER PEERS

and always was. I wish I had come over to see Minnie Foster sometimes. I can see now--" She did not put it into words.

"Well, you mustn't reproach yourself," counseled Mrs. Peters. "Somehow, we just don't see how it is with other folks till--something comes up."

"Not having children makes less work," mused Mrs. Hale, after a silence, "but it makes a quiet house--and Wright out to work all day-- and no company when he did come in. Did you know John Wright, Mrs. Peters?"

"Not to know him. I've seen him in town. They say he was a good man."

"Yes--good," conceded John Wright's neighbor grimly. "He didn't drink, and kept his word as well as most, I guess, and paid his debts. But he was a hard man, Mrs. Peters. Just to pass the time of day with him--." She stopped, shivered a little. "Like a raw wind that gets to the bone." Her eye fell upon the cage on the table before her, and she added, almost bitterly: "I should think she would've wanted a bird!"

Suddenly she leaned forward, looking intently at the cage. "But what do you s'pose went wrong with it?"

"I don't know," returned Mrs. Peters; "unless it got sick and died."

But after she said it she reached over and swung the broken door. Both women watched it as if somehow held by it.

"You didn't know--her?" Mrs. Hale asked, a gentler note in her voice.

"Not till they brought her yesterday," said the sheriff's wife.

"She--come to think of it, she was kind of like a bird herself. Real sweet and pretty, but kind of timid and--fluttery. How--she--did--change."

That held her for a long time. Finally, as if struck with a happy thought and relieved to get back to everyday things, she exclaimed:

"Tell you what, Mrs. Peters, why don't you take the quilt in with you? It might take up her mind."

"Why, I think that's a real nice idea, Mrs. Hale," agreed the sheriff's wife, as if she too were glad to come into the atmosphere of a simple kindness. "There couldn't possibly be any objection to that, could there? Now, just what will I take? I wonder if her patches are in here--and her things?"

They turned to the sewing basket.

ADVENTURES TO GO |

"Here's some red," said Mrs. Hale, bringing out a roll of cloth. Underneath that was a box. "Here, maybe her scissors are in here--and her things." She held it up. "What a pretty box! I'll warrant that was something she had a long time ago--when she was a girl."

She held it in her hand a moment; then, with a little sigh, opened it.

Instantly her hand went to her nose.

"Why--!"

Mrs. Peters drew nearer--then turned away.

"There's something wrapped up in this piece of silk," faltered Mrs. Hale.

"This isn't her scissors," said Mrs. Peters, in a shrinking voice.

Her hand not steady, Mrs. Hale raised the piece of silk. "Oh, Mrs. Peters!" she cried. "It's--"

Mrs. Peters bent closer.

"It's the bird," she whispered.

"But, Mrs. Peters!" cried Mrs. Hale. "Look at it! Its neck--look at its neck! It's all--other side to."

She held the box away from her.

The sheriff's wife again bent closer.

"Somebody wrung its neck," said she, in a voice that was slow and deep.

And then again the eyes of the two women met--this time clung together in a look of dawning comprehension, of growing horror. Mrs. Peters looked from the dead bird to the broken door of the cage. Again their eyes met. And just then there was a sound at the outside door. Mrs. Hale slipped the box under the quilt pieces in the basket, and sank into the chair before it. Mrs. Peters stood holding to the table. The county attorney and the sheriff came in from outside.

"Well, ladies," said the county attorney, as one turning from serious things to little pleasantries, "have you decided whether she was going to quilt it or knot it?"

"We think," began the sheriff's wife in a flurried voice, "that she was going to--knot it."

He was too preoccupied to notice the change that came in her voice on that last.

"Well, that's very interesting, I'm sure," he said tolerantly. He caught sight of the bird-cage.

170

| A JURY OF HER PEERS

"Has the bird flown?"

"We think the cat got it," said Mrs. Hale in a voice curiously even.

He was walking up and down, as if thinking something out.

"Is there a cat?" he asked absently.

Mrs. Hale shot a look up at the sheriff's wife.

"Well, not now," said Mrs. Peters. "They're superstitious, you know; they leave."

She sank into her chair.

The county attorney did not heed her. "No sign at all of anyone having come in from the outside," he said to Peters, in the manner of continuing an interrupted conversation. "Their own rope. Now let's go upstairs again and go over it, picee by piece. It would have to have been someone who knew just the--"

The stair door closed behind them and their voices were lost.

The two women sat motionless, not looking at each other, but as if peering into something and at the same time holding back. When they spoke now it was as if they were afraid of what they were saying, but as if they could not help saying it.

"She liked the bird," said Martha Hale, low and slowly. "She was going to bury it in that pretty box."

When I was a girl," said Mrs. Peters, under her breath, "my kitten--there was a boy took a hatchet, and before my eyes--before I could get there--" She covered her face an instant. "If they hadn't held me back I would have"--she caught herself, looked upstairs where footsteps were heard, and finished weakly--"hurt him."

Then they sat without speaking or moving.

"I wonder how it would seem," Mrs. Hale at last began, as if feeling her way over strange ground--"never to have had any children around?" Her eyes made a slow sweep of the kitchen, as if seeing what that kitchen had meant through all the years "No, Wright wouldn't like the bird," she said after that--"a thing that sang. She used to sing. He killed that too." Her voice tightened.

Mrs. Peters moved uneasily.

"Of course we don't know who killed the bird."

"I knew John Wright," was Mrs. Hale's answer.

ADVENTURES TO GO |

"It was an awful thing was done in this house that night, Mrs. Hale," said the sheriff's wife. "Killing a man while he slept--slipping a thing round his neck that choked the life out of him."

Mrs. Hale's hand went out to the bird cage.

"We don't know who killed him," whispered Mrs. Peters wildly. "We don't know."

Mrs. Hale had not moved. "If there had been years and years of--nothing, then a bird to sing to you, it would be awful--still--after the bird was still."

It was as if something within her not herself had spoken, and it found in Mrs. Peters something she did not know as herself.

"I know what stillness is," she said, in a queer, monotonous voice. "When we homesteaded in Dakota, and my first baby died--after he was two years old--and me with no other then--"

Mrs. Hale stirred.

"How soon do you suppose they'll be through looking for the evidence?"

"I know what stillness is," repeated Mrs. Peters, in just that same way. Then she too pulled back. "The law has got to punish crime, Mrs. Hale," she said in her tight little way.

"I wish you'd seen Minnie Foster," was the answer, "when she wore a white dress with blue ribbons, and stood up there in the choir and sang."

The picture of that girl, the fact that she had lived neighbor to that girl for twenty years, and had let her die for lack of life, was suddenly more than she could bear.

"Oh, I wish I'd come over here once in a while!" she cried. "That was a crime! Who's going to punish that?"

"We mustn't take on," said Mrs. Peters, with a frightened look toward the stairs.

"I might 'a' known she needed help! I tell you, it's queer, Mrs. Peters. We live close together, and we live far apart. We all go through the same things--it's all just a different kind of the same thing! If it weren't--why do you and I understand? Why do we know--what we know this minute?"

She dashed her hand across her eyes. Then, seeing the jar of fruit on the table she reached for it and choked out:

| A JURY OF HER PEERS

"If I was you I wouldn't tell her her fruit was gone! Tell her it ain't. Tell her it's all right--all of it. Here--take this in to prove it to her! She--she may never know whether it was broke or not."

She turned away.

Mrs. Peters reached out for the bottle of fruit as if she were glad to take it--as if touching a familiar thing, having something to do, could keep her from something else. She got up, looked about for something to wrap the fruit in, took a petticoat from the pile of clothes she had brought from the front room, and nervously started winding that round the bottle.

"My!" she began, in a high, false voice, "it's a good thing the men couldn't hear us! Getting all stirred up over a little thing like a--dead canary." She hurried over that. "As if that could have anything to do with--with--My, wouldn't they laugh?"

Footsteps were heard on the stairs.

"Maybe they would," muttered Mrs. Hale--"maybe they wouldn't."

"No, Peters," said the county attorney incisively; "it's all perfectly clear, except the reason for doing it. But you know juries when it comes to women. If there was some definite thing--something to show. Something to make a story about. A thing that would connect up with this clumsy way of doing it."

In a covert way Mrs. Hale looked at Mrs. Peters. Mrs. Peters was looking at her. Quickly they looked away from each other. The outer door opened and Mr. Hale came in.

"I've got the team round now," he said. "Pretty cold out there."

"I'm going to stay here awhile by myself," the county attorney suddenly announced. "You can send Frank out for me, can't you?" he asked the sheriff. "I want to go over everything. I'm not satisfied we can't do better."

Again, for one brief moment, the two women's eyes found one another.

The sheriff came up to the table.

"Did you want to see what Mrs. Peters was going to take in?"

The county attorney picked up the apron. He laughed.

"Oh, I guess they're not very dangerous things the ladies have picked out."

Mrs. Hale's hand was on the sewing basket in which the box was concealed. She felt that she ought to take her hand off the basket. She did not seem able to. He picked up one of the quilt blocks which she had piled

ADVENTURES TO GO |

on to cover the box. Her eyes felt like fire. She had a feeling that if he took up the basket she would snatch it from him.

But he did not take it up. With another little laugh, he turned away, saying:

"No; Mrs. Peters doesn't need supervising. For that matter, a sheriff's wife is married to the law. Ever think of it that way, Mrs. Peters?"

Mrs. Peters was standing beside the table. Mrs. Hale shot a look up at her; but she could not see her face. Mrs. Peters had turned away. When she spoke, her voice was muffled.

"Not--just that way," she said.

"Married to the law!" chuckled Mrs. Peters' husband. He moved toward the door into the front room, and said to the county attorney:

"I just want you to come in here a minute, George. We ought to take a look at these windows."

"Oh--windows," said the county attorney scoffingly.

"We'll be right out, Mr. Hale," said the sheriff to the farmer, who was still waiting by the door.

Hale went to look after the horses. The sheriff followed the county attorney into the other room. Again--for one final moment--the two women were alone in that kitchen.

Martha Hale sprang up, her hands tight together, looking at that other woman, with whom it rested. At first she could not see her eyes, for the sheriff's wife had not turned back since she turned away at that suggestion of being married to the law. But now Mrs. Hale made her turn back. Her eyes made her turn back. Slowly, unwillingly, Mrs. Peters turned her head until her eyes met the eyes of the other woman. There was a moment when they held each other in a steady, burning look in which there was no evasion or flinching. Then Martha Hale's eyes pointed the way to the basket in which was hidden the thing that would make certain the conviction of the other woman--that woman who was not there and yet who had been there with them all through that hour.

For a moment Mrs. Peters did not move. And then she did it. With a rush forward, she threw back the quilt pieces, got the box, tried to put it in her handbag. It was too big. Desperately she opened it, started to take the bird out. But there she broke--she could not touch the bird. She stood there helpless, foolish.

174

| A JURY OF HER PEERS

There was the sound of a knob turning in the inner door. Martha Hale snatched the box from the sheriff's wife, and got it in the pocket of her big coat just as the sheriff and the county attorney came back into the kitchen.

"Well, Henry," said the county attorney facetiously, "at least we found out that she was not going to quilt it. She was going to--what is it you call it, ladies?"

Mrs. Hale's hand was against the pocket of her coat.

"We call it--knot it, Mr. Henderson."

THE END

SUDOKU

(MEDIUM DIFFICULTY; ANSWERS IN BACK OF BOOK)

		2	6		5	7		
	2							8
	9			5	7			
		4						9
		9		8			5	
								4
2				5		8	1	
5			1	6	2	4		

quick

2 out of 3 with someone near.

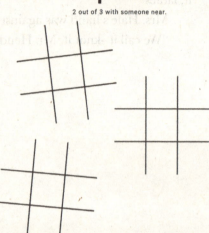

Never Miss a New Release from OffBeatReads & Receive a copy of Issue #1 of *Adventures to Go* FREE by Signing Up for Our eMail Brief at OffBeatReads.com

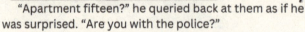

Excerpt:

"Apartment fifteen?" he queried back at them as if he was surprised. "Are you with the police?"

"Private investigator," Vegas said as she pulled out a business card that Pepper had made for her and handed it to the janitor.

He looked at it and said, "Vegas Chantly, Pie."

"That's P.I. How is everybody getting pie out of that?" Vegas asked.

"She's single," said Eleanor, which brought a stare from Vegas that contained horror and anger strangled together.

Vegas then pretended that her mother was a potted plant, so as to ignore her, and turned back to the janitor and said, "We didn't catch your name."

"Billy Sanchez."

"Isn't that the boy who made the fish movie?... I could never sit down and talk to him... because I look at him and feel like such a whore... I can't sit down and talk to the boy who did the fish movie... I couldn't even touch his hand."
Alfred Hitchcock reacting to the sight of young Steven Spielberg.

Never Miss a New Release from OffBeatReads... Receive a FREE copy of *Adventures to Go* Issue #1 by Signing Up for Our eMail Brief at OffBeatReads.com

SOUTHWEST SCENARIOS
COMMENTARIES FROM RURAL ARIZONA
BY DARRYLE PURCELL

Because humankind fails to learn from past lessons, we find that many circumstances from yesteryear are repeating themselves yet again. The commentaries that follow here and in future issues were originally published by *The Mohave Valley Daily News* between 1993 & 2013--and in many ways they apply to today.
We are grateful to republish these commentaries written by Darryle Purcell in full and unedited. His own brand of humor and style can deliver insight, provoke thought, and even boil blood.

New Arizona resident has plans to help state Fish and Game Department manage wildlife

June 29, 2001

I RECENTLY WROTE ABOUT A FERRET-FEEDING PROGRAM THAT I CONSIDERED questionable. Now, according to the Associated Press, a Marana, Ariz., resident is proposing an even more questionable wildlife-feeding program.

The AP story reports that Wallace Burford's cat, Jake, was killed by a coyote near his home. Burford, who had moved to Arizona only two weeks earlier, is angry and blames the state Game and Fish Department for his loss.

He paid $328.21 to have Jake cremated and he wants the offending department to reimburse him.

"They (Fish and Game) are responsible for all the wild game," Burford said.

The AP story reports that Burford wants the department to "post signs warning people about roaming wildlife, feed the animals so they're not hungry enough to seek out pets, or reimburse people whose pets are killed."

Since people who have smoked tobacco for many years can legally blame the tobacco companies for health problems, and get away with it, why can't someone who's not "worldly" enough to know that desert coyotes consider cats succulent morsels blame a government agency for his

| SOUTHWEST SCENARIOS

problem? After all, the Arizona Game and Fish Department is designated to *manage* wildlife.

Perhaps the agency should consider tagging all animals with warning signs. "Warning! This coyote may be hazardous to your cat's health," signs could be branded horizontally on the sides of the wild canines. Of course government diversity law would demand one side would have to be in English and the other side in Siamese. I'm not sure the signs will save all cats, especially if they are Persian or dyslexic.

I still haven't figured out how to post the warning signs on snakes.

Burford, AP reports, has a new indoor cat. I wonder if he has been warned that it may be hazardous to his tropical fish collection. Perhaps it needs a sign.

Burford's idea of a feeding program for wild animals could also save a lot of pets and bring a lot of government jobs to Arizona. I wonder how many state animal feeders it would take to keep the wildlife full and away from our frightened kitties.

For instance, how many times per day will the animals have to be fed? Can we get all the animals to agree on a specific dinnertime as a cost-cutting measure? Perhaps night-feeders, like owls, could pick up their government handouts around dusk to avoid an overtime situation.

And what could we feed them? Could we take ground meat and pat it into the shape of kittens to feed to coyotes, bobcats, snakes, hawks and other feline aficionados? And where will we get the meat? The only place I can think of that would have that many expendable carcasses to turn into coyote food would be animal shelters. Unfortunately, due to some pet owners not spaying or neutering their animals, the shelters have to "euthanize" a lot of cats. Of course, a little common sense would eliminate this as a source of coyote munchies.

And we all know the ferrets will be a problem. They are hard to organize. I'm not even sure they will meet and confer.

The AP story reports that Burford believes all residents whose pets become victims of wild animals could be reimbursed. He believes the dollars could come out of funds from hunting and fishing licenses.

Seriously, I don't believe there is enough money in that state department's budget to fund Mr. Burford's proposals. And, I'm sure the Game and Fish Department has much higher priority programs that make

ADVENTURES TO GO |

much more sense than Burford's — such as the construction of restrooms for the bears.

A LITTLE JOURNEY

BY RAY BRADBURY

ADVENTURES TO GO |

T here were two important things—one, that she was very old; two, that Mr. Thirkell was taking her to God. For hadn't he patted her hand and said: "Mrs. Bellowes, we'll take off into space in my rocket, and go to find Him together."

And that was how it was going to be. Oh, this wasn't like any other group Mrs. Bellowes had ever joined. In her fervor to light a path for her delicate, tottering feet, she had struck matches down dark alleys, and found her way to Hindu mystics who floated their flickering, starry eyelashes over crystal balls. She had walked on the meadow paths with ascetic Indian philosophers imported by daughters-in-spirit of Madame Blavatsky. She had made pilgrimages to California's stucco jungles to hunt the astrological seer in his natural habitat. She had even consented to signing away the rights to one of her homes in order to be taken into the shouting order of a temple of amazing evangelists who had promised her golden smoke, crystal fire, and the great soft hand of God coming to bear her home.

None of these people had ever shaken Mrs. Bellowes' faith, even when she saw them sirened away in a black wagon in the night, or discovered their pictures, bleak and unromantic, in the morning tabloids. The world had roughed them up and locked them away because they knew too much, that was all.

And then, two weeks ago, she had seen Mr. Thirkell's advertisement in New York City:

COME TO MARS!

Stay at the Thirkell Restorium for one week. And then, on into space on the greatest adventure life can offer!

Send for Free Pamphlet: "Nearer My God To Thee."

Excursion rates. Round trip slightly lower.

"Round trip," Mrs. Bellowes had thought. "But who would come back after seeing *Him*?"

And so she had bought a ticket and flown off to Mars and spent seven mild days at Mr. Thirkell's Restorium, the building with the sign on it which flashed: THIRKELL'S ROCKET TO HEAVEN! She had spent

| A LITTLE JOURNEY

the week bathing in limpid waters and erasing the care from her tiny bones, and now she was fidgeting, ready to be loaded into Mr. Thirkell's own special private rocket, like a bullet, to be fired on out into space beyond Jupiter and Saturn and Pluto. And thus—who could deny it?—you would be getting nearer and nearer to the Lord. How wonderful! Couldn't you just *feel* Him drawing near? Couldn't you just sense His breath, His scrutiny, His Presence?

"Here I am," said Mrs. Bellowes, "an ancient rickety elevator, ready to go up the shaft. God need only press the button."

Now, on the seventh day, as she minced up the steps of the Restorium, a number of small doubts assailed her.

"For one thing," she said aloud to no one, "it isn't quite the land of milk and honey here on Mars that they said it would be. My room is like a cell, the swimming pool is really quite inadequate, and, besides, how many widows who look like mushrooms or skeletons want to swim? And, finally, the whole Restorium smells of boiled cabbage and tennis shoes!"

She opened the front door and let it slam, somewhat irritably.

She was amazed at the other women in the auditorium. It was like wandering in a carnival mirror-maze, coming again and again upon yourself—the same floury face, the same chicken hands, and jingling bracelets. One after another of the images of herself floated before her. She put out her hand, but it wasn't a mirror; it was another lady shaking her fingers and saying:

"We're waiting for Mr. Thirkell. *Sh!*"

"Ah," whispered everyone.

The velvet curtains parted.

Mr. Thirkell appeared, fantastically serene, his Egyptian eyes upon everyone. But there was something, nevertheless, in his appearance which made one expect him to call "Hi!" while fuzzy dogs jumped over his legs, through his hooped arms, and over his back. Then, dogs and all, he should dance with a dazzling piano-keyboard smile off into the wings.

Mrs. Bellowes, with a secret part of her mind which she constantly had to grip tightly, expected to hear a cheap Chinese gong sound when Mr. Thirkell entered. His large liquid dark eyes were so improbable that one of the old ladies had facetiously claimed she saw a mosquito cloud hovering over them as they did around summer rain-barrels. And Mrs. Bellowes

ADVENTURES TO GO |

sometimes caught the scent of the theatrical mothball and the smell of calliope steam on his sharply pressed suit.

But with the same savage rationalization that had greeted all other disappointments in her rickety life, she bit at the suspicion and whispered, "This time it's *real*. This time it'll work. Haven't we got a *rocket*?"

Mr. Thirkell bowed. He smiled a sudden Comedy Mask smile. The old ladies looked in at his epiglottis and sensed chaos there.

Before he even began to speak, Mrs. Bellowes saw him picking up each of his words, oiling it, making sure it ran smooth on its rails. Her heart squeezed in like a tiny fist, and she gritted her porcelain teeth.

"Friends," said Mr. Thirkell, and you could hear the frost snap in the hearts of the entire assemblage.

"No!" said Mrs. Bellowes ahead of time. She could hear the bad news rushing at her, and herself tied to the track while the immense black wheels threatened and the whistle screamed, helpless.

"There will be a slight delay," said Mr. Thirkell.

In the next instant, Mr. Thirkell might have cried, or been tempted to cry, "Ladies, be seated!" in minstrel-fashion, for the ladies had come up at him from their chairs, protesting and trembling.

"Not a very long delay." Mr. Thirkell put up his hands to pat the air.

"How long?"

"Only a week."

"A week!"

"Yes. You can stay here at the Restorium for seven more days, can't you? A little delay won't matter, will it, in the end? You've waited a lifetime. Only a few more days."

At twenty dollars a day, thought Mrs. Bellowes, coldly.

"What's the trouble?" a woman cried.

"A legal difficulty," said Mr. Thirkell.

"We've a rocket, haven't we?"

"Well, ye-ess."

"But I've been here a whole month, waiting," said one old lady. "Delays, delays!"

"That's right," said everyone.

"Ladies, ladies," murmured Mr. Thirkell, smiling serenely.

184

| A LITTLE JOURNEY

"We want to see the rocket!" It was Mrs. Bellowes forging ahead, alone, brandishing her fist like a toy hammer.

Mr. Thirkell looked into the old ladies' eyes, a missionary among albino cannibals.

"Well, now," he said.

"Yes, *now!*" cried Mrs. Bellowes.

"I'm afraid—" he began.

"So am I!" she said. "That's why we want to see the ship!"

"No, no, now, Mrs.—" He snapped his fingers for her name.

"Bellowes!" she cried. She was a small container, but now all the seething pressures that had been built up over long years came steaming through the delicate vents of her body. Her cheeks became incandescent. With a wail that was like a melancholy factory whistle, Mrs. Bellowes ran forward and hung to him, almost by her teeth, like a summer-maddened Spitz. She would not and never could let go, until he died, and the other women followed, jumping and yapping like a pound let loose on its trainer, the same one who had petted them and to whom they had squirmed and whined joyfully an hour before, now milling about him, creasing his sleeves and frightening the Egyptian serenity from his gaze.

"This way!" cried Mrs. Bellowes, feeling like Madame Lafarge. "Through the back! We've waited long enough to see the ship. Every day he's put us off, every day we've waited, now let's see."

"No, no, ladies!" cried Mr. Thirkell, leaping about.

They burst through the back of the stage and out a door, like a flood, bearing the poor man with them into a shed, and then out, quite suddenly, into an abandoned gymnasium.

"There it is!" said someone. "The rocket."

And then a silence fell that was terrible to entertain.

There was the rocket.

Mrs. Bellowes looked at it and her hands sagged away from Mr. Thirkell's collar.

The rocket was something like a battered copper pot. There were a thousand bulges and rents and rusty pipes and dirty vents on and in it. The ports were clouded over with dust, resembling the eyes of a blind hog.

Everyone wailed a little sighing wail.

ADVENTURES TO GO |

"Is that the rocket ship *Glory Be to the Highest?*" cried Mrs. Bellowes, appalled.

Mr. Thirkell nodded and looked at his feet.

"For which we paid out our one thousand dollars apiece and came all the way to Mars to get on board with you and go off to find Him?" asked Mrs. Bellowes.

"Why, that isn't worth a sack of dried peas," said Mrs. Bellowes.

"It's nothing but junk!"

Junk, whispered everyone, getting hysterical.

"Don't let him get away!"

Mr. Thirkell tried to break and run, but a thousand possum traps closed on him from every side. He withered.

Everybody walked around in circles like blind mice. There was a confusion and a weeping that lasted for five minutes as they went over and touched the Rocket, the Dented Kettle, the Rusty Container for God's Children.

"Well," said Mrs. Bellowes. She stepped up into the askew doorway of the rocket and faced everyone. "It looks as if a terrible thing has been done to us," she said. "I haven't any money to go back home to Earth and I've too much pride to go to the Government and tell them a common man like this has fooled us out of our life's savings. I don't know how you feel about it, all of you, but the reason all of us came is because I'm eighty-five, and you're eighty-nine, and you're seventy-eight, and all of us are nudging on toward a hundred, and there's nothing on Earth for us, and it doesn't appear there's anything on Mars either. We all expected not to breathe much more air or crochet many more doilies or we'd never have come here. So what I have to propose is a simple thing—to take a chance."

She reached out and touched the rusted hulk of the rocket.

"This is *our* rocket. We paid for our trip. And we're going to *take* our trip!"

Everyone rustled and stood on tiptoes and opened an astonished mouth.

Mr. Thirkell began to cry. He did it quite easily and very effectively.

"We're going to get in this ship," said Mrs. Bellowes, ignoring him. "And we're going to take off to where we were going."

Mr. Thirkell stopped crying long enough to say, "But it was all a fake. I don't know anything about space. He's not out there, anyway. I lied. I don't

| A LITTLE JOURNEY

know where He is, and I couldn't find Him if I wanted to. And you were fools to ever take my word on it."

"Yes," said Mrs. Bellowes, "we were fools. I'll go along on that. But you can't blame us, for we're old, and it was a lovely, good and fine idea, one of the loveliest ideas in the world. Oh, we didn't really fool ourselves that we could get nearer to Him physically. It was the gentle, mad dream of old people, the kind of thing you hold onto for a few minutes a day, even though you know it's not true. So, all of you who want to go, you follow me in the ship."

"But you can't go!" said Mr. Thirkell. "You haven't got a navigator. And that ship's a ruin!"

"You," said Mrs. Bellowes, "will be the navigator."

She stepped into the ship, and after a moment, the other old ladies pressed forward. Mr. Thirkell, windmilling his arms frantically, was nevertheless pressed through the port, and in a minute the door slammed shut. Mr. Thirkell was strapped into the navigator's seat, with everyone talking at once and holding him down. The special helmets were issued to be fitted over every gray or white head to supply extra oxygen in case of a leakage in the ship's hull, and at long last the hour had come and Mrs. Bellowes stood behind Mr. Thirkell and said, "We're ready, sir."

He said nothing. He pleaded with them silently, using his great, dark, wet eyes, but Mrs. Bellowes shook her head and pointed to the control.

"Takeoff," agreed Mr. Thirkell morosely, and pulled a switch.

Everybody fell. The rocket went up from the planet Mars in a great fiery glide, with the noise of an entire kitchen thrown down an elevator shaft, with a sound of pots and pans and kettles and fires boiling and stews bubbling, with a smell of burned incense and rubber and sulphur, with a color of yellow fire, and a ribbon of red stretching below them, and all the old women singing and holding to each other, and Mrs. Bellowes crawling upright in the sighing, straining, trembling ship.

"Head for space, Mr. Thirkell."

"It can't last," said Mr. Thirkell, sadly. "This ship can't last. It will—"

It did.

The rocket exploded.

187

ADVENTURES TO GO |

Mrs. Bellowes felt herself lifted and thrown about dizzily, like a doll. She heard the great screamings and saw the flashes of bodies sailing by her in fragments of metal and powdery light.

"Help, help!" cried Mr. Thirkell, far away, on a small radio beam.

The ship disintegrated into a million parts, and the old ladies, all one hundred of them, were flung straight on ahead with the same velocity as the ship.

As for Mr. Thirkell, for some reason of trajectory, perhaps, he had been blown out the other side of the ship. Mrs. Bellowes saw him falling separate and away from them, screaming, screaming.

There goes Mr. Thirkell, thought Mrs. Bellowes.

And she knew where he was going. He was going to be burned and roasted and broiled good, but very good.

Mr. Thirkell was falling down into the Sun.

And here we are, thought Mrs. Bellowes. *Here we are, going on out, and out, and out.*

There was hardly a sense of motion at all, but she knew that she was traveling at fifty thousand miles an hour and would continue to travel at that speed for an eternity, until....

She saw the other women swinging all about her in their own trajectories, a few minutes of oxygen left to each of them in their helmets, and each was looking up to where they were going.

Of course, thought Mrs. Bellowes. *Out into space. Out and out, and the darkness like a great church, and the stars like candles, and in spite of everything, Mr. Thirkell, the rocket, and the dishonesty, we are going toward the Lord.*

And there, yes, *there*, as she fell on and on, coming toward her, she could almost discern the outline now, coming toward her was His mighty golden hand, reaching down to hold her and comfort her like a frightened sparrow....

"I'm Mrs. Amelia Bellowes," she said quietly, in her best company voice. "I'm from the planet Earth."

THE END

188

Orchard Corset

OrchardCorset.com
Ph. 1-866-456-7411

Corsets to suit your purpose: waist training, weddings, costumes, back pain relief, or just for fun.

★★★★★ 04/23/19

Customer service and sizing experts

Customer service and sizing experts are very helpful and responsive. Feeling great about my order!
koma876omen

★★★★ 04/25/19

Very comfortable

Fits like a glove and is super comfortable. Highly recommend for daily use.
Dayna L.

★★★★ 04/24/19

Gorgeous!

I knew I had to get this one when I saw the teaser picture for it. It's even more gorgeous in person. Fits well even though I have...
Read More
Amy H.

- Sizing Experts Available 7 Days a Week
- Only Steel-Boned Corsets, Never Plastic
- Interest Free Pay Over Time Option!
- Rewards program
- Men's Corsets too

A PEEK AT THE REAL GLAMOUR OF YESTERYEAR

BY ELMEDINA HOTA

Ever get caught up in a sudden wave of nostalgia, your mind wandering off into a distant past—maybe even a time period you've never lived in or known? How can we feel nostalgic for something we've never experienced, especially for a time when, as history has taught us, was (at least) slightly worse in some ways than they are now.

But the fashion!

Open the right magazine and there she is! Wearing a polka dot dress, smiling into the sun... with her hair high and wavy... red lips… beautiful cat eyes…

OR a dame with satin gloves, sultry-dark lipstick, wearing a shiny dress, and in a pair of gleaming shoes with heels not *too* big—not *too* small…

The men? Cigars pinched between their lips, a suit and hat, maybe an overcoat—looking handsome. It's easy for one to feel overwhelmed with a realization that something historic and golden has been missed.

Modern trends are dictating various looks nowadays, but can they compare to the elegance and beauty women possessed in the early to mid 1900s? When we think of "old glamour", the first couple of names that pop into our minds are Marilyn Monroe and Audrey Hepburn. I am in no way disputing their iconic existences, nor am I trying to belittle what these two achieved. I love them both! But let me assure you that there are many more names worth mentioning throughout the history of glamorous fashion and, ladies and gentlemen, we're about to take a stroll through the years when glamour was at its **absolute peak!**

Let's start with the birth of the modern woman in the Roaring Twenties.

As soon as we mention the old glamour, we immediately think of curvy women—but this wasn't the case in the '20s. The ideal body type of this era was actually quite the opposite: short, flat-chested, no waist, with a kind of boxy torso and emphasis on the hips. (Of course not all women could achieve this look, but it was the ideal.) It was a Clara Bow look; rather boyish if you ask me. How did women achieve this? With **bandeau**. It's a type of garment that streamlines the silhouette. Note the image.

An ad from a 1928 magazine for bandeau. See how it is made to not lift, but flatten the upper chest.

The women were wearing dark eye makeup, with their eyebrows drawn very thin and sloping down, and they would wear lipstick only on the front part of their lips! This was called the bee-sting or bee-stung lip, as if the lips have been stung by a bee and have swollen.

Actress Clara Bow, with Bee Sting lips

Quite strange to look at now, isn't it? To me, it also looks a little bit like they've gotten ready to perform in a tragic theater piece. My brain immediately associates this '20s makeup with a tragic scene about to be performed.

This era is also known for the Bob hairstyle. Women cut off their hair and wore the short, bob hairdo. You're familiar—and since there aren't really many things that can be done with the Bob, they used headbands as accessories.

Incidentally, several wonderful things were introduced in this era that deserve mention because they form a setting. Radio, silent movies, and the automobile industry rose to prominence. An aesthetic known as Art Deco presented itself through the use of straight lines and geometry. This was applied to seemingly every element of the '20s; furniture, graphic art, architecture, typography, and fashion! This aesthetic is gorgeous and still popular, too. Women's right to vote was an issue, and one worth fighting for. Of course it enabled women to be freer than ever before!

Back to fashion. Cloche hats were worn to minimize the look of the size of the head, and the Shift dress was the first time since Ancient Greece women in large numbers started leaving gloves in their wardrobe, and not on their hands. With this dress, women's legs were more visible than ever.

There is an article from The New York Times, dated January 29th, 1922 titled, "Flappers Flaunt Fads In Footwear". "Flappers" was a term used for women who acted in a shocking way—smoking (which was against the law prior to the '20s), hanging out with guys, wearing shorter skirts than other women—maybe even snorting cocaine. People of society were outraged by this rebellious, non-conforming behavior. Back then, you could take classes to learn how to smoke. Hard to imagine, since today people try everything they can think of to achieve the exact opposite and quit smoking.

Because of the fact that women started showing their legs for the first time in history, the stocking business started booming. The colors of clothing were bold and dramatic, with an introduction of metallic as well. It was all very new and exciting. Coco Chanel designed the very first little black dress in this era, revolutionizing the whole idea of clothing. She believed clothing should be made so that women can go to work in it, travel in it, do any single thing they wanted to, and still be comfortable doing it!

Another woman who rose to fame in this era was **Josephine Baker,** an entertainer who participated in The Harlem Renaissance. Josephine moved to France where she claimed her glory, and she was the first-ever African-American woman to headline in a movie. This was a silent movie titled, *La Sirene De Tropiques*, which means "Siren of the Tropics". Her most memorable performance might be the *Danse Sauvage*, which she did while wearing nothing but a skirt that consisted of artificial bananas.

Apart from being a dancer, an actress and a singer, Josephine Baker was also a businesswoman who created a hair product called "Bakerfix". This was, as you might've guessed, a hair gel, and it was one of the most successful hair products (in the '30s). This remarkable woman earned herself honors over the years which include: a French Resistance medal, the Croix de Guerre, and the Legion of Honor by President de Gaulle for being a spy during World War II. How extraordinary!

ADVENTURES TO GO |

For men, there was a craze for wearing golfing pants, oxford bags and raccoon coats. Rudolph Valentino was considered one of the very first sex symbols in the movie industry and so many men were trying to look like him, while women fantasized about being with him. There are many great quotes of his on the Internet, this being my favorite:

"Women are not in love with me but with the picture of me on the screen. I am merely the canvas on which women paint their dreams." Nicely put.

Valentino's sudden death at the age of thirty-one caused mass hysteria among the people. There is also a quote of his saying that he'd like to be remembered as an actor by his role in *Blood and Sand.* He grew a beard for a role, causing him to receive many letters from the fans asking him to shave! The slick-back hair, fur coats, and colorful clothing, were all objects of ridicule prior to his fame. But those things turned out to be the *very* things that helped him achieve it. A little bit of an inspiration for all of us to stay true to ourselves and wear what we love!

The '20s transitioned into the '30s with another burst of glamour. An elegant silhouette that was such an opposite to one of the '20s. The beauty ideal was very different as well. No more slopping down, tired eyebrows and eye makeup, but very high and thin eyebrows. The eye makeup relied on false eyelashes and a little bit of eyeshadow – mostly a neutral one. The lips were full and red. Hats and gloves were obligatory, only this time, the hats were much bigger than they were in the '20s. Women loved polka dots on their clothing as well.

As society struggled during the Great Depression, on-screen performers dressed to the hilt, which gave people hope of better times ahead. Backless dresses were introduced during this time. And what came out of the African safari craze? Leopard and cheetah prints.

194

| A PEEK AT THE REAL GLAMOUR OF YESTERYEAR

Actress Jean Harlow in a backless dress.

I am excited to finally talk about one of my favorite designers: Elsa Schiaparelli. She was an Italian designer who created some of the most interesting pieces of clothing I've ever seen! Elsa was aligned with the surrealists: Dali, Cockto, Magritte, de Chirico; and it shows! She created escapism from so many scary things that were happening in the world with so many incredible designs, such as her famous skeleton dress; the shoe hat, silly and unique buttons (shaped like mermaids, lips, and bugs), gloves with nail polish, furry shoes, and the famous lobster dress.

However, she was Coco Chanel's bitter enemy. This was due to the fact that Chanel believed that clothing should be comfortable and practical—whereas Elsa had fun with her designs, letting her imagination run wild. You can imagine how these two completely different views on fashion would collide and it turned into a bitter rivalry between the two. Apparently at one costume event before World War II, Chanel set Elsa's dress on fire by asking her for a dance, then steering her into a chandelier lit with candles. Luckily, the guests poured water on Elsa's dress before any real damage could occur. Malicious!

What was Elsa wearing at the party? A dress that resembled a tree! This might've been the last straw for Chanel, who just wanted to see it burn. A terrible way to act and far from glamour, don't you think?

I find two romantic stories from this time period worth mentioning. The first one is between Henry VIII and his wife Wallis Simpson. Both considered fashion icons, Wallis loved to spend money on clothing, and Henry loved to buy her things. Their relationship caused a scandal since Wallis was actually a divorced American woman, and it was unheard of for a man of his stature to be involved with a woman like her at the time. His flashy fashion sense caused trouble with the royal family. They were setting trends because the people imitated the way they dressed, and it was *too* flashy. The most interesting thing to me about this whole affair is the fact that Henry VIII was crowned the king of England after his father's death, and he abdicated his throne shortly after in order to marry Wallis! She ended up donating the dress she wore on their wedding day to the Metropolitan Museum and, since it was donated in the 1950s, the dress has faded from blue to traditional cream color. Once people saw her in this dress, it was the design everybody imitated that year. Iconic!

An ad from the 1930s

The second couple, as you may have already guessed, is Bonnie and Clyde. Such an interesting story with these two. Forced to turn to a life of crime due to poverty and they robbed banks, stole cars, kidnapped and killed people. Terrible, I know. What's the interesting part? Bonnie's love for fashion! She had a camera that she used for fashion photoshoots with her beloved Clyde. This ultimately led to their demise as that very

| A PEEK AT THE REAL GLAMOUR OF YESTERYEAR

camera was discovered at one of the crime scenes and the police used the photographs to make the 'WANTED' posters of the two.

Let's not forget that this was the era of the Great Depression, so I want to talk about the clothing that became a necessity due to the difficulties many families had to endure. There was something called a feed sack dress. It was actual cotton cloth from feed sacks that women used to make dresses! This was first done in the '20s by thrifty women who lived on farms. They wanted to have as little waste as possible, so they began using the cloth not only for clothing (especially for their fast-growing children), but for towels, underwear, curtains, quilts, and other things they needed for their households. This is why there were many different patterns and colors of the feed sacks in the '30s because they became an absolute necessity during those difficult times. It's pretty admirable what a mind can come up with, isn't it?

What is fashion to you? To me, it's everything I can see and feel. It's the mood I'm in, the action I'm about to take. I use it to respond to the world around me and express how I feel and think, whether or not it's just for that particular moment. Nothing proves this theory more than what came in the '40s: World War II. For many, it seemed like these desperate times would never end. The men became soldiers and the women volunteered as nurses, pilots, knitters – anything to help the war effort. They were all in it, all the way. There were three divisions of clothing – utility clothing, uniforms for the volunteers, and work clothing for women who took over the jobs men would be normally doing, but couldn't because they were off fighting the war.

The body ideal changed to a strong figure with broad shoulders and curvaceous legs – the women had to be strong and ready for whatever might come next. Esther Williams is one example of this body ideal, and Rita Hayworth is another. But hold on! There was a second body ideal in this era: a small, cute, curvy body type. A Betty Grable body type, if you will.

The women started wearing shoulder pads to achieve the image of broad shoulders and, to even it out, they started wearing one of my personal favorites, peplum clothing. They also wore huge hats, with many different accessories tied to them.

ADVENTURES TO GO

The women working in factories to support the war effort were required to wear head scarves. Why? So the hair wouldn't get caught up in machinery. This led to another trend: turbans! Women wore turbans in so many different, wonderful ways and in so many bright colors. Easy to see how fashion responds to the things happening in the world!

There was rationing because of the war—food, clothing, nearly everything was rationed. But President Roosevelt decided not to ration accessories for morale, since women were doing such a great job on their side. Women were wearing hairstyles called victory rolls. Elizabeth Arden launched the "Victory Red" lipstick for women to wear while fulfilling their war-time duties. There are reports that Hitler hated red lipstick, so this was a way for women to give him a middle finger.

Most men were wearing uniforms, as you know, but civilian clothing consisted of high-waisted pants, short and wide ties, and huge jackets. It looked wonderful, at least to me. I love a guy in a good suit.

Cab Calloway in a Zoom Suit

What was known as the Zoot suit did not go over well. Zoot suits were these huge, oversized suits worn mainly by Latin men. Believe it or not, the suit even caused riots, and men in uniform would beat up any man found wearing one. Hard to believe, especially since today we can see people wearing all types of clothing; from fabrics that barely cover their private parts to oversized clothing completely covering the figure. But—**not** excusing the violence—because of the war rationing, wearing a Zoot suit was considered unpatriotic because it wasted fabric.

The post-war world brought an end to the rationing, and with it the reemergence of the hourglass figure. Many women wore it wonderfully: Marilyn Monroe, Elizabeth Taylor, Jane Mansfield, Sophia Loren to name some. After the era of women taking the role of men in their line of work, the fifties became about returning to femininity. Men took back their roles upon returning from the war and women took theirs: and the hourglass was the silhouette reflecting it. Whoever didn't have this particular body type would wear a girdle. This is something mid-century fashion couldn't work without. The girdle was an absolute must! It wasn't about being skinny, but curvy, with a tiny waist—and that's what wearing a girdle achieved. Skirts got longer and there was a new type of clothing everyone had to have called the, "New Look". This particular style was inspired by the clothing of the 1850s when women were dolled up, with so much fabric in their dresses and it quickly became an obsession in the 1950s. It was wide and long, very elegant and glamorous! Who designed it? Christian Dior. Coco Chanel responded with the Chanel cardigan suits, which were boxy and comfortable. She hated Dior's creations, claiming that he takes women back to the 19th century with his ridiculous clothing. These rivalries between Chanel and other designers could make an article on their own!

Actress Louise Brooks

ADVENTURES TO GO |

There were two types of clothing for teenagers, which was a new thing as there wasn't any type of junior clothing prior to this time period. There were teenagers that were considered nice teenagers and there were also naughty ones. The nice ones would be wearing similar clothing to adults, with an exception of a motif on the clothing, such as a photo of the Eiffel tower on a skirt, or Mickey Mouse—you get the gist. This was also the period of time when teenagers started wearing blue jeans rolled up at the bottom. Why? Because children grow quickly – so kids would wear longer jeans they'd fit into months later and, until they did, they'd roll them up. Rolling them up became an actual trend. Nice teenage boys would wear jeans, and they'd dress up as adults in suits when they'd go to a party. Sort of like modified adult clothing.

The naughty teens would wear leather jackets and jeans, and they'd grease their hair which led to them being called greasers! There was another type of naughty teens called the Teddy Boys, with their greased hair and Edwardian-style jackets which were considered rebellious at the time. Teddy is short for Edwardian, hence the nickname. These guys were non-conformists. There were also Teddy Girls who wore Teddy jackets with their jeans. They were the "cool" kids no one wanted to mess with!

For me, the most interesting thing about these time periods is the uniformity. The women wore girdles because not wearing them would be considered outrageous. Of course, that's not the only reason. The girdles worked wonders for the hourglass figure they wanted to achieve. Think about it, they wore such an uncomfortable item to achieve this particular look because it was set as a fashion trend. This shows the incredibly high standards that were set for women throughout time. Even now, when we've accepted so many different things and ideals, we still have trends that are impossible to achieve. Women get surgeries to achieve perfect bodies and facial features. The men were uniformed in their suits and these were acceptable clothes in the past. Sleeveless tops on men were considered outrageous, but they were worn by the Beatniks – a subculture of people who were considered to be hipsters. Men are now free to wear whatever they want, aren't they?

The beauty standards throughout the eras were distinctive and were the ones everyone followed, whereas now everyone has their own idea of beauty and people create different things and share them on social media.

| A PEEK AT THE REAL GLAMOUR OF YESTERYEAR

The best thing about the clothing then was that most of it had glamour written all over it—even if it was a simple dress, the women would accessorize their looks in such a way that each one had its own charm. I find this particular charm lost today, as women prefer a plastic look rather than natural and charming. They want to achieve bigger lips than they have by injecting them, using makeup to draw lines where they shouldn't be, and contouring themselves so much that, when they take the makeup off, they look like a completely different person. And what is the end result of this? Everybody looking the same. Not having any authenticity. There is a fine line between adding a dash of glamour and looking like a plastic doll.

I hope this was as fun for you to read as it was for me. What was your favorite period, fashion-wise? I think mine was the style from the '30s. The way fashion responded to the events happening in the world throughout these time periods is evident, and I truly hope that this message will stick with you: use clothing to declare what you feel, for fashion is a response to what's happening around you and is a direct expression of who you are. Instead of romanticizing the old glamour, why don't we look within ourselves and channel it? Let's forget about nostalgia and live in the moment because the world has always been and will be a scary place to survive in – but it can be a lot easier if we feel better about ourselves. How can we feel better? If we look better. Wouldn't it be wonderful if we stopped chasing these impossible standards and simply bring our already existing charm out in the open? Think about it. How can we appear interesting if we all look the same? Beauty lies in individuality. Be yourself!

THE INCIDENT IN GALLOWAY'S QUARTER

DR. HENRY LYDO

ADVENTURES TO GO |

Nestled in a forest of cypress trees and live oaks sheltered by Spanish moss, sits the small town of Nikina, North Carolina. The place presently has 5435 people, and is growing. According to local elders the town has been steadily growing for the past 100 years. From the Big Swamp area runs a creek referred to by locals as *Panthere' Folle Creek*. This somewhat narrow flow of water moves slowly behind the small settlement, meandering passed old West Indies styled buildings in a quiet tinkle of bourbon tinted liquid.

One of these old buildings happens to be a locally famous, or infamous watering hole known as *The Patriot*. This pub dates back to the 1700's according to local tradition. It sits on an inward bend of the creek. Almost every person living in the area had an ancestor who was slain there in some gun or knife fight over the years. Several enterprising people have poked around in the creek bank behind the bar over time, discovering valuable elegant antique wine, beer, and liquor bottles; since through the ages patrons inside the pub simply sat up underneath the eve on the back porch, tossing their empty beer and wine bottles into woods toward the creek. Until around ten years ago in the past, few heritage residents spent much time worrying about trash being found somewhere in the woods by people walking around looking for it. There were far too many more important things for a person to do back then, especially in an agricultural community.

The spring door on the front porch suddenly explodes open. Out stumbled two men, well known by the locals. Both stepped off the front porch nearly tripping in their stagger, then one followed the other off to the side, as if searching for a place to engage in a bit of private conversation.

The one initiating the conversation was an elder known as *Mason McPherson*. He was a large boned, rather muscular man, with skin tanned dark as an Indian's from a lifetime spent out in the sun. His teeth were chipped to a slight degree in the front, and his lips were chaffed to the point of peeling. He seized the other man by the front of his shirt with a powerful sun scarred right hand, speaking through his tightly clenched teeth as he did so.

The one listening was none other than a local conservation official known as *Richard King*. He was much younger than Mason, being of slighter build, with much less tan in his skin. Even though he wore plain clothes

| THE INCIDENT IN GALLOWAY'S QUARTER

and a large straw hat upon his closely trimmed reddish brown head, every local clearly recognized who he was. He had a worried expression on his face as Mason closely spoke, punching Richard in the chest with his left index finger to give emphasis in his words. Mason had no expression upon his face as he continued speaking, being concealed by golden rimmed, dark sunglasses and a large, very expensive river boatman's straw hat. His complete demeanor and general aura was one of a commanding, indisputable authority.

"You boys understand one damn thing around here right now. Its a war going on in Galloway's Quarter, and soon to be full scale at that, I'm afraid. Out-landers don't comprehend the fact that The Freebooters simply ain't goin' to give in, Richard. They can bring the Fed into the Quarter, the Mounties, The Green Barrett, Elvis, and who ever the damn-hell else they wanna bring, and they'll still never back down."

This iconic phrase "*The Freebooters*" was simply a localized slang term for mega-wealthy landowners and local business people, controlling virtually every aspect of the whole *Tide Water* region, from politics, to business, and taxes. No person could ever hope to accomplish any ambition without first going through them, then he was required to uphold a rigorous moral expectation to pass their inspection, and on Freebooter terms to define morality. Any who failed had better pack up and move at least three states over to escape their broad influence, if these people ever desired success at any endeavor in life. *That's just the way it is, and the way it always has been, and the way it shall forever be,* the locals are fond of saying. *Live in it, love it; or pack-ass and get the bloody hell out! Its all just that simple.*

"But the law is the law, and nobody anywhere stands above it," gasped the young officer, Richard. Sweat rolled off his face as he spoke with a clear Seppo-accent, betraying the fact he originated from somewhere far outside state boundaries, and consequently assumed to live according to an opposing belief system. Automatically he was an object of mistrust.

"I don't cotton to repeating myself, Richard. Like I said earlier, this is a three hundred year old life style around here, and these locals ain't going to forego on it just because of some poo-boy do-gooder law dreamed up in Raleigh, Columbia, or Washington; which might as well be fairyland out here in the Greene Swamp, as far as everybody is concerned. All that I have to tell you, or anybody, but especially any out-lander; is don't push

ADVENTURES TO GO |

your luck in these parts, for God's sake, fellow," spat old man, Mason, with a firm inflexible face. "The locals take it as a person throwing his weight around at their expense, and them having such a feeling ain't good for any-bodies health."

"The law shall be enforced, even around here, Mason," promptly retorted Richard as he struggled to stand his ground. "That die has already been cast. Our move is being made, even as I stand here speaking. What must be done, shall be so, even if we have to bring in Federal troops. Right now we have three elitist government men on the ground marching out there, who will shirk at nothing to see their job through . They are headed out to visit the chief-Formy and the Duval clans, even as we are speaking, with a very curt message for them and everybody else out there, and all of Galloway's Quarter."

Mason took a deep breath, then released it slowly before speaking. He turned his head to spit a mouthful of tar black juice onto the ground, then snapped back around.

"I just don't know what to tell ya, except I told ya so, Richard. I was asked to deliver that specific message to you, personally. I am not at liberty to say specifically who told me to tell ya, but he is a man who knows how to get things done around here; and more than that, he jolly-damn well means what he says," Mason roared out of a growing frustration.

The place in Galloway's Quarters where the Formy and the Duvall clans claim their estates, lies is in an out of the way spot called *Crusoe Island*. The great Waccamaw River divides, then branches outward, only to merge again some thirty miles away down stream. The isolated land tract in between this loop divide in the river is known as *Crusoe Island*.

Nobody knows if this name, Crusoe, came about after Defoe's tale of Robinson Crusoe was published or not; but it might be possible, as the conclusion is deduced from historical dates. According to legend, the people who now occupy Crusoe Island originated with the great Hispaniola planter class. The famous slave revolt took more than twenty years to develop. The ides for a crushing revolution were on the wind, even ten years prior. During that time intelligent planters with plenty of foresight, sold their massive wealth producing properties to break even, or even reap a small profit. Many planters who doubted tales of future harbinger were eager to cash in on these often bargain property deals. Those thousands

206

| THE INCIDENT IN GALLOWAY'S QUARTER

who saw the light and exited out while they could, scattered, going many places all across America, and into Canada. Several hundred made their way down the Waccamaw River, and onto Crusoe Island, among other places.

According to the legendary account, descendants of Portuguese sailors escaped from a ship wreck in the mouth of the Waccamaw, already occupied the island for more than 100 years. The cash laden planter refugees offered to buy them out, but kindly allowed any single Portuguese women to remain, at no charge. Since these French planter colonists often did not bring any women with them, the wealthiest members of their community found an easy bargain talking these women into marriage, thus the colony grew quickly.

The Portuguese were already living off the land, building cabins, cutting wood, planting gardens, harvesting fish from the river, and game from the woodlands. These planter Frenchmen simply carried on with this tradition, where they still do to this day. These people spend their days fishing, planting, sowing clothes, weaving gill nets, or carving four feet diameter by twenty feet long cypress logs into canoes with hatchets and glowing coals. When they are not engaging in any of this activity, they are sitting neath the shade of some huge live oak tree, quaffing down beer by the keg and eating home cut steak over fresh pan cooked corn bread.

These people have many customs borrowed from the old French and the Hispaniola planter culture. One example would be the great October bonfire ceremonies, where hard drinkers and story tellers gather around, listening to a local bard sing stories of past and present heroic deeds. Some of these deeds may or may not always be in agreement with the established present day laws of the surrounding area. There is also a heroes portion of pit roasted pork for any person brave enough to claim or take it, and often there might be rough housing to accompany a variety of riotous late night activities.

The area referred to as Galloway's Quarter was an old borough district once occupying the areas of three adjacent present day counties. These areas included vast parts of Columbus County, parts of nearby Robinson County, in company with portions of Horry and Marion counties in South Carolina. All of these areas claimed by Galloway's Quarter were and still are parts of the great Green Swamp, and the Big Swamp basin areas. In

ADVENTURES TO GO |

some areas the swamp covered tracts of land continue, but have different identifying local names; like *Spinster's Swift*, *Old Fiddler's Foot*, and a personal favorite, *The Crazy Woman's Back Side*.

Crusoe Island is the chief section dominating other areas of Galloway's Quarter. The headmaster was a wealthy tobacco plantation, and big-time mercantile business owner named Mijj Bo Greene. The Greene clan stood among the chief planter class, and among the wealthiest in the area, going all the way backward to the earliest days of first settlement. Mijj Bo Greene was not only the chief headmaster of the entire district, he also had powerful connections reaching all the way upward into the governor's mansions, in both North and South Carolina.

Nothing going on inside the area did so without Mijj Bo Greene's permission. One of his right hand assistants was none other than Mason McPherson, but there were other big fish who were part of the time-honored gilded Crusoe Dynasty. A mega-wealthy planter, business man, speculator, and local state politician, was none other than Adonias Parker. Adonias Parker had three brothers. One was named Dooley Parker. The second one was named Rascal, and the third named Ebeneezer. These brothers were known by locals as the Parker Brothers Business Enterprise executives; or more simply put, the PBBEE crew.

Their entity at large was legally a broad based business title referred to as *Parker Brother's Inc*. This long revered clan was into everything from owning heating and air companies, mobile home and RV construction firms, to residential and commercial construction companies, apartment rentals, tobacco farms, hog and turkey houses, herds of goats a thousand head in size, real-estate sales enterprises at large, and so forth. There was also some low key back door money lending going on. Sometimes the shark was thrown in, sometimes not, depending on who the debtor was.

This quiet reality of cash lending was also common place among the Crusoe Dynasty at large, who operated as a proxy in addition for lending operations, from the governor mansions of North and South Carolina, to certain enterprising citizens knowing how to conduct a proper appeal. No business ever conceived by mankind may increase wealth like lending money for value appreciating collateral can. That fact of being is why government regulators in the *Land Of The Free* are so firmly adamant about keeping individual citizens from engaging in it.

208

| THE INCIDENT IN GALLOWAY'S QUARTER

The last thing desired is for some poor sap to raise himself up by his own boot straps, to the point that he can directly compete with the banks, not to mention work his way into state or federal congress; then change laws only serving to repress individuals, who otherwise only exist with their necks beneath inflexible boot heels of corporations, banks, and greed laden government officials desiring that the citizen population remain in lifetime servitude to the State and Federal tax system.

After all, people paying a never ending tax was how these congressional members maintained the high interest installment fees on unsupervised loans taken out by themselves to the Federal Reserve. They collected their portion of an undefined cost of living allowance by serving on the board of directors in some large corporation, Ivy League University, state based college or public entity that supposedly gets its funding from donations. Thus, payment for their new Lamborghini, their personal corporation or business entities, and their elegant mansions on the hill depended on citizens being compelled to half all earnings with them.

Adonias possessed a huge mansion sitting out in the middle of swampland a mile back from Beaufort's Inlet. The grandiose two story, classic styled, thirty room luxurious home had six, two feet diameter Doric columns supporting a huge front porch. Every room had massive elegant crystal chandeliers plated with pure gold, and hanging in the center of the front porch above an elegant foyer entrance. On the outside was a huge kitchen room maned by totally dedicated, career minded hired servants, who constantly prepare food and transported it inside the mansion estate. Some of these people, however, were rumored to be people indebted to Adonias for favors of various sorts, who were employed with him at payment plus interest.

In the yard were various animals such as goats, chickens, cows, and even hogs; but the hogs were kept on a tract of land way off in the distance, somewhere far out of sight and smell range, and strictly fed a daily diet of freshly harvest acorns. A huge garden filled with every variety of vegetable was planted behind the home, since Adonias, his clan and his associates, loved a large variety of fresh vegetables and meat on the hoof. All of this possession required constant maintenance, assuring ongoing employment opportunity to the locals.

ADVENTURES TO GO |

The entire estate sat in the midst of a hundred acre land tract, surrounded by a twelve feet high masonry wall, topped by razor wire angling toward the outside, and a massive black iron bared gate at a front estate driveway lined with blossoming roses, azaleas, tulips, chrysanthemum, magnolia and live oak trees. Often paid guards were standing on either side of the gate, as they were in specially designed towers spaced every forty yards up and down the wall. No expense was spared because Adonias and his clan could well afford it.

In addition to this, the Crusoe Dynasty had hundreds of smaller fish working the rat lines for them. These smaller fish included everybody from school principals, area business men, local policemen, and state politicians; to rogues of every sort who were ever willing to engage in any request made to them from members of the ruling dynasty and their motley company of associates. Nothing was ever going to make it passed any of them, or their minions.

The reason why is because everybody wanted a piece of the golden pie and the luxurious lifestyle lived by the ever prominent Crusoe Dynasty, not to mention the fact that they and their minions held solid gate keys in at least two entire states, in virtually every area of aspiration. Being on positive terms with the entire legion, if you will, determined one's successes or failures in life; not skills, qualifications, education, the lack thereof, nor work ethic. Even the crime labs in two states were financed, if not owned outright, by this untouchable dynasty. Fighting the system was a fool's errand, since individual people didn't have a leg to stand on, regardless of their status. Those speaking out too loud also tended to have mysterious unfortunate experiences, and worse.

Things were changing in Galloway's Quarter, so they were seeming to local people, and not for the better. Many an out-lander from areas surrounding had commenced to question and criticize a few matters at hand. For example, it was long known where there was only one way in and one way off the island, back to the mainland. The only alternative option was to wade across one of the few low points in the river, and then swag across the swamp, until one could make it out to the hill on the opposite side.

For this reason it was long said where the isolated residents kept an army of ghosts posted all around the island at various strategic points.

210

| THE INCIDENT IN GALLOWAY'S QUARTER

People back in the larger town of Whiteville, on the mainland, were saying now that it was no army of ghosts, but an actual army of well camouflaged sappers; who would shoot with silent, poisonous darts or arrows, if an unfortunate did not fall into one of their hole traps down into the swamp. In any case the many alligators found throughout the river and in the surrounding swamps would quickly dispatch of any remaining evidence, and do so very thoroughly.

This situation was only one of the many concerns brought to light by the newly complaining locals in the surrounding areas. Out-lander crowds from very far away were filling up these previously isolated areas, and bringing with them their questioning, vexing ways; and bizarre alien ideas about politics, and the way life should be lived in general, according to them. The county authorities might as well be the local school principal, joked many of the long time residents in regard to the petty, whining complaints continually raining down upon them from above. "God forbid if a person had no choice but to work around one of these belly aching, coo-coo, cock-a-doodle-dew, sons of bitches!"

One of these idealistic do-gooders determined to force his opinions for change on all who might oppose it, claimed to be a sportsman. Since his retirement he now was a grossly overweight man, who wore a large silver band from the Mason's lodge down in Loris on his left ring finger. He was retired ex-military; and because of this sole fact alone, thanks to the local veteran's administration handing him a job above all other local contenders, had secured employment at the court house in Whiteville as an arrogant IRS agent, employed by both the State and Federal government. He was assigned with harassing the provincial folk for every hard earned dime that he could savagely wrest from their grasp, since it was common knowledge residents of North and South Carolina survived only by working cash gig-jobs on the side. Unfortunately for these folks, on-the-books wages from public employment were far below what it cost to live in these two states, especially when the revenuers finished with extorting more than half of whatever amount they struggled to bring back home.

This man thought that he had hit a true jackpot when he purchased two large homes on the eastern edges of Whitevile, North Carolina, and Florence, South Carolina, with a ten acre tract of land for only $150,000.00; a mere fraction of what it would have cost him in his native, Jersey State.

ADVENTURES TO GO |

Cash saved up in mere months easily secured his ownership rights to the properties. People in the area knew all too well where he managed to make this purchase in hard cash stolen from the citizen base, since people were always being singled out and commanded to hand over horrendous money sums they never owed to begin with. *The IRS wasn't required to support their claims of citizens being indebted to them by hard facts; so this man had a perfect cover for crime, galore*, brazenly declared many among the proletariat masses in Galloway's Quarter.

His name was *Roger Borkowski*. He joined a local hunting club, many of whom were also of the out-lander stripe, that had somehow leased a partial land tract over on Crusoe Island. He became a subject of hearth-side community derision when he stormed through the brush like a Sherman tank, with hundreds of dollars worth of unnecessary equipment such as hand warmers, special overalls and fancy camping equipment, not to mention government ordained licenses and expensive club fees on top of that; all for the very simple purpose of harvesting meat and fruit from the surrounding woodlands. Needless to say, he never even got a single shot even after two years of hunting, although the land tract was readily known by most old timer heritage inhabitants to support a huge deer population.

One still clear day while he was sitting high up in a fancy store-bought tree stand, he caught a glimpse of resident islanders slinking around on the club's rented land tract, and he was utterly appalled for lack of more descriptive words. Here these people were, wearing faded jeans and home-stitched denim dyed with black walnut hulls; and shooting deer three and four at a time over piles of pears, Indian corn, or salt, like nothing was ever supposed to be said about it. To make matters worse, when Borkowski approached one of these people, asking about his lack of an orange hat, or his neglect for placing tags on the carcasses of deer he had recently slain, he and the crowd this man was accompanied by glanced over at him as if he was out of his mind for questioning anybody. Matter of fact, not one of them had any confounded idea what on earth this strange fat man with the attitude, who they barely understood, was even talking about!

Roger quickly informed his fellow club members about this matter to behold. A number told him they were aware that the land was being hunted, but went on to say nothing was occurring that had not always

212

| THE INCIDENT IN GALLOWAY'S QUARTER

been so. This was how the resident islanders made their living, and all was perfectly understood and accepted without further questioning.

Two other club members volunteered to take him on a tour of the island. He simply could not believe the sight of people hauling literal fish loads onto the river bank in home knitted gill nets, salting fish, living outside of the utility system and the standard range established by the county zoning commission, not to mention scrounging and gathering off the land in general. *If these people could live like this, then why couldn't he do the same?*, Roger screamed in outrage with the voice of a spoiled brat, punk boy, when he and the other three made it back to their truck.

"Because this is the only life these people know," came the curt reply.

"Well, something needs to be done about this matter," Roger snapped back to the others, with a noticeable flushed tint in his cheeks. "These people need to learn about the same laws the rest of us in this country have to live by," he continued to whine and bellow.

"You are not from around here, fellow," the three replied in a rather cautious low pitched voice. "You had better pipe things down, and watch your step in Galloway's Quarter."

"Well, we'll see!," the man snapped with an air of crass arrogance to the other three. "We'll soon see who had better watch their step around here!"

On that note, quickly as he could make it back home, he called the state conservation commission and the county zoning board, informing them of every infraction he bore witness to. He also screamed that if these people were allowed to live in such a fashion, then he could do so as well, and so could anyone else.

"If things were always done in such a way, then some form of change was long overdue," he continued to cry over the phone. "This was 1981, for crying out loud here!"

With this clearly implicating information on hand, the three men reported by Richard King were on their way toward the island. They were all unshakable in their confidence. They had their two way radios bouncing on their left hips, and their order papers proudly held in hand. The local police readily agreed to back them up, if indeed they needed any backing. All the imposing three had to do was make the special prearranged emergency call.

213

ADVENTURES TO GO |

The three were instructed to wade onto the island through a low portion of the river and the swamp. While there they were instructed to seek out signs of any illegal activities; from hunting and fishing on the sly, to people living without being hooked up to the utility municipality, and home construction done outside of code. When they found any of this horrible criminal activity, they were commanded to curtly inform the offenders of their violations, collect all proper identification, then issue prompt citations for maximum penalties to be collected. Any person offering resistance, or found to lack identification credentials would be immediately arrested, then transported to the jails back in Whiteville and Loris. The same rules would apply to any person hunting without proper licenses, and equipment. If needed be, the national guard could even be flown in; so never fear giving us an emergency call, they were politely informed.

The three officers headed down toward the bridge, then carefully parked their jeep in safe cover on the mainland side. From there they walked approximately a half mile eastward, until they arrived at a knee deep portion of the river, at a point in the slow moving river somewhere around seventy yards wide. Carefully and quietly they radioed their exact location identification back into headquarters, where a bead was taken on a newfangled electronic map.

The agents in the office back in Whiteville carefully recorded every step as the bead on the map slowly moved from the river onto the island mainland. The bead appeared to go some twenty percent inland, then pause. The pause held for at least thirty minutes before any type of question was made in regard to the matter. The HQ commander quickly snatched a radio from the desk top.

"What's going on? We see a pause here on our electronic map, holding for the past thirty minutes. Copy?"

Some fifteen seconds passed before a broken reply came in.

"This is CO10. We are questioning seven locals here in regard to some hunting violations. There is a fresh deer kill on the ground, but no tags. Not one of these people are admitting to the kill. They are all wearing jet black homemade overalls, with bandannas across their faces, and none of them claim to be in possession of proper identification, over.."

214

| THE INCIDENT IN GALLOWAY'S QUARTER

"This is HQ. We all copy that report. Be ever cautious with these people. None of us can stress that fact too lightly, over?"

There is a stir on the radio and a rather long pause.

"HQ requesting situational analysis here! Do you copy?"

Nothing but static for a moment.

"CO Core, do any of you copy?"

"HQ, this is CO12 reporting. We attempted to make arrest, but the seven scattered and vanished into the swampy backdrop. We are in the process of giving pursuit, copy..?"

"This is Command Center in reply," spoke a different voice. "Give pursuit for an hour only. Take careful notes on what occurred, reactions, your possible unanticipated motivations, etc, then head on out. We need a complete observational analysis on the entire situation out there CO Core."

"This is CO12 in reply. We all copy that directional order loud and clear."

The three conservation officers moved on out into the swamp lands. Even though it was supposedly winter time, as they moved about in the slow moving bourbon tinted water they could hear the eerie slide and splash of what must have been three inch diameter water moccasins, a vigorous deadly snake in the king cobra family. When the officers gazed outward into the landscape all that they could behold was an endless forest of closely packed cypress trees, with a heavy screen of Spanish moss hanging from what must have been every limb, and every space in between packed with cat-claw briers and bramble in a thick screen of yuopon bushes.

As the officers moved along the air above the quagmire hung heavy with the feeling of hostile eyes gazing upon them from an unseen distance in the vegetative backdrop. In virtually no time an hour had passed. A powerful motivation for exiting this morass onto the hill loomed heavily inside the three, as visions of horrifying death traps concealed in the dark water, and pitiless snarling beasts encircling about unseen around them, danced in their heads.

The bead on the electronic map moved slowly along, then paused after what seemed like a mile or more away. From the map it was known to be a local point or small village community known as Duval's Wake. Thirty minutes passed and no location analysis report. Time for a call back.

"This is HQ calling for a situational analysis, copy that?"

ADVENTURES TO GO |

"HQ, this is CO11. We see a dozen or more property zoning violations. We are informing the residents all around here, who glare at us through hard narrowed eyes, as if failing to comprehend our words. I fear that they may not even be able to understand us when we speak, and we certainly can hardly understand them, copy HQ?"

"This is HQ, CO11. We all copy loud and clear. Take good notes on everything, and be extremely cautious around there above all else, copy that CO11?"

"This is CO11 again, and we copy. We are writing citations out left and right, worth every amount from $100.00 to $5000.00. We certainly are getting some hard angry stares now, I can tell all of you. What I can't comprehend is how the courthouse is going to collect on anything here, since these people don't even work public jobs for the most part. Those that do work at all only work part-time, for cash, copy HQ? They do seem to make decent money, strangely enough, in spite of their broken employment chain."

There was static on the radio, then it suddenly cleared.

"This is HQ. We copy that. You and the CO Corp write out the tickets. Be sure to collect proper ID, with complete addresses that have been confirmed. The courthouse will concern itself regarding collections on all of this. Those tickets have a very finite life span, only a month, I think. After that time an interest increase is activated. The total on this doubles every week after that time. When the value amounts of these tickets exceed property values, a virtual army of officers will descend from the hill here onto that island, to enforce eviction notices. To be honest about it, it shouldn't take long for that to happen, copy?," asked a broken chuckling voice on the radio.

A long pause preceded only a static return. A stressed broken voice finally replied after some forty minutes or so.

"HQ, this is.." (*static fuzz*). "Situation out of control! Emergency call! Situation out of..! (*static fuzz*).

The red bead on the electronic screen moved backward in the direction of the swamp, then turned going northbound, before pausing a half mile into what seemed like swamp land a few hundred yards upward from the point where the three entered in.

216

| THE INCIDENT IN GALLOWAY'S QUARTER

"This is HQ. Give us a situational analysis! We demand a situational analysis immediately!"

There was no reply but static for thirty more minutes, then the static suddenly cleared.

"Stay away from de i-land territory BO," spoke an unknown growling muffled voice. "Dis is whut happns to nosy out-landers." Then a continuing line of static.

"HQ! HQ! We copy! Give us a report immediately."

Nothing but static on the radio.

"I'm calling this in as an emergency rescue. Do you copy CO Corp? I am calling this scene in as an immediate emergency, over and out!"

The captain over at the headquarter grabs a phone, calling the sheriff's office at the Whiteville courthouse. He carefully explains the situation in detail, gives the logistical locations recorded on the electronic map in his office, then requests an investigation unit of twelve well armed troops. The sheriff on duty at the time immediately grants the request, and includes three detectives to accompany the troop of twelve.

Quickly the troop rides out to the bridge connecting Crusoe Island with the mainland side. They proceed eastward from the bridge in search of the jeep in which the three had driven in and made their first report from. When they arrived at the specific point indicated in which the jeep had been parked, the jeep was no longer there; but tire tracks and human foot prints in the mud from that point down the bank, toward the water, indicated that the vehicle had more than likely been taken out of gear and pushed over into the river. Notes were made regarding the observation and plastic casts were taken of the strange foot prints.

These foot prints were strange since they possessed no tread of any sort. Upon close examination, however, on some prints stitching was observed around the edges. Obviously these boots were home-made. Once the jeep had been confirmed as being underneath the river, then the conclusion could be made that islanders were responsible for the deed, since virtually nobody anywhere else were known to wear home crafted boots and shoes. The information was gathered and the reports promptly stashed, as the troop continued onward in its foregoing mission.

They slugged through what felt like a thousand miles of mud, water, and outright muck as they battled mosquitoes constantly, even though it

ADVENTURES TO GO |

was during the midst of winter. Then suddenly the land came to a rise. The swamp transformed into a thick dry hardwood forest, with a tree covered hill in the center, blanketed by a fine yellow grass. As the twelve proceeded upward onto that hill, an outspread live oak tree dominated the summit with a thick limb approximately twelve feet up, upon which hung the bodies of four men, upside down. Three wore the very noticeable uniforms of conservation officers. Their throats had been slit from ear to ear. One, dressed in faded jeans and a white tee-shirt with the words written across the front, *Eat More Kitty Cat, It Keeps Us Dogs More Competitive* , was a rather overweight corpse with a large silver Mason's band on his left ring finger. This corpse had been completely decapitated.

To the far right of this petrifying spectacle, a four foot bamboo staff had been driven into the soil. Upon this bamboo was thrust the blood drenched severed head of this hanging corpse. A note hung underneath, with huge Gothic letters painted red on an aged cypress wood board , which said; *Abandon hope, all ye out-landers who enter herein.*

The twelve searched all round for any sign of evidence, while the detectives snapped pictures of the murder scene. One of the officers, who was from the Whiteville area, shook his head from side to side.

"This is it. This occurrence tops them all off thus far. There really is a war going on out here, boys. I don't know how much any of you realize it?"

Another officer with a firm demeanor snapped around. He spoke with an accent revealing him to be from somewhere way out of state.

"There is certainly going to be a firm call for war now, if one there ever was before," he spouted. "I would hate to be from anywhere around in these parts right about now, myself. Situations could get real sticky, and quick, as people get all emotional and start wanting us to pull the guilty out of our hats, or from out of a cypress stump somewhere."

Another officer suddenly raised his head to the ongoing conversation. He put his radio down from his mouth, back into the sling on his left hip.

"Well I just reported this scene to the department," he spoke in his own alien accent. "They're calling in the US Marshal service, who will more than likely get an elite Marine Corps attachment to accompany them in. Somebody said war? This stuff is serious, and it well may be an all out war, until justice is promptly served."

218

| THE INCIDENT IN GALLOWAY'S QUARTER

In two hours time a Chinook Helicopter over passed the area, pausing down from where the twelve police troopers stood. Out parachuted ten persons. As they slowly drifted to the ground, thirty more followed. As the first ten were taking off their jump suits, the other thirty landed. As they undressed, the group of ten began walking toward the twelve troopers and the crime scene at hand.

One specific individual walked up to the troop of twelve, removing his jump helmet, face cover and goggles. He was a rather tall man being some six feet three in height. He walked with a confident, well conditioned stride.

"Who is the commander on duty among you twelve?"

One of the twelve officers approached him.

"I am officer 4397-3 at your service, sir. Most people in the organization call me MacArnold."

The large US Martial relied.

"I am Supervisory Deputy US Martial, Rolland Wiseman, who has been assigned to this entire case. We are going to observe the incident of this crime scene, observe the incident of the jeep being shoved downhill into the river, arrive at our own conclusions, then proceed on into this island community in pursuit of the guilty.

"Well we're glad to have you," spoke Arnold to the man. "None of us quite know what we are dealing with here."

"Mr. Arnold," the tall man replied as he swept his right hand through his tangled dark hair.

"Just for the record, every one of my men are seasoned military veterans. We have been exposed to blood drenched scenes of every stripe, on a daily basis. Rest assured, Mr Arnold, none of our investigative platoon could ever become so startled that we couldn't function. All of this tragedy is only another day at work, and we will get to the bottom of it, no matter what. Matter of fact, I am going to divide my troop up and allow one half to proceed on with the investigation, then the other half shall accompany me and the Marines there with us, as we march onward toward this community, Duval's Wake."

Five US Martial's and thirty Marines from the elitist units marched undaunted through the briers, bramble tangle, the mud and the muck for about a mile, until the woods finally dried and cleared up somewhat on

ADVENTURES TO GO |

higher ground. In thirty minutes the thirty five men noticed a clearing in the woods, and twenty apparently aged shacks up on the hill summit. On the front porches women with sun browned hard faces donned in faded home made gowns dutifully repaired gill nets, while long bearded men dressed in tattered blue jean overalls repaired horse drawn plows, sharpened machetes, or dressed out fish and hanging pigs. Slowly they raised their heads as they put down their tools to pause in their work, as the marching troop approached. Rolland approached a man sitting on his porch chewing tobacco, appearing to be an elder with authority.

" I am Supervisory Deputy US Martial, Rolland Wiseman, sir. I have eviction orders to immediately evacuate every man, woman, and child from these premises. The charges are that these homes are not up to code, and neither have the taxes been paid on the homes, or the land. Tickets were issued earlier ordering every person in this community to get his or her property up to code, or else pay a fine. Since none of these fines have been paid, then interest was applied to the dollar amounts until the value of the fine exceeds that of the property.

"My final word to all of you is that none of you own your property anymore. Your land and any of your valuables now belong to the county of Cumberland, the state of North Carolina, and the authority of America. On that note, sir, I am ordering every person on this land tract to exit out of his or her home, or else we are coming in to take you on suspicion of murder until we can get evidence verification. Is that understood Mr.-?"

The man appeared to be somewhere in his sixties. His body was browned from a life out in the sun, his gray hair short above his ears, but his beard hung down to his naval. He wore faded blue jean overalls with a chest bib, and a plain tee shirt.

"Just wait a cotton tailed minute here, fellow. I don't give a flying flapjack who you claim to be. You can't just huff in here and order people around like that."

"Sir, you are not comprehending what I am telling," commanded Rolland. "I don't have time for debate. I need you and all of your neighbors here to vacate these premises immediately. Either that eviction is commenced, or we are coming in to take you."

The old man turned his head to left, spitting a mouthful of black juice upon the white sand by his side.

220

| THE INCIDENT IN GALLOWAY'S QUARTER

"If you want us and what is our'n, then you'll have to take us.., and be damned!," the man yelled. The others quickly raced back into their shacks, locking the doors upon these words being yelled by the elder. Obviously it was some sort of coded message for defense.

"Whats your name, sir?," asked Rolland.

"Name 's Jivus Duval," the elder retorted as he turned to spit another wad.

Rolland suddenly grabbed Jivus by the left arm, forcing him around while handcuffs were slapped upon both his wrists.

"Have it your way, Jivus. You'll be the first to go down here in Duval's Wake."

After the cuffs were placed upon Jivus, he was handed to another officer who cuffed him onto a chain around fifty feet long. The opposite end of this chain was anchored to a small dogwood tree nearby.

"Move out men, its door to door. All weapons on guard, and remember your basic training. Don't fire unless fired upon, then promptly return fire with all due efficiency. All members of this community are potential murder suspects and deemed hostile, especially in light of their present rejection of the evacuation order given."

The thirty Marines quickly positioned themselves on the front porch of the 29 cabins. The other five US Martial's proceeded to ransack Jivus's cabin, emptying the drawers, turning over the beds, emptying the refrigerators and closets. The contents of all were carelessly dumped onto the floor.

The thirty Marines hammered the front doors of the cabins with their fists, screaming at the top of their lungs;

"Open up, we are members of the United States Marine Corp. Open up now or else we are coming in. Do you comprehend? Open up immediately, or else we are coming in on you!"

There was no reply from inside the cabins. Rolland nodded his head in signal, and the officers proceeded to kick in the cabin doors. When the wooden doors exploded open, to every officer's astonishment the cabins all appeared to be empty, not only of their human inhabitants, but also of their most cherished personal property.

Every officer had now entered into one of these cabins. An extremely tense search was conducted for the inhabitants, which failed to yield

ADVENTURES TO GO |

anything. The old man in chains laid down on the soft grass at his feet. A teen aged youth arose from the tall yellow grass some distance behind the cabins, noticing that the old man had laid down; then placed both hands upon a plunger, pushing it all the way down with what appeared to be every ounce of might that he had to give. The cabins suddenly exploded into flames and a thousand fragments. When the wind from it all settled back down, there was peace once more again on Duval's Wake. Gradually the residents arose from the yellow grass a hundred yards behind the cabins and the round of the hill, to survey the damage done to their homes and the effectiveness of their attack.

Back in Whitevile the HQ office knew something was afoul when his radio messages came back as dull static. For three hours this type of response had been the case. But look at the military and law enforcement professionals who had vanished seemingly into thin air! The possibility of negativity defied all logic, as every person in the office shook their heads in disbelief. A new Supervisor Deputy Marshal driving all the way from Raleigh, burst through the double doors at the office in the courthouse.

"Would somebody around here tell me just what in the ten tales of hell is going on here?," he roared without even introducing himself, since he had been called in only an hour and a half ago. "I was interrupted from having my midday ham sandwich and coffee."

"Something has gone afoul," snapped the HQ supervisor, Jack Penny, a sun and liquor dried up lifetime Whiteville resident somewhere in his late 50's. Probably the most excitement in his life he ever had was drinking liquor and chasing worn out whores around town, all the way to North Myrtle Beach on a dismal Friday night. He was also guilty of periodically slipping off into the Lime Light bordello down in Bennetsville, when his old lady of 35 years turned her back on him for a day or so; but he had given all of it up more than ten years ago now. He really was a happy man just being clean, he loved to boast. All he did now was work, and go to church on Wednesday nights and Sundays.

"Give me more information, please here!," fired the US Marshall. "Why are you so certain that something has run afoul? Based on what are you making that conclusion? Show me the evidence, Penny," the US Martial berated.

222

| THE INCIDENT IN GALLOWAY'S QUARTER

"Well I just know it. I always receive prompt response from my men when they are in the field. There hasn't been a response for more than three hours now. I have your men on call out there who are law enforcement experts, but I also have elite Marines who have accompanied them, and who are battle savvy on top of that. Something is just not right, I am telling you."

"Didn't you even bother to send in a confirmation detachment, Penny?," thundered the US Martial.

The US Martial took a deep breath, shook his head, then exhaled as if in disgust.

"I utterly despise incompetence," he snapped.

A noticeable flash of sudden anger passed through the body of Penny.

"I know that you are with the US Martial Service, and that you are a supervisor, but you never gave me your full title.

"Yeah? Why does it even matter at this point?," the Martial returned with his own display of disgust and anger combined.

"Look," leveled Penny with the martial, "if you, are any damn body else is going to storm in here just because myself or another person bothered to call and request assistance, then proceed to speak down to me and verbalize your opinion regarding my qualifications just because of it, then the very least that you could do is tell me who you are."

"Yeah? I can do that, if doing it matters any. My name is Albert Vollstrecker. My rank and title is Chief Supervisor Deputy US Martial. I have been a veteran of law enforcement, first with the US Army beginning at 18, whereupon I retired. I was acting veteran of nine major US battle engagements. I have seen it all in my time, practically speaking here. I have never seen anything resembling this situation, however. I have been with the US Martial Service now for 10 years."

Penny smiled as the man spoke his title and name.

"Well if you have all of this detailed experience and title, then why don't you begin doing something to produce a valid solution to this situation, rather than berate me, the man in charge at the moment?"

Vollstrecker paused, glaring hard at Penny, then moved toward the phone on Penny's desk. He punched in a number, then placed the phone to his right ear, continuing to glare at Penny with a firm expression on his face. A few minutes passed, then he began to speak.

ADVENTURES TO GO |

"Yes Mam, this is Albert Vollstrecker, Chief US Martial Supervisor. Could I please speak with the central command officer for the US Marines? The situation is rather urgent, to say the least."

He paused for five minutes, then began speaking.

"Yes sir, this is Albert Vollstrecker, Chief US Martial Supervisor, rank number 30773-A. You are aware of the thirty Marine Corps men assigned to this Crusoe Island situation, aren't you?

Another pause for a minute.

"You haven't heard from them, you mean?"

Another pause then a tart comment coming from Vollstrecker.

"The person assigned to take charge is a local named Jack Penny, and he hasn't called you yet?

Vollstrecker glared at Penny again as he stood with the phone hard against his right ear.

"I tell you what. I am going to take over this case now, and it will be me and you working this case into its conclusion," fired Vollstrecker as he continued to glare at Penny.

"Yes sir, we'll take fifty more of your elitist, with clear instructions that this situation has reached a point of no return, and must be dealt with just as any other battle situation should," spoke Vollstrecker into the phone.

A pause for a maybe five minutes, then Vollstrecker's face lit up.

"Yes sir, then it is a return confirmation. Fifty elite specialist will be on site inside of two hours, meeting right here in this office."

He paused again as his face shown brighter.

"Its a proud go ahead!"

He walked back over to the desk of Penny, then placed the phone back on its hanger. Vollstrecker never spoke a single word to Penny as his eyes seemed to growl at him.

Vollstrecker walked back over to the electronic screen with the map on it, typing location coordination indicators as fast as he could punch the key pad. When these men arrived in a few minutes, every minute detail would be placed in possession of their commanding officer. They would possess a complete geographical, terrain, and population layout of the entire island and the area surrounding it back on the mainland. Matter of fact, the entire area and history of Galloway's Quarter would be held underneath a microscope. This situation was on now, for better or worst,

224

| THE INCIDENT IN GALLOWAY'S QUARTER

with Vollstrecker assuring himself, and all confident that fate would be on his side. He would be the victorious hero in this backwoods tale of rebellion.

Vollstrecker and his minions were not the only people aware of seriousness in the mounting scenario. None other than Mijj Bo Greene himself had raised his eyebrows, and drawn a few deep breaths. Suddenly he felt motivated to intervene, and for good reason. Quickly he called up the Parker brothers, and old Man, Mason. Adonias had invited them all to his mansion estate over at Beaufort Inlet.

"We can fly from over at your place, Adonias, and visit Governor Sealgair at his mansion in Raleigh. I would say that we drive there, but we simply haven't the time. Everything around here is that urgent," spoke Bo Greene to Adonias Parker over the phone.

Within two hours time of the phone conversation, this motley crew had met over at the mansion estate of Adonias outside of Beaufort Inlet, and without hesitation. With few words between them, they loaded up onto a small, twin engine plane behind the mansion home there. Adonias done a maintenance check and the general pre-flight inspection, and soon they were lifting off.

In seemingly no time the dynastic crew had landed in a small airport less than a mile from the Governor's personal mansion estate in Raleigh. A cab was already parked and waiting outside the small terminal building. When the plane pulled into the hanger area, the crew exited and entered into the cab, while paid attendants moved the plane into a lock down at its proper station. Three minutes later the cab pulled up to the heavy black iron gate before the entrance way at the mansion. The cab driver spoke a few unintelligible words, and in an instant the guard in front of this gate allowed them to enter, without questioning to any extent.

These same words were spoken by Greene to the guard at the top of the outside mansion stairway, with the exact reaction. The only reaction witnessed by the Parker Brothers or Mason were smiles and nonverbal welcoming indications of relaxation in company with complete solitude. A college aged, well built female mansion attendant, wearing a low cut, almost skin tight gemstone satin dress, escorted the crew into a back parlor room.

ADVENTURES TO GO |

The figure of a six foot four, man with well groomed gray hair, donned in a Stuart Hughes Diamond Edition suit and tie, arose from an elegant sofa seat in red cushioned satin over foam and rhinoceros leather. He turned toward them, smiling. He approached Greene first with his right hand fully extended. Greene returned the handshake, then Sealgair stepped forward to extend his hand toward the others.

"I swear it has been so long since I have seen all of you together in the same company," he gasped as he smiled. "Come on toward the seat here, and relax. I have a gnawing feeling that there is some sort of situation at hand," he said as the crew took their seats upon the huge couch. "I speak with great interest in knowing the details."

Before them stood a heavy coffee table of teak wood, carved with elegant depictions of scantily clad native women and pirate captains lounging around in a tropical oasis. Many of these men were rowing in boats on lakes with these native women, or women donned in long dresses and gaudy luxuriant sun bonnets. Others were laid out by the lakeside with scantily native women on blankets, where picnic baskets filled with a variety of tropical fruit stood between them. The male seemed to be pouring the female a chalice of wine, as the two lay on an outstretched blanket underneath a large saw tooth palm in the cool shade.

The room itself was trimmed in pure gold, with stunning, nearly three dimensional paintings of tropical scenes depicting the luxury and elegance of life on some Caribbean plantation estate during an age of glory, enlightenment, and wealth, hanging upon the walls above glass tables with silver legs on lions feet, trimmed in pure gold. In the corner to the far right stood a glass, silver, and crystal pedestal with an elegant marble bust of Marie Antoinette, trimmed in pure gold guarding the room and the palace interior. Before this marble bust seven under-clothed belly dancers donning veils of mist moved delicately with complete silence, in a perfect beckoning rhythm for the carnal entertainment of the governor and his guests. The Parker Brothers and Mason glanced all around, saying nothing at the moment while Greene continued speaking with the Governor.

"Yes, indeed we have a situation that is both urgent and serious at the same time. I'm sure you have heard of the matter over in Galloway's Quarter, haven't you, sir?"

226

| THE INCIDENT IN GALLOWAY'S QUARTER

The Governor smiled warmly as he gloated at the alluring dancing display before him. He swallowed hard as he suddenly shifted his eyes toward what resembled a pool in the rear quarters of the mansion. The pleasant rustle of a whirlpool from the same area seemed to carry throughout the entire palace interior. The girls raced with smooth silent organized precision toward the pool areas on cat-like feet. The smiling governor chuckled lowly as he shifted his attention back in the direction of his guests.

"I just got wind of a concern involving Galloway's Quarter a few minutes before you entered. Otherwise I know no specific details."

Greene sighed, then began to speak.

"The locals have been harassed by these aliens for a long time now. One of them didn't like the lifestyle they lived, and called the Fed on them. The conservation officers then raced out there in a frenzy to write citations for hunting violations, zoning codes, and anything else they could find to include. These citations had huge fines, that doubled with large interest charges when the locals couldn't pay. When the value of the citations exceeded their property values, the locals had to be evacuated from their long cherished land holdings, and hard won homes."

"Oh, I see," sighed the Governor. "So that is when the trouble began, I presume. Was there any violence involved?"

"Yes, and deaths. Matter of fact, I haven't had a confirmation on every detail of the situation at the moment involving the Marine Core elites and the US Martial troop who were sent in earlier, but what I did hear wasn't good at all," spoke Greene to the Governor.

"A hammer man I use when I need him, named Yarborough, who also ventures into the general area periodically for the purpose of helping me move backlog, radioed back that a troop of thirty marines and ten US Martial Servicemen were slain by the locals today. I know Harlan Yarborough's reputation, governor, a career criminal with a detailed prison history and violent past; but to speak the truth he has always been dead on honest with me, in every way. Probably its because when I need a job done, I speak directly, and I always pay out on time. Being careful to take such simple measures is how I built my business reputation. This reputation is how I always succeed in getting chores completed, governor."

The Governor smiled again with his warm sleepy sheepish grin.

"Yes, oh yes indeed, sir, to speak the truth about it, probably you wish that he was lying this time. I am sure you could dislike him much less for it right about now."

Greene hung his head slightly, then picked it back up, almost becoming agitated as he commenced speaking.

"What are we going to do? You well know everything that's at steak here. These marines going in this time will be ultra thorough in their search."

The Governor gazed momentarily at the wall, glancing back in the direction of the pools, then took a deep breath.

"I'll call Washington and see what we can arrange. I will work for you through lawyer, C.R. Loes. We will use judge Brunne Sealgair, a distant relative of mine, you know. No matter what happens, all of you and your associates will be eased back down onto your feet. All of you have done far too much for me to simply ignore your increasingly imposing situation, even if it means that I must sacrifice my own cousin, the judge; who indeed is trustworthy, but only to an extent of requests not threatening his peculiar idealistic sense of ethics. When we have a job to do, Greene, we both are aware that we simply don't have time for impracticality. Direction for action must be definitively determined, swift, and above all else, successful. I can't say any more than that at the moment. Let me get on ASAP with this call. Once business is efficiently and thoroughly concluded, then we all can get on with more warmly accommodating pleasures and pass times."

The new troop had already met at the HQ office in Whiteville, then stormed back out toward Galloway's Quarter, beginning with Crusoe Island. Local people were forcibly arrested at machine gun point, and loaded up onto huge trucks for transporting personnel. They would be relocated to the mass containment facility at Camp Lejeune.

There had been much exchange of gunfire, with people dying on both sides. Most of the locals vanished into the swamps, in spite of the persisting determination in their persecution. More troops had been called in for reinforcement, and to assist in eradicating all local resistance from the swamps. This war in Galloway's Quarter was gaining momentum.

As the troops stormed through Crusoe Island, they made their way intending to push through every inch of Galloway's Quarter, beginning with the Horry County realm. Here an expansive field of pot plants

| THE INCIDENT IN GALLOWAY'S QUARTER

standing twenty feet tall, with sticky purple buds all over was stumbled upon. As the exasperated troops patrolled cautiously, they found cocked rat traps spring loaded with shot gun shells, sitting in waiting to make a kill. Fine fishing wire running across entrances going into these fields would engage the instantaneous murder. There were swinging spike traps, pit falls, and spear sets, all anxiously awaiting their victims.

As the patrol cautiously eased along, a plan developed in the mind of their commanding officer. Instead of destroying the field and the root cellar found in the center of the field, where millions of dollars in processed cocaine was stashed, they would simply stake it out to discover whose it was. Head Quarters had long heard of rumors from informing locals speaking of such realities, but nothing like this had ever been discovered in, or even near Galloway's Quarter.

Certain locals had also informed them of other eerie occurrences. According to claims, Bo Greene owned dozens of tobacco warehouses throughout North and South Carolina, not to mention the ones in the counties where Galloway's Quarter extended. For several years now these warehouses had been mysteriously going up in flames at night time. For years the Federal tobacco program had been playing out, everybody was aware of that, but there was still big money to be found in warehouse insurance collections. Over the years, when these informants were sought out for further questioning, they could never be found. No person in their locality seemed to know of their whereabouts.

A twin engine airplane landed in broad daylight near the huge dope plantation on a shockingly narrow runway. Fourteen men dressed in black denim and caps rushed out of the airplane toward the center of the field. A high collar had been pulled up over their noses and mouths to conceal their identity. These men raced toward the root cellar type storage room with military precision. In less than five minutes they were seen moving back toward the plane carrying huge burlap type bags filled with something.

The commanding officer didn't have to ask any more questions, he knew what was inside the bags. He also got a solid ID on the twin engine plane as he continued to watch through a set of binoculars. He radioed the information back to HQ for an ID check, but it came up empty. Vollstrecker failed to give clear reasons as to why this was so, saying instead that he simply didn't know. Before the day was over, the military troop

ADVENTURES TO GO |

would locate seven more pot plantations, and storage cellars filled with other types of contraband, primarily cocaine, not to mention the huge amounts of small arms and stashed ammunition.

When darkness finally enveloped the land, Galloway's Quarter was being patrolled from the air by light, almost completely silent, police helicopters. Numerous structures were a flame throughout The Quarter, and even beyond, especially below the South Carolina line. A radio call was made to determine the source of these fires and to develop a situational analysis. Virtually all of these structures turned out to be tobacco warehouses, or buildings linked back to the industry. When the identity for ownership of these buildings was investigated, a majority turned out to be none other than ole Mijj Bo Greene himself. The others were owned by the Parker Brothers, or through what was appearing more under investigation to be an established proxy.

As far as the fields of pot were concerned, under the cover of darkness the light twin engine planes returned. In some cases a light helicopter took their place. To discover the root source of these fields, only one move could be made that would work. The transport vehicle itself must be captured. To the surprise of the pursuing platoon, there was absolutely no resistance. When asked to give identity, none captured had spoken a word as of yet.

A few planes heavy laden with bales of marijuana and large plastic bags filled with cocaine, had caught sight of the pursuing troops and taken to the air in an act of escape. Military choppers from the national guard center in Whitevile were called in to pursue. When the drug smugglers realized their capture was soon eminent, they began tossing their stash out as they passed over the three or four county area of Galloway's Quarter, and even beyond into Marion County.

Later on the locals would find some of this heavy laden stash, cut it up and sell it for five times the going price, because of its high quality. The street name for this booty was *Airplane*, propeller weed, or propeller dust. When the law enforcement branch back at the courthouse in Whitevile caught wind of this, they immediately placed an unusually heavy penalty and fine on any charge of possession or distribution.

The troops moving through Galloway's Quarter formed a straight line, staggering individual troops thirty yards apart as they crept along through the swamp. When the resistance attacked the center of the line, the two

| THE INCIDENT IN GALLOWAY'S QUARTER

ends would loop around to enclose the insurgents. If one end or the other was attacked, then the free end would loop around to make an enclosure. In any case, when an enclosure was made, the resisting insurgents would be promptly eliminated. There was one exception to this fact, however.

Once the platoon had been marching steadily for some four days without provisions. On the fifth morning when the commanding officer demanded the slumbering troops to arise and resume the march, they refused, proclaiming that they couldn't do so without provisions. The commanding officer smiled, declaring that he would give full provision at the first opportunity. The platoon then agreed to resume marching for the purpose of full filling their duty assignment to eradicate all resistance.

No sooner had they exited camp and gone a few hundred yards outward, they encountered new resistance. These insurgents were soon encircled. To the astonishment of every person present, these insurgents only consisted of three teen aged boys and seven girls of the same age. They were all long time residents of Crusoe Island, so they informed the platoon commander as they begged for mercy.

The platoon surgeon was brought in who promptly ordered them all stripped. He closely examined their teeth, their tongues, and their bodies in general, pronouncing them all healthy. With agreement of the men, the three boys were taken to another area out of ear shot, and simply liquidated, while the young girls were transported to more open woods on higher dry ground. Here they were all tied to trees.

Seven pits were dug into the ground some ten feet long and two feet deep. Hickory wood was thrown into these pits and burned into glowing coals and ashes. Pieces of rebar were laid across the pit as the wood continued to burn. While the fire was going the girls were hanged on a tree limb by their ankles, and their throats were cut. Their bodies would be opened and eviscerated so they could drain in this fashion while the fires burned.

When the coals were ready the heads, hands, and feet were removed, and their body cavities opened and lain on the rebar over the glowing coals. On these bodies would be poured the juices of scrounged fruit. One man even had some molasses from a used up MRE container, while another had a bit of mustard on hand and a jar of honey, another some salt and vinegar. These substances were mixed to form an excellent sauce,

ADVENTURES TO GO |

then dutifully spread over the seven bodies on the fire pit with a field made folded leaf brush.

After a day of laying around the fires and enjoying each other's company, every man in the entire platoon feasted until he reached his complete contentment. No person spoke a word of complaint in regard to his rations for the day, nor did a single man appear to possess any feelings of rejection, or animosity toward being given such fare. This was an unspoken measure fully allowable by military rules, to be determined according to individual situations by the commander himself, for the purpose of alleviating stress in his fighting men while moving through enemy territory. Rules were severe and secrecy was adamant, being commanded from every person involved. Penalties were harsh and unforgiving for violating this code. In the light of this final atrocity, the terrible situation on Crusoe Island had finally been brought to an unstable closure. In the whole of Galloway's Quarter, the matter was another story.

Harlan Yarborough was a shady character of question, being seen in company with Ananias Parker, and two of his sons. Several from the HQ office in the Whitevile courthouse could attest to this. It was a well known fact among the inner circle that Harlan was capable of fulfilling virtually any request, if enough money was involved. He could be trusted to defend ones claim with his life, as long as he who expected these gracious services did according to the prearranged agreement.

Yarborough was a 275 pound man of solid statue and well built, perfectly toned muscle. A thick yellow mustache completely covered his upper lip. He wore his long blond hair parted back in the center of his head, and braided up into a tight queue that hung down between his shoulders in the back. Often he wore brand new Levis blue jeans, perfectly starched along every crease. His favorite shirts were various styles of Polo, or maybe a high fashioned Texas brand of western styled shirt. On his head he always wore a perfectly white, Stetson Fedora, with at least a $200.00 price tag.

In his pocket he carried a shop made hawk bill pocket knife. He always kept this blade razor sharp. He could retrieve this folded blade from his pocket with his right hand, opening it like it was spring loaded. Every person who knew him claimed he would slice the insides out of a person's torso in about as much time as it took to glance over at them. He has also

232

| THE INCIDENT IN GALLOWAY'S QUARTER

been sent to the brig more than once for stabbing or cutting people who ran afoul with him. A number of local people in Galloway's Quarter had the scars around their throats, or across their stomach to prove it.

Harlan was a prodigious drinker and cocaine user. He was said to consume an entire pint of 90 proof whiskey in a single gulp. When the money flow was good, the liquor flowed inward just as deeply. He tended to trade in both bootleg liquor, powder, and weed, when other business was slow. Any request made involving violence or moving contraband, he was usually up for. He was straight up in business and despised any person who wasn't, forever vowing to see that they got their dues.

Yarborough lived to brawl, often getting into scrapes for no apparent reason other than a person's sour look, or no reason at all. He could be loyal, however, very loyal, and he highly admired bravery, coming to a person's rescue who stood strong in a fight with multiple people, if he felt that the person was to be respected.

There was more about Yarborough that only a few others knew. He was actually a trained fight master. He lived for the death match, which has been outlawed in every country on earth, save only a few. Japan, under certain conditions, and Brazil, are two of only a few. Supper wealthy foreigners from Germany and France in particular, loved to watch the bloody display, and were willing to pay no less than $10000.00 per ticket, and to place bets. Every year around Christmas time, for about four months, Harlan would vanish from Galloway's Quarter, always returning unannounced, and loaded down with cash.

A man who traded cocaine with him claimed that he traveled to Brazil every year, engaged in a challenge, returning home with more than 6 figures for accepting the contest. The single adult daughters of these ultra wealthy patrons were also known to literally throw themselves at a consistent winner, often supporting him for an entire year, with their father's permission. It was said that only the greatest fighters from the *Clan Of The Wasp* were allowed to compete. Having a child from such a consistently valiant contestant was considered a badge of honor. This specific instance was the only known variant from the father's usual rigid demeanor in questions of choice and morality, since all marriages and relationships were prearranged by parents.

ADVENTURES TO GO |

The way Yarbourough brought the money back tax free and unquestioned from offshore was simple. He loaded the wealth up onto an unlimited debit card. The type he used was untraceable, and acquired when offshore for greater secrecy insurance. When he made it back home he simply called up Mijj Bo Greene, Ananias Parker, or Mason McPherson, who always made certain that Harlan could walk over to the local Wachcovia Bank teller machine and withdraw his cash, no questions asked. When he couldn't, should all else fail, he could simply motor on out to Masons or Ananias Parker's estate, and one of these individuals would pay it all out to him directly. Either person possessed the means to simply take back their money from the card; there again, no questions asked.

When the Crusoe Island Dynasty needed a certain type of handy man, Harlan was in, without questions. He was one of the first men the HQ detectives approached to question. Several threats were made from past allegations being pursued and punitive actions taken. When enough cash was placed before him, Harlan commenced speaking, but with great hesitation and only so much, no matter how much money they handed him.

"Tell us what ya know!," raged the biker detective as he tossed three more thousand in cash down in front of him.

"Look, I've already said what I need to say. Hooker Ainsley asked me to be his torch man. He offered to hand me twenty grand in cold cash for doing it. He paid me half upfront. When the warehouse went up in flames last November night, I collected on my other half."

The heavily tattooed detective glared down.

"There's only one problem with that story, Harlan, and you know it. Ainsley's warehouse wasn't the one that burned on November 12th, 1980. That is the one, right?"

"It was last November night! I can't recall which one after a year now, but I do clearly recall that it was last November night."

The detective drew a deep breath on his rum soaked cigar. A cloud of black smoke went up above their heads.

"Come on, Harlan here, don't munk around with me about this. There was only one damn warehouse that went up last November, at least in Galloway's Quarter. That warehouse was Bo Greene's on November 12th. Did you burn one outside of the old Quarter here? We need to know

234

| THE INCIDENT IN GALLOWAY'S QUARTER

more in regard to this? So fess up and tell us all about it!," the detective fired with a sinister laugh.

Harlan maintained an expressionless face, saying nothing in reply.

The detective took another puff, then glanced over toward Harlan

"Come on man, start talking. You've already admitted to burning down a tobacco warehouse on November 12, 1980. You claimed it was for Hooker Ainsley. Once we connect the dots on this you're looking at 15 to 20 long, and hard ones, for arson. You know what prison life is like in these parts, don't you?," the detective sneered. "You've heard of Caledonia Work Farms down in Georgetown, South Carolina, haven't you? That's the place where a hired arsonist like you, and especially with a record like yours, winds up. What have you got to lose right now? We are all waiting for you to begin talking."

Harlan still maintained a hard expressionless face, giving no reply. He was well acquainted with Caledonia. He had never been there, but he had spoken with plenty who had. Simply put, Caledonia Work Farms was a hell on earth. Inmates were forced to live in tents, to labor in the fields and underneath a torrid blazing sun 6 days a week, twelve hours a day. They lived in pup tents, grew their own food, and hand pumped their own water, while they existed underneath a 24hr shotgun guard.

Worse than these overall conditions, they were subjected to abuse from the guards themselves, not to mention other inmates. This abuse included random lashings, beatings, being placed into solitary confinement with only bread and water for weeks on end, then being forced to room with multiple known sodomites. Fortunately for him in this department, he could fight well. Most other inmates were not so lucky. Still, he had rather remain on the outside of Caledonia Work Farms.

"Lets be level on this, Harlan. We already know the deal here. You did torch the warehouse on November 12th, 1980. Hooker Ainsley was only Bo Greene's proxy. Greene had better things to do the night Ainsley met with you. He only handed Ainsley ex amount of cash, and Ainsley negotiated the deal, confirming this with a quick call to Greene. After he handed you your amount, he already had his own, and the deal was done."

Harlan still said nothing, only glaring, then glancing away.

"Look at me, boy, when I speak to you," growled the biker detective. Harlan glared directly into his eyes. "The tobacco warehouse that you

ADVENTURES TO GO |

burned was Mijj Bo Greene's. Bo Greene and Governor Sealgair have an owner partnership in many of those warehouses. This stuff is serious kimchee here. When we get finished picking around in Galloway's Quarter, we'll have a beeline running all the way up to D.C., directly into the presidential palace itself! You'll wind up making history around here," the biker detective and the other four in his company suddenly burst out laughing.

Harlan had no expression on his face, remaining silent. The detective took another deep breath.

"Lets be up front about all this? What's it gonna take? Name your price."

"I don't need money!," Harlan fired.

"What a you want then, if not money? Just let us know here, so we can be on with it."

"Give me immunity," Harlan snapped.

"Is that really what you want? You want immunity here? Is that it?"

Harlan made no reply.

The detective glanced around the room at the other expressionless faces, then turned to face Harlan.

"You want immunity, do you? Well then, you have it! Now start talking."

Harlan slowly leaned inward toward the detective.

"You have all the answers, and I have already told you the rest! Now lets be strait on this matter right now. I have places I need to be, and people I need to see, if you will."

Harlan abruptly arose from his seat, huffing out of the interrogation room. The five detectives merely sat glancing around at one another without speaking a single additional word.

With that word from Harlan three detectives motored on over to the burn site outside of Chadborn, NC. There were also burn sites near Loris, SC, and just outside of Fairmont, NC. When the three reached the site in Chadborn, all that remained were ashes, cinders, concrete blocks, and a tangle of smoldering tin and metal. Investigators were already onto the scene, sifting through the ash in search of any evidence that might connect with the suspects, or make another lead.

Several of the elder warehouse workers surveyed the scene, walking about casually. One was a frequent laborer from the local black community,

236

| THE INCIDENT IN GALLOWAY'S QUARTER

named James Jessup. Most locals knew him as Dr. Jake, the creator of a local juke-joint dance known as Dr. Jake's Shake. This dance stood somewhere between a mo-town midnight special, and *The Shag*. Local black and white folk relished the moves and the accompanying music. Dr. Jake was rather bent by the years a bit, being somewhat reserved, but would freely carry on a conversation when he felt moved to. Generally speaking, he was well liked. Much more than that, as it concerned the detectives, Dr. Jake tended to know lots about events occurring in the area.

One of the three detectives was a thin man dressed in new jeans and a fresh Izod shirt. His name was Bartleby Shaw. He was a quick witted man and bore the skill of being able to interact with all local people on their level in way that courted their trust. He was also well known by the locals throughout the general area, so cementing a relationship might be more readily accomplished when he approached people, more so than the other two.

"Dr. Jake, tell me something now," smiled Bartleby.

"I'll show tell ya anything ya want to know," laughed the elder.

"How's that shake comin' along these days?," both men laughed loudly for a bit.

"It has come along really good for many long years now. I think the years are catching up with me. It'll still come around, but its much slow, and not quite as hard these days."

Both men gazed at the pile of smoldering ruins laying before them.

"What a you think about this mess here?"

Dr. Jake shook his head.

"Hmm, you said the right word, mess it is."

"But this isn't the only such mess," clipped Bartleby. "We have the same mess in Loris, Fairmont, and maybe five other areas."

"What I think about it is that all this mess is just icing on the cake!," Dr. Jake laughed. "That's what I think about all this."

Bartleby suddenly firmed up in a cautiously serious way.

"What a ya mean there, Dr. Jake? What are you referring to here?"

"You might need to check out Bo Greene's and Ananias hog parlors. Somethings a stir there, from what I am hearing."

"You have any idea what it could be?," Bartleby asked with reserved caution.

ADVENTURES TO GO |

"People round here have been scared to death, to speak the truth, for a long time now," whispered Dr. Jake in a low tone of voice. " Basically the rule was hear no evil, see no evil."

"I see, Jake," replied Bartleby.

"Well, many who saw things, things out in the woods, things here with these warehouses, things that have been going on for the past nine years, and even earlier; tended to up and disappear if they spoke out. Local people have long known it and stayed mum. These out-landers are different."

"I'm listening," replied Bartleby, "but I still don't quite pick up on what you are saying."

"Well what I am saying is this, to put in simple words; rats get killed by traps, and wooden base ball bats."

"That certainly explains lots about informants suddenly not being available for questioning, and locals in the area not knowing anything about their whereabouts," replied Bartleby.

"I think you 'uns just might need to motor on out to the hog farms over on Old Red Hill Road, and those just outside of Loris," Dr. Jake spoke as he turned to face the detective. "There were three right here who tried to sound the alarm, and are now nowhere to be found. Their families are wondering, their wives, sisters, mothers and daughters are crying."

"Thanks for the tip," Dr. Jake there, "I guess that we have our day cut out for us," Bartleby spoke as he headed over toward the other two men standing off closer to the burn site. He picked up pace as he neared the other two.

"Lets go, and now!," he fired. "We'll speak as we head out onto the road."

The three race over toward a brand new 1981 Lincoln, then sped off the property and onto the highway.

"We might be only a short few miles from resolving this entire horrendous situation," spoke Bartleby to his comrades. Within fifteen minutes the car was speeding down a narrow paved road. A green sign ahead confirmed the location as Red Hill Road. Three curves were rounded, then a dirt road branched off to the left. Quickly Bartleby turned the wheel and the car began to bump along over the roots, holes, and gravel stone. Ahead was a series of twelve hog farms. Some thirty men

| THE INCIDENT IN GALLOWAY'S QUARTER

were walking all over the dirt on one these farms, while others were sifting through the soil in search of something.

Bartleby and the other two detectives walked over toward the man writing notes and watching carefully as teams of two and three men sifted through the muck and soil.

"Hello sir, I am Bartleby Shaw, one of the detectives from the central county office at the courthouse in Whitevile. I have word that something was up."

"Yeah, well you heard right about this mess, something was definitely up here."

"I haven't heard any more though. That's why I rode over here."

"There was a pile of what was presumed to be extremely fragmented human bone discovered by a worker here in the pig manure. He became suspicious late one night when he spotted two unidentified men throwing what he took to be a human corpse to the pigs. He was standing more than a hundred yards out, so he wasn't clear about it, but was enough to be concerned, " the man spoke as he carefully recorded more bone fragments being pulled from the mud.

"What made him so convinced that these bone fragments were human?," asked Bartleby?

"Claims he found a few human teeth. Some of our investigators here on scene have made some possible discoveries of the same. All of this matter is being sent in to Raleigh for further confirmation."

"No firm confirmation on the fact yet?," Bartleby snapped. He quickly scribbled something on a note pad he kept in the vest pocket on his suit, then snatched the paper up, handing it to the man.

"None," the man replied, "nothing affirmative yet."

"There's is my office number. Call me when something comes up that's a definite hit."

Slowly the links were merging. The two governors and the Crusoe Island dynasty had some nasty dirt on their hands. The problem with connecting the suggestions was that the line of evidence didn't run out far enough to connect and form the link. For any sort of claim to ever hold up in court it would have to. Not only that, before any sort of slam could be initiated other than what had already occurred, one would have to root out

ADVENTURES TO GO |

all of the connections supporting what was appearing more as some sort of backwoods big time criminal association.

Detective Bartalby leaned back into his leather bound office chair as he gave thought to the overall situation. He packed a brier wood pipe full with new Raleigh tobacco, lit it up, and eased backward in deep contemplation. Five hours had passed since he met with the investigator down at the burn site. The phone suddenly blared from the desk to the left of the room. It was Randal Bowmen from the fire investigation team.

"Bartleby, we have a new lead in this case."

"Well I'm all ears, lets hear it."

"We've discovered that three torch men were involved. One of them was Harlan, the ruffian, you know the one I am speaking of. The other two were Ricky Leech, Pat Bass, two who are almost in the same league as Harlan."

"I'm not familiar with the other two," replied Bartleby.

"We spoke with Harlan," Bowman continued. "Harlan seemed to be the most intelligent of the three."

"Harlan confirmed that he had been a hired hand in this, but Leech broke down and revealed the name of their employer. You're not going to believe it. It was senator Don Layton, a right hand associate to the cat daddy, Mijj Bo Greene, himself; the man who is said to swing the really big meat around in these parts."

"You're kidding me!," fired Bartleby in surprise.

"No, no, this stuff is real. Others are in the process of questioning Don right now."

"What about our big league suspects, the Parker brothers, Mijj Bo Greene, and Mason McPherson? Made any solid connections yet?"

"We're following through. We haven't made any solid connections, but I am telling you, even if we do I am not sure we can make a snag in all of this."

"This mess on Crusoe has finally ended. The people have been allowed to enter back onto the island. At long last we finally have our suspects on the four murders opening up this massive can of worms that followed. We are making some progress in finding those who were responsible for murdering those forty officers who tried to make the property evictions.

| THE INCIDENT IN GALLOWAY'S QUARTER

Maybe we are finally heading somewhere," Bartleby replied. He puffed on his pipe in between word exchanges.

"This entire situation will drag on for some time still yet, possibly years. Then there is that lawyer and politician in with all of the big boys, C.R. Loes. This man has powerful connections way up into Washington D.C. Once we all get to poking around in that ka ka, we still may yet find out that it's hasn't any bottom to it. Like I said, even though we have goods that are getting better in quality, it will be a long fight," Bowman assured.

Fifteen years passed. A few key elders were suspected according to scant circumstantial evidence, and pulled time on Caledonia Work Farms; but got off on reduced sentences, thanks to the help of Mijj Bo Greene via Mason McPherson. Not one served over five years time, even though they were implicated in the murders of Federal officials. After those citizens who were evacuated from Galloway's Quarter returned, an unsteady rhythm of life continued on for some time, often putting government officials and citizens on edge. That tenseness has continued on down through time .

Senator Don Layton eventually would up being sentenced 20 years in Federal prison for arson. His right hand man, Harlan Yarborough, was in the can with him. Harlan's mafioso connections allowed the senator to live a king's lifestyle while there behind bars, according to local rumors. Some in the area of Gallaway's Quarter suspect that both of them agreed to do some mysterious, dark job for the mob in exchange for their cushy lifestyle and respect garnished from the inmates, but no specifics have yet to come into light. Thanks to the connections of McPherson, Ananias Parker, and Bo Greene, with the help of C.R. Loes, Harlan and Layton were out free and clear after serving only two years.

As for the Parker brothers, McPherson, and Governor's Sealgair, and Elire, from South Carolina; after three years of battling in federal court, all charges were finally dropped due to lack of evidence, thanks to the help of lawyer C.R. Loes, said to be the best in three states. Their eldest sons, however, were nailed on drug smuggling charges, found to be with connections reaching all the way down to great Gulf Coast cartel in Columbia, South America.

Rascal Parker owned an R.V. manufacturing company, and was found stashing the pipes in the kitchen and bathroom full with cocaine, and the space between the upper and lower floors full with the same powder. Several

ADVENTURES TO GO |

rooms in these R.V.'s were said to contain bales of hash and marijuana. The bales had been linked back to the huge fields of the weed discovered in Galloway's Quarter. His eldest son took the fall for it.

In three short years the young man was back out onto the streets. His time in prison was said to be basically a stint in a high classed hotel room, where the man could come and go as he pleased. There again, a result from having connections; yet suspicions of fulfilling some yet to be discovered, tarnished orders fly out on the streets.

None of these sons who took the fall had to serve a single moment down in labor fields. The guards were said to have catered to them, rather than dared to harass. They were never in the company of other inmates; so no negative situations occurred due to interaction, as does with the average person who is forced to submit to the power structure among inmates out on the prison floor. Basically every sentence served was a slap on the wrist, and a ride on the gravy train. So it goes when people have solid connections with the right tycoons. Knowledge that a person is in possession of, is only secondary at best in the secular order of reality.

Back on Crusoe Island all of those accused were eventually released by the Fed on lack of evidence. The locals swear to this very day that all of these people who really were guilty simply allowed themselves to be swallowed up by the cypress swamp. When the dirt in all of this business finally settled down, they eventually eased back out, only to be absorbed back into the established communities, living out their mortal lives in complete contentment.

According to resident stories, the last out-lander made his exit off the island back in 1988, running with every fiber of his being up to Boston, vowing to his dying breath he would never again bother with traveling back to the South-land, anywhere. To this day the moment of that final exit is celebrated exuberantly in the streets of Duval and Formy with great elaboration and excitement. The celebration is called the *Le Jour De La Seconde Libération*, held on the thirteenth day of every April since '88. To this very moment the name, Crusoe Island, sends shivers up the spine of every out-lander back on the mainland, from Whitevile all the way up to Maine.

On clear nights during the harvest moon, if one stands on the high side back a ways from the bridge going into the island, he can still hear an arousing midnight song of the Blue Tick, and perceive distant bravado cheers of a highly individualist culture set to endure the ages forward into infinity, on its own terms, as its many long buried skeletons continue to molder down in the swamp mud.

THE AUTHOR

Dr. Henry Lydo is a national & international academic/ ESL Instructor. He has been a writer for over thirty years. His latest publications have been two books of nonfiction with Algora Publishing, a fictional novel by Atmosphere Press, and fictional publications with combo e-zines and print magazines; Leaves of Ink, CC&D Magazine, a novel with Atmosphere press, Short Story Lovers, The Fear of Monkeys, and Frontier Tales. He recently signed three contracts with Pen it Publications. *Ludlow's Daughter, Das Konto, and They Called Him Ringo Arenas* are novels recently published by Reverend Crown Publications.

Facebook: Rowdy Living Press
https://rowdylivingpress.home.blog

"FOR ADDISON"

KYLE OWENS

ADVENTURES TO GO |

Stirs of sound brought her out of her slumber as her eyes slipped open and adjusted to the outline of a woman dressed in white standing over her.

The nurse smiled, "Good morning, Addison."

"It's too early for there to be anything good about it," Addison replied while rubbing her eyes with the sides of her fists.

"I don't see too many little girls wearing Spider-Man pajamas."

"Probably even fewer bald little nine-year-old girls wearing them, too."

Addison lay in bed for a few seconds then sat up and stretched her arms above her head with a silent yawn.

Suddenly she spied a man standing in the doorway. He had dark hair, a prominent nose, probably in his mid thirties. He was wearing a white short-sleeved shirt, a dark-colored tie, blue slacks and brown shoes. He stood in the hallway as if he was uncomfortable about walking inside.

"Hi," he mused.

"How ya doing, buddy?" Addison asked without hesitating.

He gave a gentle laugh as he asked her, "How are you today?"

"I'd be better if I didn't have cancer."

The man was taken aback by her comment and stumbled to try to figure out what to say or do next. But Addison had no trouble continuing the conversation.

"What's your name?"

"I'm Wilson Potter."

The nurse smiled, "He comes by here often."

"I've never seen him."

"I'm usually on the other end of the hospital," informed Wilson.

The nurse said, "You two should talk and get to know each other."

"What in the world will we talk about?" asked Addison.

"You've never had any trouble talking about anything before. Now he's a very nice man so don't scare him. I'll be back later."

The nurse left and Wilson stared at Addison in which he felt overwhelmed by her gaze. He glanced down at his feet.

"Wilson Potter sounds totally like an old man's name."

"Sometimes I feel like an old man."

"Totally I bet. My name is Addison Brockwell," she told him as she maneuvered out from under her bed covers and sat with her legs crossed.

| "FOR ADDISON"

"Addison? I've never heard of a girl named Addison before."

"I'm glad to enlighten you. Are you a doctor?"

"No. I'm a volunteer. I come by a few times a week and help out around the hospital and such."

"Why?"

He struggled for a reply, "To- well, you know, give back to the community."

Addison just shook her head, "You're not giving back to the community."

"I'm not?"

"No. You're searching for something."

Wilson slowly walked into the room intrigued by this little girl's comment. "What am I searching for?"

She thought about his question for a second. "You're not sure yet. But you're looking for an answer."

"What's the question?"

"Why?" she replied, again without any hesitancy.

The two were quiet for a moment when Addison said, "It seems totally drab in here doesn't it?"

"It is a hospital room. I guess that's how they all seem."

"It needs some color, maybe some yellow roses. I saw some in a magazine one day and they were totally beautiful. There's a vase in the kitchen on the top cabinet near the window. It looks like purple glass. I saw it there yesterday when I was wandering around when I wasn't supposed to be and thought that would look perfect with yellow roses in it. I'd set them on the window sill there. When the sun rises it would reflect through the vase and fill the room with rainbows. I have to say that I think I have pretty good decorating tastes for a nine-year-old."

"I agree," said Wilson.

She got down from the bed and went over to the window. She raised the blind with a pull of a dirty white string. She then opened the window and listened.

Wilson watched her lean out the window as she cupped her hand to her ear to which he had to ask, "What are you listening for?"

She turned to him and put her left index finger to her lips.

247

ADVENTURES TO GO |

After a few more seconds she then seemed to come out of her intense listening trance and said, "I can totally hear the fair."

"Yeah, they have one every Labor Day weekend. It's pretty popular."

"Did you go to it?"

"No. I haven't been to a fair since I was a kid."

"I've never been to a fair before," she said as she climbed back onto her bed.

Wilson was surprised as he said, "Maybe your parents can take you out there one evening."

"I don't have any parents. My Mom is a drug addict living out in the Seattle streets and I never knew my Dad. I just got passed around between family members and then when I got sick nobody wanted me. I cost too much to have around. So I became a ward of the state. Seems like everybody I care about turns against me. Even my own body."

Her voice trailed off then she asked, "Are you married?"

Wilson was quiet for a second then said, "No."

"Me neither," she said with a big grin that made Wilson's somber face shatter into a smile.

She stared down at her hands, rubbing her right thumb over the fingertips of her left hand when she blurted out, "Do you like baseball?"

"I like baseball."

"Do you have a favorite team?"

"I always liked the Cincinnati Reds," he said. "That was my Dad's favorite team so it became my favorite one through genetics."

"They have a TV in the gathering room, well that's what I call the room, and they show a lot of New York Mets games so they have become my team, I guess. Man, they lose a lot, too. I guess I didn't think cancer was bad enough so I became a Mets fan, too."

Wilson tried to keep from laughing out loud but couldn't hold it in. He began to comprehend her spunk and that she wasn't going to let cancer or her life's circumstances get her down. He was starting to worship her like a fan's awe for a baseball player idol.

"What do you do for a living, Wilson?" Addison asked.

"I'm a writer."

"A writer? So you're unemployed," she smiled.

Wilson couldn't help but to laugh, "You're fun to talk to."

248

| "FOR ADDISON"

"I get that a lot. So what kind of writing do you do?"

"Short stories mostly."

"Have you been published before?"

"Yes."

"You do know that having someone just post one of your stories on a website and saying they'll pay you in exposure isn't publishing don't you? That's totally a scam."

"I get paid for my work, though I may hire you as my literary agent."

"Have you written a novel?"

"I'm working on one."

"What's it about?"

"A coal strike in the Appalachian Mountains in which a young boy and a girl fall in love and are on opposite sides of the strike."

"That sound totally boring," Addison said as she rolled her eyes.

"Hopefully it reads better."

"Do you know what your next short story will be about?" Addison asked.

"Not for sure yet. Do you have any ideas?"

"How about one about me?"

Wilson nodded his head as if he seemed to be contemplating the idea, "That's something for me to think about."

"I'm more exciting than a coal strike."

"I'm sure you are."

"What's that in your pocket?"

Wilson looked down at his shirt pocket, patted it then said, "That's my notebook. When I come up with ideas for stories I write them down. My memory isn't the best anymore."

Addison then got down from the bed as she seemed to be in constant motion unable to be still. She ran her hand across the desk in the corner then over the luggage then she stood at the window and listened to the distant echoes of the fair.

"How far down is it to the ground here do you think?" asked Addison as she stared at the grass beneath the window.

Wilson got up, walked over to the window and looked over her shoulder, "About five feet I guess. Why?"

She turned to him, smiled and humped her shoulders as she then said, "I was just wondering was all. How tall are you?"

249

ADVENTURES TO GO |

"I'm six foot two."

She thought about it a little more and whispered out, "That's totally interesting."

Wilson was a bit bewildered about what she was doing as she walked over again to the desk that was beside her bed. She opened up a drawer and pulled out a Spider-Man action figure then got back onto the bed and began fiddling with it.

"Can I have a drink of water?" she asked.

"Sure," replied Wilson. "I'll go get it."

Wilson went out of the room and headed to the small kitchen area at the end of the hall. He got a paper cup from the cabinet when he spied Addison's vase, which caused him to smile. Then he walked over to the water fountain, filled the cup and headed back to Addison's room. When he got there she was standing at the window looking down at the ground.

"Here's your water."

Addison looked up at him, "I dropped my Spider-Man out the window. Could you get it for me?"

"Sure."

She took the cup of water and Wilson headed out of the room then down the hallway and out the rear entrance. He turned left, walked through the grass until he arrived at Addison's window. He bent down to pick up the tiny action figure when he saw Addison near the window sill as she said, "Catch me."

Wilson went into a panic as she put his hands up to keep her from jumping down.

"What are you doing?"

She put her index finger to her lips then said in a whisper, "I'm escaping for the day and you're going to help me."

"We can't do that."

"Yes we can. I want to go to the fair."

"You can't go out in your pajamas."

"A lady can dress how she pleases. Now I've got my flip-flops on and I'm ready for action."

"But you're sick."

250

| "FOR ADDISON"

"No. I'm dying. There's a difference. This is the day I have to go to the fair because I feel my strongest. If I don't go today I may never get to go."

Wilson's mind began racing. He couldn't take her. But she was dying. This was her wish. She had made him her own private Make-A-Wish Foundation.

"I'll take you, but we have to leave a note."

"Where's your sense of adventure?"

"Look at me Addison. Do I look adventurous?"

Addison stared him up and down and whispered out, "You totally have a point."

We have to leave a note or I can't take you."

"You're such a Wilson."

He helped her down and she stood beside him as he took his notebook out of his pocket and scribbled down that he had taken Addison to the fair, placing it inside her room by the window sill.

"Okay, we can go," said Wilson.

She took him by the hand and they walked toward the parking lot.

"Which one is your car?" Addison asked in a bit of anticipation.

"This one here," said Wilson as he pointed toward a 1984 short bed, two-door, Chevy pickup truck.

Addison stopped and stared at the truck with her mouth agape as if she was looking at a squashed bug on her dinner plate.

"That's your vehicle?"

"Yes. What's wrong with it?"

"I thought a writer would be driving a better vehicle than that. Maybe a Ferrari or a Lamborghini, you know- something along those lines."

"I can't afford anything like that. I'm not Stephen King for crying out loud."

"Obviously."

Wilson helped her into the passenger side of the pick-up then got into the driver's side and they headed out to the fair. They got there in about fifteen minutes and Addison quickly got out, grabbed Wilson's hand and led him to the fairgrounds' front gate. Wilson paid their admission and she pulled him over to a ticket booth.

ADVENTURES TO GO |

"We want a book of tickets," said Addison to the woman inside a small trailer.

The woman gave Wilson the tickets, he paid for them and then Addison grabbed his hand and led him straight toward the Ferris wheel.

"Wait a second," said Wilson as he realized their destination.

"What is it?"

"Where are you taking me?" he asked in a very nervous voice.

"To the Ferris wheel."

"I can't ride a Ferris wheel."

"You're not that heavy, Wilson," said Addison as she tried pulling him forward.

"You don't understand: I'm afraid of heights," Wilson told her with a hint of embarrassment.

She looked at him and said, "It'll be okay, Wilson. Because I have a belief that no matter what a person is afraid of in life they will be able to conquer it when they need to the most."

Wilson drank in her words with the realization that she was facing cancer and seemed to be doing it pretty well. He thought if she can do that then he should at least try to defeat his fear of heights- even if it was just for a day. If he couldn't muster the courage for himself then maybe he could for her. After all this was her day. Totally.

"Okay. I'll get on the Ferris wheel with you," said Wilson in a deflated voice.

"Hooray!" shouted Addison. "It's going to be totally fun fun fun. "You'll see."

They got into line as Wilson's anxiety began to rise. The wheel turned and stopped in front of them. The ride operator opened the bar, Addison and Wilson climbed into the seat and the bar was closed with a loud clank. Their pod slowly moved then paused for the next set of passengers to get on.

"How are you doing, Wilson?"

"I'm not going to lie: I'm terrified right now."

"Stop worrying. It's won't fall over until we get to the top."

"What?"

Addison started laughing as she tried to get him to relax. "It'll be okay. Look how far you can see. It's like flying."

252

| "FOR ADDISON"

Then as the Ferris wheel was filled with passengers the ride began spinning around at a quicker pace. Addison held her arms up over her head while Wilson never let go of the bar.

The two of them rode the ride until it stopped. Wilson was relieved it was over, but before he got a few feet away from the ride Addison pulled to his hand and told him, "Let's ride it again.""No," said Wilson as he removed her hand from his wrist. "I don't have any courage left to ride it again."

"You don't need courage, you just need me. Now come on."

"Can't I just watch you ride it while I stay down here on this beautiful flat ground. I promise to wave at you every time you pass by."

"You can't conquer your fear of heights on the ground. That's not how life works. To conquer your fear you have to get on it and ride it hard! Now come on, I'm tired of fussing at'cha."

She pulled to Wilson's hand until he surrendered to which they got back in line and rode the Ferris wheel again…and again… and again. Wilson never conquered his fear of heights, but with each ride his fear became more tolerable. Then one last time after they rode it they went back to get into line and Wilson looked at his watch and Addison saw him.

"Why do you keep looking at your watch for?" asked Addison. "Are you not having any fun?"

"I'm having fun. It's just that I usually-" Wilson then stopped himself as he realized Addison was more important at this moment.

"Don't worry about the hospital. They won't do anything to you. I mean the worse they can do to you is kill you, right?"

Wilson gave a quiet smile and Addison knew something else was consuming him.

"You have to be somewhere don't you?" queried Addison.

"I don't have to be, I guess."

"Yeah, you do. Where do you need to be?"

Wilson was hesitant to tell her, but she kept pulling to his hand and demanding to know where he needed to be until he finally told her.

"Every day at five I go see Margaret."

"Is she your girlfriend?"

"She's my wife."

253

ADVENTURES TO GO |

Addison was surprised by his answer as she quickly added, "I thought you said you weren't married."

"She's at the cemetery."

Addison stared at him then said softly, "Then let's go see Margaret."

Addison led Wilson by the hand through the crowd of people, out into the parking lot and to his truck. They got in and Wilson drove the ten-minute ride to the cemetery that was on a hillside on the east side of town.

They walked toward the grave that was placed beneath a large oak tree. A concrete bench was beneath it where they sat down and stared at Margaret's tombstone.

"So this is Margaret?" asked Addison.

"Yeah, she was my wife for ten years."

They were quiet as Addison stared out at the row of tombstones peaked out of the grass and her mind began to piece things together.

"She died of cancer didn't she?" asked Addison.

Wilson was surprised that she knew that because he was trying to do everything he could to keep her from finding out for fear it might disturb her. So he simply nodded that she had.

"She died in the same hospital I'm in, didn't she? That's why you volunteer there."

"Yes."

"Don't you see? You're not there to do good for the community: You're there to see Margaret."

"I don't believe in ghosts. I know she's not there."

"But it was the last place you saw her alive. That's why you go there. You want to be where the last place she was alive."

Her words made sense to him.

"What room was she in?" asked Addison.

"She was on the top floor, room fifty-five."

"I've been in there before. I've been in all of the rooms before. I like meeting everyone to let them know that cancer doesn't have to depress you. I think it's important to have a good attitude just for your loved ones to be able to sustain themselves. Providing you're not like me and don't have any loved ones. But if you accept it with courage and grace, everyone deals with it better, I think. We can't make life fair, Wilson, so we'll just have to try to make it better."

| "FOR ADDISON"

Wilson drank in her words. She seemed so much older and wiser than a nine-year-old should be. She seemed to know how to adjust to a crisis with an intimate attitude, which was something he hadn't been able to accomplish on his own.

"How did you two meet?" asked Addison.

"At a dance."

"You dance?" asked a surprised Addison.

"Not well. But I can dance. Well, sort of."

"What song was playing when you danced with Margaret?"

"*Peggy Sue* by Buddy Holly. It was a sock hop dance after one of the football games."

"A sock hop dance?" Addison said as she shook her head in disapproval. "I'm glad that I didn't go to your school."

They sat for a few seconds longer before Addison had to have more details, "Did you ask her or did she ask you to dance?"

"She asked me."

"Way to go Margaret," Addison said as she gave a thumbs-up to Margaret's gravesite. "Was it a slow dance?"

"No. *Peggy Sue* is kind of an up-tempo song, so I have to move."

"I'm guessing that Margaret was a better dancer than you were."

"What makes you think that?"

"Because your name is Wilson."

"I don't see what that has to do with it."

"Were you named after the ball company?"

"No. At least I don't think I was. I never really asked my parents why they called me Wilson. But I'm sure it wasn't after a ball that they saw bouncing around in the neighbor's yard. At least I hope not."

The sun was warm as it paraded the landscape. Birds called out to one another and the distant sound of traffic in the distance slowly slipped in.

"Let's dance," suggested Addison.

"Dance? But we don't have any music."

"Margaret will provide the music. Won't you, Margaret?" Addison said as she went over and patted the tombstone and then walked back over to Wilson.

Addison then took Wilson's hands and stood in front of him as he became a bit uncomfortable.

ADVENTURES TO GO |

"I guess I should confess that I really can't dance at all."

"Nobody taught you?"

"No."

"I'll teach you. I'm sure you're a good dancer."

"No I'm not. I'm a Wilson, remember?"

"What kind of dancing do you like?"

"I don't know- jumping jacks?"

"Jumping jacks aren't a dance, Wilson. I know what we'll do," said Addison as she took her flip-flops off.

"What are you doing?'

"We'll do a father-daughter dance," she said as she placed her bare feet onto his shoes while holding his hands.

Wilson then slowly began moving his feet around as she held his hands in hers. He felt himself wanting to cry for this was the first moment since his wife's death that he didn't feel alone.

"You're a good dancer, Wilson. We might have to change your name to Travolta," Addison said with a smile. "You're doing good with the music, too, Margaret," she quickly added.

"You know, Margaret always wanted a daughter."

"Well, I'd be the perfect choice. I like dancing so me and Margaret would hit it off just great. Plus you'd save a ton of money on not having to buy me shampoo."

Wilson laughed, "You're a character."

"I try to be."

They danced for a while then sat back down on the bench. Wilson noticed that Addison was looking tired.

"Are you ready to go back?" asked Wilson.

Addison looked at Wilson and asked, "Can I be buried next to Margaret?"

Wilson was surprised by her question as she further added, "I'd like to be next to her so we can talk about you. You're fun to talk about."

Wilson smiled, "I'm sure Margaret would like that."

"Me, too."

Addison lovingly placed her head against his shoulder while holding his hand. Then inside the quietude, time seemed to stop beneath a wide

256

oak tree branched over a small hill as two former strangers found their composition of place.

Wilson's cell phone rang. He looked at it and a somber look crossed his face. "It looks like the hospital found our note. We better get back."

Wilson and Addison got back to the hospital and Addison sat in her room alone. Then Wilson walked in.

"I got it all smoothed over."

"So they're not going to kick me out?" asked Addison.

"No. Did you have fun today?"

"Totally," she smiled.

"I'll let you go on to sleep and I'll see you again tomorrow."

"Can you come around noon? I have to do tests in the morning."

"I can do that."

She reached out her open arms and asked, "Hug?"

"I insist," Wilson smiled and hugged her. "Thanks for a great day."

"You bet."

As he pulled away he felt tears well up in his eyes. He looked down upon her smiling face then she closed her eyes and quickly fell asleep. Wilson then turned and walked out of the roomThe next day Wilson went about his many errands, writing his word quota for the day then heading to a flower shop and picking up some yellow roses for Addison.

He made his way to the hospital at noon and walked into the room and was surprised Addison wasn't there. The bed was made and all her belongings were gone. He walked out into the hallway and saw a nurse.

"Excuse me, is Addison still having her tests done?"

"No," said the nurse sadly. "She passed away last night. I'm sorry."

Wilson felt ill. He wanted to run. Hide from the world. He just looked at the flowers clutched inside his hand.

"Do you know where she was taken?"

"They sent her to Seattle where her mother lives. They'll make all the funeral arrangements there. I'm sorry, Wilson."

Wilson then turned and walked away. Then he stopped. He headed to the kitchen and got the vase off the top cabinet. He placed the yellow roses inside then left the hospital with the vase at a quick pace.

He got into his truck and drove straight to Margaret's grave. He placed the vase of the flowers beside Margaret where Addison wanted to be buried then sat on the bench crying. This little girl had come into his world for one day and it was the most beautiful experience he had ever had since the days with his wife. Now he had lost both of them to the same disease.

Wilson stared out at the blue sky with its wash of ivory colored clouds sliding over its face with a melting softness. Then he reached into his shirt pocket and pulled out his notebook. He folded the cover back onto itself, retrieved his pen from the same pocket and began scribbling down some lines, finally taking control of his emotions.

Stirs of sound brought her out of her slumber as her eyes slipped open and adjusted to the outline of a woman dressed in white standing over her.

Be Sure to Read Kyle's Entertaining Vegas Chantly
Mystery, *Checkmate a Killer*

SODUKO ANSWERS

4	1	8	2	6	9	5	7	3
7	2	5	1	3	4	6	9	8
3	9	6	8	5	7	4	1	2
8	5	4	6	7	3	1	2	9
1	3	9	4	8	2	7	5	6
6	7	2	5	9	1	8	3	4
2	6	7	3	4	5	9	8	1
9	4	1	7	2	8	3	6	5
5	8	3	9	1	6	2	4	7

Thanks for Reading!

Watch for Issue #8 this Summer
and a Special Edition This Fall.

Following is an excerpt from the wildly entertaining
Vegas Chantly Mystery, *Checkmate a Killer;*

Available everywhere books are sold.

CHECKMATE A KILLER

CHAPTER ONE

On the outskirts of Blue Falls, Georgia, in the Pine Sap Camper Park (which had the catchy slogan "Come and stick around"), Vegas Chantly was sound asleep in her nineteen seventy-two silver Airstream camper. It was set up on lot twenty-one and had a giant painting of Woody Woodpecker on the right rear quarter panel.

Inside, everything was nearly quiet, with only the whispers of bird calls intertwined with rustling leaves seeping through the thin walls. At seven o'clock, the radio came on and awakened the warm August morning.

| CHECKMATE A KILLER

"Good morning, sleepy heads. Here's your quick rundown of the news on this fine day. A body was found at the Rhinehouse Apartments complex on Fifth Street. The police said it appeared to have been accidental, and the case is closed. In literature, local professor Oliver Kimball's essay on how to feed the hungry through cannibalism has now won both a Nobel Prize and a Bram Stoker Award. Also, it's National Pig Day. So go out there and eat a wiener, America! Last up is the weather forecast — like they're going to get that right — brought to you by Fitness Plus and Diet Center, located at the Plaza Shopping Mall right beside Big Tony's Pizza. Rear entrance advised ..."

Vegas slowly opened her eyes, reached out with her left hand, and turned off the radio. The twenty-seven-year-old sat up in bed, her shoulder-length blond hair tangled and sticking up as if she had been shocked.

She rubbed her eyes with her fists, let out a big yawn like a lioness after eating a tourist, and suddenly noticed that standing at the foot of her bed was a short, redheaded round-on-both-ends woman with her hands on her hips and big, oval, black-framed eyeglasses perched on her nose.

"We need to continue our talk from last night," she said.

"Good lord, Mom. You scared me to death," Vegas said, her hand clutching her heart. "No wonder I never get the hiccups."

Vegas leaned against the back wall of the camper while she continued to try to rub the sleep from her eyes.

Vegas' mom, Eleanor, looked around the camper, shook her head, and said, "I can't believe my only child is living in a camper in a camper park. If your father was alive, he'd roll over in his grave."

Vegas cocked an eyebrow as she digested her mother's words. "I think you said that wrong, but I'm too sleepy to know for sure or not."

"Why don't you move back in with me? There's absolutely no reason for you to be living in a place like this," pleaded her mother.

"No," said Vegas as she stared up at the ceiling in despair. "Last night my answer was no, and it's the same today. Now if you'll excuse me, I really need some coffee. And maybe that guy who plays Thor on a sweet roll."

Vegas slowly slid out of bed. She was wearing an extra-large red T-shirt with a drawing of Frankenstein's monster printed on it, and a pair of gray jogging pants cut off at the knees. She made her way to the kitchen counter, which took all of two steps.

ADVENTURES TO GO |

"Why don't you want to move back in with me?" her mother implored.

"Because you're crazy, Mom."

"You live in a camper and you call me crazy. Look around you, sweetie. It's obvious that the private investigator business isn't working out for you."

"I'm doing fine, Mom."

"Do you have any clients lined up?"

"Tons."

Eleanor shook her head. "I didn't know you measured clients by weight now."

"Okay, hundreds then."

"Hundreds?" asked a doubtful Eleanor. "Am I supposed to believe that you actually have hundreds of clients?"

Vegas got the coffee can off a shelf and began unscrewing the lid when the can slipped out of her hands, bounced off the floor, and sent coffee grounds everywhere.

"This morning isn't starting off well," Vegas said as she bent down to pick up the can, and on her way back up hit her head on the underside of the counter, which sent her back to her knees.

"Ow. I think I'm dead," Vegas said as she rubbed her head. "I admit I could be off in my client count." She placed the can on the counter from her kneeling position and then used her hands to scoop the coffee off the floor and back into the can.

"You're not going to drink that are you?" her mother asked in a state of horror.

"It doesn't matter. I don't like this brand of coffee anyway," Vegas said.

"Are these clients ever going to pay you?"

"Stop worrying about my financial situation, Mom. The camper's paid for."

"Of course it's paid for. Your father paid it off in ninety-six."

Eleanor sat on the bed, shook her head, and tried to keep from crying as she said, "I just don't like you being a private investigator. It's dangerous, you know? If anything ever happened to you, I don't know what I would do. Well, I'd probably sell the camper."

Vegas began placing several fistfuls of coffee grounds into the machine. "Mom, I'll be okay. I'm a big girl now. I can iron my pants and everything."

| CHECKMATE A KILLER

Eleanor noticed some business cards on the tiny kitchen table. She picked them up and began shuffling through them as if they were playing cards.

"Vegas Chantly, pie? What's that?" Eleanor asked.

"That's P.I., Mom. This coffee maker isn't even working."

Eleanor reread the cards, "I need to get these glasses changed. Where did you get these?"

"Pepper made 'em for me on his computer," Vegas said as she walked to her tiny red refrigerator, opened the door, and retrieved a root beer. She popped open the can and took a big swig.

"Pepper? I'm not sure I like you hanging out with him."

"He's fine — in his own way."

"Doesn't he think he was once probed by aliens or something?"

"It could have happened," Vegas said with an unsure look on her face and took a seat in a patio chair pushed into the corner. It sat beneath a shelf that held a thirteen-inch black-and-white television from the nineteen-seventies and a Pink Panther plush toy.

"What's all this on the back of the cards?" asked Eleanor.

"Those are my rates."

"Do you think you can get that much just for looking into people's windows?"

"I do a little more than that. And yes, the rates are competitive."

Eleanor put the cards down, then turned to her daughter and asked in her serious voice, "I want you to be honest with me now. Do you need money?"

"I've got money, Mom," Vegas said as she drank her root beer.

"Oh, my God! Are you hooking?" Eleanor said as she threw her hands in the air in despair.

"Yeah, that's how I can afford all of this. Enough of this now, Mom. Every time we get together, you end up talking about me and my life. Let's talk about you for once. What's new with you?"

Eleanor appeared to be a bit taken aback by her daughter's query, "Me? What did you hear?"

"Nothing, Mom," Vegas said through a sigh as she stared at the ceiling, then back at her mother. "Just tell me what you did yesterday."

ADVENTURES TO GO |

Eleanor's eyes indicated she was trying to retrace her life from yesterday. "Oh, the other day I was watching *The Wheel of Fortune*, and before the lady contestant said a letter, I yelled out S, and do you know that there were three S's in the puzzle? I was so excited. That's never happened to me before — or since, for that matter. But for one moment in a long day, I was Lady Action."

A proud look was etched on Eleanor's face as Vegas asked, "What was the answer?"

"Answer to what?"

"To the puzzle. What was the answer?" Vegas asked in a frustrated voice.

"I think it was Rain Maker or something like that," Eleanor said.

"There are no S's in Rain Maker."

"Well, Mommy can't remember what it was. I just remember being excited that I got the S's right. You know, if I'm ever on *The Wheel of Fortune*, that's going to be my strategy. I'm going to say, 'Give me an S, Alex.'"

"The name of the host is Pat."

"No, I'm pretty sure it's a man," Eleanor said.

"Whatever you say, Mom," Vegas said in surrender. "I'm going to regret asking this, but what if the contestant before you asks for an S?"

Eleanor thought it over, and a plan of strategy seemed to reveal itself to her satisfaction. "Well, I guess I'll go with R then, in case it's Rain Maker again. You know, I'm pretty good at these game shows during the day. My mind is always working. I'd love to be on one. Do they make you take a test first before you can be a contestant?"

"You better hope not," Vegas said.

The payphone situated beneath a large oak tree some twenty feet from Vegas' camper suddenly rang.

"I'll get it," Eleanor shouted as she rushed out of the camper.

"No, you won't!" Vegas yelled as she sat her can of root beer down and tried to beat her mother to the phone. The tail of her shirt caught on a sharp point on the tiny kitchen counter, and her mother made it to the phone as she finally freed herself.

"Hello? Yes, this is Vegas Chantly's residence. I'm her partner," Eleanor said, much to the chagrin of her daughter.

264

| CHECKMATE A KILLER

Vegas took the phone from her mother. "Give me that," she said to her. "And you're not my partner, you're my Brutus."

Vegas composed herself, then began speaking into what was probably the last payphone in all of Georgia — and perhaps in all of civilization.

"Yes, this is Vegas Chantly. I can do that. Give me your address." Vegas then whispered to her mother, "Get me a pen and a piece of paper."

"Who is it?" asked Eleanor.

"Get me a pen and a piece of paper," repeated Vegas.

"Who is it?"

"Get me a pen and a piece of paper."

"But who is it?"

"Work with me here, woman," Vegas said in annoyance.

"Okay, okay," Eleanor mumbled as she reached into her purse and dug her hand into it like it was a backhoe. She somehow found a pen and a scrap of paper and handed them to Vegas.

"He's a chess champion?" Vegas continued as she spoke with the person on the other end of the line. "Wilson Hopkins. I think I heard about him on the news. Was he the one that played a whole class of second-graders and they tied him up and painted him purple? Interesting. Bosco Hopkins … Rhinehouse Apartments … Apartment fifteen. Okay. I'll be right there. Bye."

Vegas hung up the phone.

"Is that a new case?" asked Eleanor.

"Yeah. A chess champion died, and the police said it was an accident, but the brother believes he was murdered."

"Murdered?" Eleanor said in a voice drowned in worry.

"That's just what he thinks," Vegas said in an attempt to calm her mother's worries. "I'm sure the police were right in saying it was an accident."

"If you believe the police are right, then why are you taking the case?"

Vegas tried to deflect the question and mumbled, "I'm just curious, is all."

"You don't have any other cases lined up, do you?" Eleanor replied in what Vegas called her "interrogation tone."

"Everything's fine," Vegas said, hoping her mother would miraculously just move on. "I'm just going through a slow time right now. Not a lot of

ADVENTURES TO GO |

people need detectives in August. Solar wind patterns and all. Besides, maybe I'll learn about chess when I get there."

"You know, your father tried to teach me chess, but I was afraid of the horse."

"I really don't have time to try and understand you right now. I've got to go change," Vegas said as she headed back to the camper.

"We can take my vehicle," Eleanor said.

Vegas stopped at the camper door, turned to her mother, and shouted, "You're not coming with me!"

"I'll be your backup."

"I don't need a backup. I don't want you coming with me. That's final!"

"But your minivan is in the shop. Remember?"

Vegas' self-assurance seemed to collapse into itself when her mother reminded her of that fact. "I forgot about that. The battery wasn't charging."

"That's why I only drive vehicles that run on gas."

"I really wish you'd run away from my life," Vegas said.

Eleanor took Vegas by the hand, kissed it, stared into her daughter's blue eyes, and said, "Mommy would never do that."

Depressed, Vegas went inside her camper, changed her clothes, combed her hair, and came out twenty minutes later to find Eleanor waiting for her by the door. She grabbed her daughter by the hand and led her to her ivory-colored GMC Yukon.

"This reminds me of my taking you to kindergarten class on your first day of school," Eleanor said with a smile.

"I'm going to investigate a possible murder. How does that remind you of taking me to my first day of kindergarten?"

"You weren't appreciative then either."

As they got in the car, Vegas picked up a book that was in the passenger's seat.

"What's this? D.B. Cooper? Why do you have a book about D.B. Cooper?"

"Now, I don't want to scare you, but I think your Uncle Ray was D.B. Cooper," Eleanor casually informed her as she slid her key into the ignition.

"I have an Uncle Ray?" Vegas asked with a snarled lip.

"You can call him D.B."

266

| CHECKMATE A KILLER

"What makes you think he's D.B. Cooper?"

"Honey, it has to be somebody."

"Being alive doesn't make you a D.B. Cooper suspect, Mom."

"He was in the military. He parachuted in the Navy."

"Was he a fighter pilot?"

"He was stationed on a submarine."

Vegas stared at her mother in disbelief and couldn't help but say, "He parachuted from a submarine?"

"It was very hush-hush."

"Sounds like it would be very drown-drown."

"I'm sure the government gave him an air tank and a fishing pole when he jumped."

Vegas cocked her elbow to rest it on the opened window, placed her head in her hand, and said, "That doesn't make any sense, Mom."

"Oh, it will. Believe me, I know what I'm doing," Eleanor said and started rummaging through her purse.

"What are you looking for?" Vegas asked.

"My keys."

"They're in the ignition, Mom."

"Oh, that's handy, isn't it?"

Vegas just shook her head and wondered, "How in the world did I ever get to kindergarten class on time?"

CPSIA information can be obtained
at www.ICGtesting.com
Printed in the USA
BVHW031951180523
664414BV00015B/908